"Come, you need *Havelock said with a sincerity that made her wish she could trust him.*

Made her wish she could let go of her habitual distrust of the entire male sex, just once.

"I won't let you fall."

It wasn't falling she was worried about. It was the increasing frequency with which she was having foolish, feminine thoughts about him. Foolish, feminine reactions, too.

There were skaters of all ages, shapes and sizes twirling about on the ice. All looking as though they were having a splendid time. Life didn't offer many opportunities like this, to try something new and exciting. And the ice probably wouldn't last all that long. Mary might never get another chance to have a go at skating.

When had she last let herself go, the way they were doing? Living in the moment?

Having fun?

When had she got into the habit of being too afraid to reach out and attempt to take hold of the slightest chance at happiness?

She reached out and took the hand Lord Havelock was patiently holding out to her, vowing that today, at least, she would leave fear on the bank, launch out onto the ice and see what happened.

* * *

Lord Havelock's List
Harlequin® Historical #1200—September 2014

Author Note

Some of you may have read my Christmas novella "Governess to Christmas Bride" (*Gift-Wrapped Governess* anthology), in which the hero, Lord Chepstow, flees London when his good friend Lord Havelock suddenly decides to get married. He wouldn't have found it so scary had Lord Havelock not asked for his help compiling a list of wifely qualities. The next thing, he was sure, would be expecting him to scour society drawing rooms for a woman who matched them. And once marriage-minded ladies scent husband material, there is no saying who they won't get their claws into.

Well, Lord Chepstow stumbled into love anyway. But what, readers have wanted to know, happened to Lord Havelock, the man who so startled him by asking for help compiling the list of what makes a perfect wife?

Here, at last, is his story....

Annie Burrows

—

Lord Havelock's
List

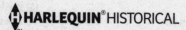

Recycling programs
for this product may
not exist in your area.

ISBN-13: 978-0-373-29800-6

LORD HAVELOCK'S LIST

This edition published by arrangement with Harlequin Books S.A.

For questions and comments about the quality of this book, please contact us at CustomerService@Harlequin.com.

Printed in U.S.A.

HARLEQUIN®
www.Harlequin.com

My lovely new editor, Pippa—
such a pleasure to work with.

ANNIE BURROWS

has been making up stories for her own amuse-ment since she first went to school. As soon as she got the hang of using a pencil she began to write them down. Her love of books meant she had to do a degree in English literature. And her love of writing meant she could never take on a job where she didn't have time to jot down notes when inspiration for a new plot struck her. She still wants the heroines of her stories to wear beautiful floaty dresses and triumph over all that life can throw at them. But when she got married she discovered that finding a hero is an essential ingredient to arriving at "happy ever after."

Chapter One

December 1814

'Ho, there, Chepstow! Need some advice.'

Lord Chepstow, who'd been sauntering across the lobby of his club, paused, recognised Lord Havelock and grinned.

'From me?' He shook his head ruefully. 'Lord, you must be in the suds to want *my* advice.'

'I am,' said Lord Havelock bluntly. Then glanced meaningfully in the direction of the club's servant, who'd stepped forward to take his coat and hat.

Chepstow's grin faded. 'Need to find somewhere quiet, to talk in private?'

'Yes,' said Lord Havelock, feeling a great weight rolling off his shoulders. Not that he had much hope that Chepstow, of all men, would come up with any fresh ideas. But at least he was willing to listen.

As soon as they'd passed through the door to the library—the one room almost sure to be deserted at this, or any other, time of the day—he said it.

Out loud.

'Got to get married.'

'Good grief.' Chepstow's jaw dropped. 'Would never have thought you the type to get some girl into trouble. Not one you feel you have to marry, at any rate.'

Havelock clenched his fists in automatic repudiation of such a slur on his honour, causing Chepstow to raise his own hands in a placatory gesture.

'Now I come to think of it…' Chepstow said, carefully moving a few feet out of his range, 'sort of thing could happen to anyone.'

'Not me,' Havelock insisted. 'You know I've never been much in the petticoat line.' He lowered his fists as it occurred to him that, actually, Chepstow might be the very chap to help him, after all.

'You have been though, Chepstow. You've had some really high-flyers in keeping, haven't you? And still managed to stay popular with ladies of the *ton*. How d'ye do it, man? How d'ye get them all eating out of your hands, that's what I need to know.'

'By opening my purse strings to the high-flyers,' said Chepstow candidly, 'and minding my manners with the Quality. It's perfectly simple….'

'Yes, if all you are looking for is something of a temporary nature. But if you had to get married, what kind of woman would you ask? I mean, what sort of woman do you think would make a good wife? And how would you go about finding her, if you only had a fortnight's grace to get the knot tied?'

Chepstow froze, like a stag at bay. 'Me? Married?' He slowly shook his head. 'I wouldn't. The trick is avoiding the snares they lay for a fellow, not deliberately walking straight into one.'

'You don't understand,' Havelock began to say. But Chepstow wasn't listening. He was looking wildly round the room, like a hunted animal seeking cover. And then, with obvious relief, he found it in the form of a pair of young men just barely visible above an enormous mound of books on one of the reading desks, engaged in earnest conversation.

'Let's ask Ashe,' he said, grabbing Havelock by one arm and towing him across the floor with an air of desperation. 'Kind of chap who reads books when he don't need to is bound to know something worth knowing about matrimony.'

Which was rot, of course. But Chepstow was clearly panicking. Anybody who thought they could get away with manhandling him across a room, whilst babbling about books, had obviously lost his wits.

But then the topic of matrimony was apt to do that to a fellow. He wouldn't willingly put his head in the noose if there was any alternative. But, having racked his brains for hours, Havelock simply couldn't find one.

So he'd decided that the only thing to be done was to see if he couldn't somehow sugar-coat the pill he was about to swallow. Find some way, unlikely though it seemed, to find a woman who wouldn't oblige him to alter his entire way of life.

Who wouldn't try to alter *him*.

'Ashe, and, um…' Chepstow floundered as he shot a blank look at the second man at the table with Ashe.

'Morgan,' said the Earl of Ashenden, waving a languid hand at his companion. Havelock had seen Morgan about, at the races, Jackson's, this club and various social events, though had never had cause to speak to him before. Son of some sort of nabob, if memory served him. Nothing wrong with him, so far as he knew. Just not out of the top drawer.

Not that he cared a rap for any of that. Not at a time like this.

Introductions dealt with, Chepstow thrust Havelock into a chair, then perched on the edge of his own as though ready to take flight at a moment's notice.

'Havelock has decided he wants to get married,' he announced, rather in the manner of a man who has just tossed a hot potato out of his burnt fingers. Then he practically pounced on the waiter, who'd ventured into the library to see if any of the young gentlemen needed refreshment.

'We need a bottle of wine,' declared Chepstow with feeling.

'Not *want* to,' Havelock explained once the waiter was out of earshot. 'Have to. Need to. And before you start questioning my *ton*, no, it isn't because I've suddenly started seducing innocents,' he growled, shooting Chepstow a resentful look. 'That's not it at all.'

'Steady on,' said Chepstow, pushing enough books aside that the waiter would have room to put a bottle and some glasses down when he returned. 'Sort of mistake anyone could make. With you looking so…out of sorts. And then broaching the topic the way you did.'

'Gentlemen,' said Ashe in that quiet way he had that somehow made everyone listen. 'Perhaps the best thing to do would be to let Havelock explain, in his own words, just what his problem is and how he thinks we may be of assistance? Before he feels compelled to call on his seconds.'

At Morgan's look of alarm, Ashe chuckled quietly.

'It is a foolish man who casts a slur on Havelock's honour these days.'

'I don't, and never have, challenged my friends to duels.'

'You shot off half of Wraxton's ear,' put in Chepstow.

'He wasn't my friend.' Havelock folded his arms over his chest and glared across the table at Ashe. 'And it wasn't me he insulted. But…a lady.'

'Oho! And I thought you said you weren't in the petticoat line.'

'I'm not. Never have been. It wasn't like that—'

'From what I heard,' put in Ashe mildly, 'if it hadn't been you, it would have been her husband who challenged him.'

'He should have done,' snapped Havelock. 'Only…' He sighed, and pushed his fringe out of his eyebrows irritably. '*I* lost my temper with him first.'

'Never mind,' said Ashe soothingly. 'At least *someone* shot him. That is the main thing.'

'I shouldn't have done it,' admitted Havelock, as the waiter returned with a tray of wine and clean glasses. Meeting Wraxton had been nothing like the first duel he'd fought. Wraxton would have killed him stone dead if his pistol hadn't misfired. And therefore he'd wanted to kill him right back. If it hadn't been for a freakish bout of hiccups throwing his aim off, causing him to nick the man's ear rather than put a hole through what passed for his heart, he would have done. And would then have had to flee the country or face charges for murder.

Seeing how close he'd come to bringing dishonour on his family through sheer anger had pulled him up short. Since then, he'd made much more effort to keep a rein on his temper.

Although few people were foolish enough to think they could get away with goading him, after the affair with Wraxton. The tale had got about that he'd deliberately marked the man. That he was a crack shot.

Which just went to show what idiots most people were.

'I only wish,' he said, pouring himself a generous measure of wine, 'my problems now could be solved by issuing a challenge, picking my seconds, then putting a bullet into…someone. But the fact is I need to get married,' he said glumly. 'And soon. But I don't want to end up shackled to some harpy who will make my life a misery by constantly nagging at me to reform. And the thing with women,' he said, lifting the glass to his mouth, 'is that you never can tell what they're really like until *after* they've got you all legally tied up.' He took a gulp as he recalled just how many times he'd seen it happen. One minute they'd been blushing brides, tripping down the aisle all sweetness and light, and the next they'd become regular harpies, henpecking the poor devil who'd married them into an early grave.

'Well, the answer, then, is to make sure of the woman's character before you wed her,' said Ashe with infuriating logic.

'And just how am I supposed to do that in the limited time I have available?'

'Marry someone you know well,' said Morgan as though it was obvious.

'God, no!' Havelock seized his glass and threw the rest of its contents back in one go. 'I can't face the thought of actually *living*, in the *same house*, with *any* of the girls I know really well. And anyway, they wouldn't oblige me by marrying quickly. They'd want a big society affair.' He shuddered. 'Not to mention a massive trousseau, and so forth.'

'So, to be blunt, you want a girl who will take you exactly as you are, and won't demand a big society wedding.'

'Exactly.'

'You are looking for a mouse,' put in Morgan. 'A mouse so desperate for matrimony she'll take what little you're prepared to offer.'

'That's it,' he cried, startling the sneer from Morgan's face. 'That would work. Morgan, you are a genius.'

'You'd better be prepared to accept someone plain, then,' returned Morgan, somewhat taken aback by his enthusiasm for a suggestion he'd made with such sarcasm. 'And probably poor, as well.'

Havelock leaned back for a moment, considering. 'Don't think a plain face would put me off, so long as she's not a complete antidote.'

'Just a moment,' put in Ashe. 'Though, for whatever reason, you have decided to marry *now*, and in such haste, you must not forget the matter of succession. All of us, except perhaps you, Morgan,' he said, giving the nabob's son a dry smile, 'have a duty to marry and produce sons to take over our responsibilities in their turn.'

'Point taken,' said Havelock before Ashe could state the obvious. It went without saying that he'd have to find someone it wouldn't be too much of a hardship to bed.

'I notice you haven't denied needing a girl with a sizeable dowry,' said Morgan, looking at him through narrowed eyes. 'Is that why you need to marry in such a hurry? In need of an heiress, are you?'

At that point Chepstow, who'd got through two drinks to Havelock's one, let out a bark of laughter.

'Just because I'm not one of the dandy set,' said Havelock, self-consciously putting his hand to his neckcloth, which he'd knotted in a haphazard fashion much, much earlier that day, and no doubt looked even further from the apparently effortless elegance attained by the other men about the table, 'that don't mean I haven't a tidy income.'

Morgan eyed the pocket of Havelock's jacket, which had somehow got ripped half off during the course of the day, and then lowered his gaze to his muddied boots, which he hadn't stopped to change after the devastating interview with his lawyers. He'd walked and walked whilst trying to come up with a solution, before he'd noticed he was passing his club, and decided to come in and see if anyone else could come up with any better ideas.

'I don't need a woman to bring anything but herself to the union,' he finished belligerently.

Once again it was Ashe who defused the tension, by summoning the waiter who'd been hovering at a discreet distance, and asking him to fetch ink and paper.

'What we need to do, I think, is to make a comprehensive list of exactly what you do need, before we set our minds to the problem of how you may acquire it.'

'There,' cried Chepstow triumphantly. 'Didn't I say that Ashe was the very fellow to help? I'll just…' He half rose from his chair.

Havelock only had to glare at him for a second or two to take the wind out of his sails. A gentleman didn't bail out on his friends when they'd gone to him for help. Havelock had stood by Chepstow every time he'd needed help getting out of a scrape. Now the boot was on the other foot, he expected a similar show of loyalty.

Chepstow subsided into his seat with an air of resignation and, in a hollow voice, asked the waiter, who just then arrived with the writing materials, to bring them another bottle of wine.

'So,' said Ashe, dipping the pen into the ink, 'you do not require beauty, or wealth, in your prospective bride. But you do require a compliant nature—'

'A mouse,' repeated Morgan derisively.

Ashe shot him a reproving look over the top of his spectacles.

'Undemanding. And not one of the circle in which you habitually move.'

At Havelock's shudder, Ashe wrote, *not of the upper ten thousand* on his list.

'Any other requirements?' He paused, his hand hovering over the paper.

Havelock frowned as he considered.

'Quite a few, actually. That's what makes it all so damned difficult.' He ran his fingers through his hair, for what felt like the thousandth time that day. Not that it made any difference to the style, or rather lack of it. It was fortunate he wasn't obsessed with his appearance, for his thick, curly hair did whatever it wanted. Impervious to comb, or pomade, the only thing was to keep it short and hope for the best.

'I don't want a woman with *any* family to speak of,' he said with feeling.

'You mean…no titled family?' The nabob's son shot him a glance loaded with sympathy. 'Wouldn't want them looking down on you.'

Before Havelock had a chance to get up, seize the fellow by the throat and give him a shaking, Ashe put in mildly, 'Morgan is not aware of how very well connected you are, Havelock. I am sure he meant no insult.'

No, Havelock sighed. He probably didn't. And anyway, he'd already decided to forgo the pleasure of indulging in a decent set-to with anyone within the walls of this club.

'Look, I'm related to half the bloody *ton* as it is,' he explained to the bemused Morgan. 'What with stepbrothers, and stepsisters, and all the attendant stepcousins and aunts and uncles and such like all thinking they have a right to poke their nose into my affairs, I don't want someone bringing yet another set of relatives into my life and making it any more complicated, thank you very much.'

He saw Ashe write the word *orphan* on the list.

Morgan nodded. 'Makes sense. And an orphan, a girl with no family to support her, is all the more likely to agree to the kind of bargain you seem determined to strike.'

'What do you mean by that?'

Chepstow poured a large measure of wine into Havelock's empty glass and nudged it towards him.

'I am sure Morgan meant nothing you need take offence at, Havelock,' reproved Ashe in the reasonable tone that so many men found damned supercilious.

He was beginning to understand why.

Havelock folded his arms and glared across the table.

To his credit, Morgan met his look without blinking.

Ashe removed his spectacles and set to polishing them with a silk handkerchief he produced from an inner pocket of his tailcoat. 'May I make a suggestion?'

'I wish you would. It's why I came in here, after all. See if anyone could help me find a way through this… morass,' said Havelock.

'Well, for myself,' said Ashe diffidently, 'I could not

stand to be married to a woman who did not possess a keen intellect.'

'Lord,' said Havelock, aghast. 'I wouldn't know what to do with a bluestocking!'

'Oh, come,' said Lord Chepstow, his devilish grin returning for the first time since they'd sat down. He then proceeded to offer a variety of suggestions about what exactly a man could do with a bluestocking, her garters, and various other items of apparel before descending into a spate of vulgarity that, though a little off the topic at hand, did at least serve to lighten the atmosphere.

When they'd stopped laughing, had wiped their eyes, topped up all their glasses and called for another bottle of wine, Ashe brought them all back to the point.

'You mustn't forget that this woman, whoever she may be, will be the mother of your children, Havelock. So, as well as considering what kind of woman you could tolerate living under your roof, you should also ask yourself what kind of children do you want to sire? For myself, I would hope my own offspring would have the capacity to make me proud. I would hate to think,' he said, giving Havelock a particularly penetrating look, 'that I had curtailed my own freedom only to produce a brood of idiots.'

Havelock ran his fingers through his hair yet again. 'You are in the right of it.' He sighed. 'Must think of the succession. Very well, put that on your list, Ashe. Not completely hen-witted.'

Since Ashe was taking a sip of wine it was Morgan who picked up the pen and wrote that down.

'I want her to be kind, too,' declared Havelock with some force. 'Good with youngsters. Not one of these women who think only of themselves.'

'Good, good, now we are really getting somewhere,' said Ashe, as Morgan added these further points to the steadily growing list.

'It's all very well making a list,' put in Morgan, tossing the pen aside. 'But how do you propose finding a woman who meets all your requirements? Put an advertisement in the papers?'

'God, no! Don't want the whole world to know how desperate I am to find a wife. I'd have every matchmaking mama within fifty miles of town descending on me with their simpering daughters in tow. Besides...' he shook his head '...it would take too long. Much too long. Only think of having the advertisement put in, then waiting for women to reply, then sifting through the mountain of responses, then having to interview them all...'

Morgan let out a bark of laughter. 'You are so sure you will have hundreds of replies, are you?'

'Oh, yes,' said Havelock testily. 'I've had women flinging themselves at me every Season for the past half-dozen years.'

'And during summer house parties,' put in Chepstow.

'There was that Christmas house party, wasn't there,' Ashe added, 'where—'

'Never mind that!' Havelock interrupted swiftly. 'I thought we'd agreed never to speak of *that* episode again.'

'Then there was that filly at the races,' said Chepstow.

Morgan laughed again. 'Very well. You have all convinced me. Havelock is indeed one of those men that society misses regard as a matrimonial prize.' Though the way he looked at Havelock conveyed his opinion that there was just no understanding the workings of the female mind.

'And you wouldn't believe some of the tricks they've employed in their attempts to bag me,' he said bitterly.

'Couldn't you simply settle with one of these women who've shown themselves so keen to, um, bag you? That would save you time, wouldn't it?'

Havelock gave Morgan a cold stare, before saying, 'No. Absolutely not. Can't stand women who flutter their eyelashes and pretend to swoon, and flaunt their bosoms in your face at every opportunity.'

Modest, he noted Ashe write on the bottom of the list, out of the corner of his eye.

'And anyway, the girls I already know, the ones who have made it plain they want me, have also made it plain they want a damn sight more from me than I'm willing to give. I'd make them miserable. So then they'd make damn sure they made me miserable.'

Ashe dipped his pen in the inkwell one more time, and wrote, *not looking for affection from matrimony*.

Morgan frowned down at the list, sipping at his drink. 'What this list describes,' he said thoughtfully, 'is a woman who is willing to consider a businesslike arrangement. Someone from a respectable family that has fallen on hard times, perhaps. Someone who would like to have children, but has no hopes of gaining a suitor through the normal way.'

'Normal way?'

'Feminine wiles,' supplied Morgan helpfully.

'Oh, them,' huffed Havelock. 'No. I definitely don't want a wife who's got too many feminine wiles. I'd rather she was straightforward.'

Honest, wrote Ashe.

'Good grief,' said Chepstow, peering rather blearily at the list. 'You will never, ever, find a woman who has all those attributes, no matter how long you look.'

'Oh, I don't know,' said Morgan. 'There are any number of genteel poor eking out an existence in London right at this moment. With daughters aplenty who'd give their eye teeth to receive a proposal from a man of Havelock's standing, from what you tell me. I'm tolerably sure that he could find one or two amongst them who would have at least a couple of the character traits he finds important. Particularly if he's not going to be put off by a plain face.'

Havelock leaned forward in his seat. 'You really think so?'

'Oh, yes.'

'And do you know where I might find them?'

Morgan leaned back, crossing one long leg over the other, and stared hard at the wall behind Havelock's head. The other men at the table waited with bated breath for his answer.

'Do you know, I rather think I do. I could probably introduce you to a couple of likely prospects tomorrow night, if you don't mind—' He broke off, eyeing Havelock's less-than-pristine garb, and laughed. 'No, you don't look like a chap who stands on ceremony. And I have an invitation to a ball, given by people who will never be accepted into the very top echelons of society, for all their wealth. Yet, amongst their guests, there are always a number of people in the exact circumstances to be of use to you. Good families, fallen on hard times, who have to put up with what society they can get. I dare say every single female there of marriageable age will look upon you as a godsend.'

'And you wouldn't mind taking me to such a ball?'

'Not in the least,' said Morgan affably. 'Is that not what friends are for? To help a fellow out?'

It was. He'd been on the verge of being disappointed in Chepstow. But really, the fellow had done what he could. He'd brought him to Ashe, who'd helped him to get his thoughts set down in a logical fashion, and introduced him to Morgan, who was going to give him practical assistance.

'To friendship,' he said, raising his glass to the three men sitting round the table with him.

'And marriage,' said Ashe, lifting his glass in response.

'Let's not get carried away,' said Lord Chepstow, his glass stopping a mere inch from his lips. 'To Havelock's marriage, perhaps. Not the institution as such.'

'Havelock's marriage, then,' said Ashe.

'Havelock's bride,' said Morgan, downing his own drink in one go and reaching for the bottle.

'Yes, don't mind drinking to her,' said Chepstow. 'Your bride, my friend.'

And let's hope, thought Havelock as he carefully folded the list and put it in his pocket, *that the woman who possesses at least the most important of these attributes will be at the ball tomorrow night.*

Chapter Two

'Can you really do nothing better with your hair?'

Mary lowered her gaze to the floor and shook her head as Aunt Pargetter sighed.

'Couldn't you at least have borrowed Lotty's tongs? I am sure she wouldn't begrudge them to you. If you could only get just a *leetle* curl into it, I am sure it would look far more fetching than just letting it hang round your face like a curtain.'

Mary put her hand to her head to check that the neat bun, in which she'd fastened her hair earlier, hadn't already come undone.

'No, no,' said Aunt Pargetter with exasperation. 'It hasn't come down yet. I am talking in generalities.'

Oh, those. She'd heard a lot of those over the past few months. Generalities uttered by lawyers about indigent females, by relations about the cost of doing their duty and by coach drivers about passengers who didn't give tips. She'd also heard a lot of specifics. Which informed her exactly how she'd become indigent and why each set of people she'd been sent to in turn couldn't, at present, offer her a home.

'Now, I know you feel a little awkward about attending a ball when you are still in mourning,' Aunt Pargetter went on remorselessly. 'But I just cannot leave you here on your own this evening to mope. And besides, there will be any number of eligible men there tonight. Who is to say you won't catch someone's eye and then all your problems will be solved?'

Mary's head flew up at that, her eyes wide. Aunt Pargetter was talking of marriage. Marriage! As if that was the answer to *any* woman's problems.

She shivered and lowered her gaze again, pressing her lips tightly together. It would solve Aunt Pargetter's problems, right enough. She hadn't said so, but Mary could see that keeping her fed and housed for any length of time would strain the family's already limited resources. But, rather than throwing up her hands, and passing her on to yet another member of the family upon whom Mary might have a tenuous claim, Aunt Pargetter had just taken her in, patted her hand and told her she needn't worry any longer. That she'd look after her.

Mary just hadn't realised that Aunt Pargetter's plan for looking after her involved marrying her off.

'You need to lift your head a little more and look about you,' advised Aunt Pargetter, approaching her with her hand outstretched. She lifted Mary's chin and said, 'You have fine eyes, you know. What my girls wouldn't give for lashes like yours.' She sighed, shaking her head. And then, before Mary had any idea she might be under attack and could take evasive action, the woman pinched both her cheeks. 'There. That's put a little colour in your face. Now all you need to do is put on a smile, as though you are enjoying yourself, and you won't look quite so...'

Repulsive. Plain. Dowdy.

'Unappealing,' Aunt Pargetter finished. 'You could be fairly pretty, you know, if only you would…' She waved her hands in exasperation, but was saved from having to come up with a word that would miraculously make Mary not sound as though she was completely miserable when her own daughters bounced into the room in a froth of curls and flounces.

Aunt Pargetter had no time left to spare on Mary when her beloved girls needed a final inspection, and just a little extra primping, before she bundled them all into the hired hack they couldn't afford to keep waiting.

'We have an invitation from a family by the name of Crimmer tonight,' Aunt Pargetter explained to Mary as the hack jolted over the cobbles. 'They are not the sort who would object to me bringing along another guest, so don't you go worrying your head about not receiving a formal invitation.'

Mary's eyes nevertheless widened in alarm. She hadn't any idea her aunt would have taken her to this event without forewarning her hosts.

Aunt Pargetter reached across the coach and patted her hand. 'I shall just explain you have only recently arrived for a visit, which is perfectly true. Besides, the Crimmers will love being able to boast that their annual ball has become so popular *everyone* wants to attend. But what is even more fortunate for you, my dear, is that they have two sons to find brides for, not that the younger is quite old enough yet, and I've heard rumours that the older one is more or less spoken for.'

As Mary frowned in bewilderment at the contradictory nature of that somewhat rambling statement, her aunt explained, 'The point is, they have a lot of wealthy friends with sons who must be on the lookout for a wife, as well. Especially one as well connected as you.'

'What do you mean, Mama?' Charlotte shot a puzzled glance at Mary. It had clearly come as a shock to her to hear there might be anything that could possibly make Mary a likely prospect on the marriage mart, when all week they'd been thinking of her as the poor relation.

'Well, although her poor dear mama was my cousin, by marriage, her papa was a younger son of the youngest daughter of the Earl of Finchingfield.'

Mary's heart sank. Her well-meaning aunt clearly meant to spread news of her bloodlines about tonight as though she were some…brood mare.

'But if she's related to the Earl of Finchingfield, why hasn't she gone to him?' Dorothy, Charlotte's younger, and prettier, sister, piped up.

That was a good question. And Mary turned to Aunt Pargetter with real interest, to see how she would explain the tangle that had been her mother's married life.

'Oh, the usual thing,' said her aunt with an airy wave of her hand. 'Somebody didn't approve of the marriage, someone threatened to cut someone off, people stopped speaking to one another and, before you knew it, a huge rift had opened up. But Mary's mother's people still know how to do their duty, I hope, when a child is involved. Not that you are a child any longer, Mary, but you know what I mean. It isn't fair for you to have to suffer the consequences of the mistakes your parents made.'

Charlotte and Dorothy were both now looking at her with wide eyes. Mary's heart sank still further. In the few days she'd been living in their little house in Bloomsbury, she'd discovered that the pair of them had a passion for the kind of novels where dispossessed heiresses went through a series of adventures before winding up married to an Italian prince. She was very much afraid they'd suddenly started seeing her as one of those.

Still, since the Crimmers, who were in trade, weren't likely to have invited an Italian prince to their ball, she needn't worry they would attempt to push them into each other's arms. Actually, she needn't worry that either Lotty or Dotty would push her into anyone's arms. They were both far too keen on eligible bachelors themselves to let a single one of them, foreign or not, slip through their own eager fingers.

She pulled her shoulders down and took a deep breath. No need to worry. Aunt Pargetter might talk about her suitability for marriage as much as she liked, but that didn't mean she was at risk of having some marriage-minded man sweeping her off her feet tonight. Or any night. She wasn't the type of girl men did want to sweep off her feet.

Men didn't tend to notice her. Well, she'd made sure they wouldn't by developing the habit of shrinking into the background. And by dint of following just a few steps behind her more exuberant cousins, she very soon managed to fade into the background tonight, as well. It was never very hard. Most girls of her age actually *wanted* people to look at them. Especially men. So there was always someone to hide behind.

Mary found a chair slightly to the rear of her aunt and cousins when they all sat down. By shifting it, only a very little, she managed to make use of a particularly leafy potted plant, as well.

Though she was now shielded from a large percentage of the ballroom, she had a good view of the main door through which other guests were still pouring in, greet-

ing one another with loud voices as they flaunted their
evening finery. If she hadn't already decided to keep out
of sight, the wealth on display in this room would have
totally overawed her. Dotty and Lotty scanned the crowd
with equal avidity, whispering to each other behind their
fans about the gowns and jewels of the females, the fig-
ures and incomes of the males.

'Oh, look, it's Mr Morgan,' eventually exclaimed
Lotty, as a pair of young men entered the ballroom. 'I
really didn't think he'd be here tonight.'

From that comment, and the fact that she and Dotty
immediately sat up straighter, their fans fluttering at a
greatly increased tempo, she guessed the man in question was what they termed 'a catch.' She could, for once,
actually see why. The shorter of the two men was extremely good-looking, in a rugged sort of way, besides
being turned out in a kind of casual elegance that made
him look far more approachable than others of his age,
with their starched shirt points and nipped-in waists.

'Who is that with him?'

Following slightly behind the handsome newcomer
was a taller, rather rangy man with ferocious eyebrows.

'He must be a friend of his from school, or somewhere,' whispered Lotty. 'See the way Mrs Crimmer
is smiling at him, giving him her hand and sort of...
fluttering?'

Mary joined her cousins in watching the progress
round the room of what must be decidedly eligible bachelors, given the way the ladies in every group they approached preened and fluttered for all they were worth.

By the time they reached their corner of the ballroom,
Dotty and Lotty were almost beside themselves.

'Good evening, Mrs Pargetter, Miss Pargetter, Miss

Dorothy,' said the tall, slender man, somewhat to Mary's confusion. *This* was the man who'd set her cousins all aflutter?

He must be very wealthy then, because he certainly didn't have looks on his side. Not like his companion.

'Allow me to present my friend,' Mr Morgan added. 'The Viscount Havelock.'

Dotty's and Lotty's heads both swivelled in unison as they tore their eyes from the man they considered the prize catch of the night, to the man they'd just discovered to be a genuine peer of the realm. They both pushed their bosoms out a little further, fluttering their fans and eyelashes at top speed.

The viscount, apparently unimpressed by their ability to do all three things at once, accorded them no more than a curt nod.

Then his gaze slid past them, caught her in the act of biting back a smile and stilled.

'And who is this?'

'Oh, well, this is my…well, almost a niece, by marriage,' said her aunt. 'Miss Carpenter.'

Mary's cheeks heated. She really shouldn't have been mocking the ridiculous way her cousins had been preening just because a titled man was standing within three feet of them. But he didn't look as though he minded. On the contrary, that bored, slightly irritated look he'd bestowed on them had vanished without trace. If anything, she would swear he looked as though he shared her view that they were being a little silly.

And then he smiled at her with what looked like… Well, if she didn't know better, as if he'd just found something he'd been looking for.

'Do you care to dance, Miss Carpenter?'

'Me?' Her jaw dropped. She closed her mouth hastily, then shook her head and lowered it.

'N-no. I couldn't…' Lotty and Dotty would be furious with her. And insulted. And rightly so. It was almost a snub, to ask her, in preference to them, after they'd made their interest so blatant.

Could that be the reason he'd asked?

You never could tell, with men. What looked like an act of charity could be performed deliberately to spite someone else, or in order to put someone in their place. She stared doggedly at her shoes, her spirits sinking to just about their level. You couldn't judge a man by the handsome cast of his features. And she'd been foolish to have been even momentarily deceived by them and that rather…heartening smile.

It was a man's actions that revealed his true nature.

'My niece is in mourning, as you can see,' her aunt was explaining, waving her hand towards Mary's plain, sober gown.

'Really?'

She couldn't help looking up at the tone of the viscount's voice. It was almost as if he… But, no, he couldn't be pleased to hear she was in mourning, could he? That was absurd.

And there was nothing in his face, now she was looking at it, to indicate anything but sympathy.

'Perhaps,' he said, in a rather kinder tone of voice, 'you would be my partner for supper, later?'

'Oh, well, I…' The look in his eyes made her tongue cleave to the roof of her mouth. It was so…intent. As though he wanted to discover every last one of her secrets. As though he would turn her inside out and upside down, until he'd shaken them all from her. As though nothing would stop him.

It made her most uncomfortable. But at the exact same moment Mary decided she would have to somehow refuse his invitation, her aunt accepted it on her behalf. 'Mary would be honoured. Wouldn't you, dear?' She poked her with the end of her furled fan, as if determined to prod the approved response from her.

When she still couldn't give it, the viscount smiled again, then turned his attention to her cousins.

'And in the meantime,' he said, with surprising enthusiasm, 'would either of you two lovely young ladies show pity on a stranger, by dancing with me?'

Fortunately, before they could elbow one another out of the way in their eagerness to get their hands on him, the tall thin one held out his hand to Charlotte.

Mary sighed with relief as the foursome made their way out on to the dance floor. But her relief was short-lived.

'I believe you have made a conquest,' breathed her aunt in rapturous tones as she sidled closer, pushing a palm frond out of the way. 'Lord Havelock seemed most interested in you.'

'I cannot think why,' said Mary. She'd practically hidden herself behind a potted palm, she was wearing a plain gown that did nothing for her pale complexion and she'd turned down his offer of a dance. 'Perhaps he needs spectacles,' she wondered aloud. 'That might account for it.'

'Nonsense! He can clearly see that you have good breeding. My girls may be prettier than you,' she said with blunt honesty, 'but neither of them would know how to go on in his world.' She nodded towards the viscount, who was leading a glowing Dotty into the bottom set.

'Well, I don't suppose I would, either,' retorted Mary. 'It's not as if I've ever been a part of it.'

'No, but your mother was far more genteel than I've ever been. And your father, too—I dare say he taught you how a real lady should behave.'

Mary did her best not to react to that statement, though something inside her shrivelled up into a defensive ball at the mere mention of her father.

'Papa was…very strict with me, yes,' she admitted. Not that she would ever mention the form his strictness took, not to a living soul. Particularly not as he directed most of it firmly, and squarely, at her mother, rather than her.

'And he certainly did have strong opinions about how a lady should behave,' she also admitted, when her aunt kept looking at her as though she expected her to say something more. And he enforced those opinions. With loud demands, interspersed with terrifyingly foreboding silences, when he was sober, fists and boots when he was not.

'I really do not want,' she said tremulously, 'an eligible *parti* to prefer me to either of my cousins. Especially not when they seem so taken with him.'

'Well, that's all very well and good, but he's plainly only got eyes for you. Besides, both my girls would be far more comfortable with Mr Morgan. Not out of their reach, socially, you see, for all his wealth.'

Mary took a second look at her cousins as they skipped up and down the set. Though Dotty looked as though she was enjoying herself, Lotty was positively glowing. And had Dotty just shot Mr Morgan a coy glance over her shoulder while the viscount's back was towards her?

She frowned. How could either of them prefer that great long beanpole of a man to the dashing viscount? Not only was he much better looking but he had a more amiable expression. She'd even thought she might have detected a sense of humour lurking in the depths of those honeyed hazel eyes. When he'd caught her smiling at the way Dotty and Lotty had reacted on learning he had a title, it had been like sharing a private joke.

Only, she reminded herself tartly, to suspect him of snubbing them rather unkindly a moment later.

She was in no position to judge him. Or think her own observations could have any sway over Dotty's or Lotty's decisions. Lords were notorious for being as poor as church mice. If his pockets were to let, then he'd be looking to marry an heiress. Which ruled them both out.

Besides, they knew Mr Morgan was wealthy. Which must make him terribly tempting.

Anyway, she was not going to harbour a single uncharitable thought towards them. Not when they'd been the only ones of her extended family to make room for her in their lives. The girls could have protested when their mother told them Mary was to share their room. But they hadn't. They'd just said how beastly it must be for her to have nowhere else to go and emptied one of the drawers for her things.

Mary had tried to repay them all by making herself useful about the house. And until tonight, she'd thought she was beginning to make a permanent place for herself.

But it was not to be. Aunt Pargetter, who wasn't even really an aunt at all, but only a distant connection by marriage, might be kinder than most of the relatives she'd met so far, but it was absurd to think she would house her indefinitely.

Even so, she was not going to tamely submit to her misguided plans to marry her off. No matter how kindly meant the intention was, such a scheme wouldn't do for her.

In the morning, she would find out where the nearest employment agency was located and go and register for some kind of work. Not that she had any idea what she might do. She darted a look at Aunt Pargetter, wishing she could ask her advice. But it would be a waste of time. Aunt Pargetter, though kindness itself, was also one of those females who thought marriage was the height of any woman's ambitions and wouldn't understand her preference for work.

Well, then, she would just have to, somehow, discover where the agency was on her own. Although what excuse she could give for wishing to leave the house, she could not think. Everyone knew she had no money with which to go shopping. Besides, since she was a stranger to London, either Dotty or Lotty, or probably both, would be sent with her to make sure she didn't get lost.

She became so wrapped up in formulating one plan after another, only to discard it as unworkable, that she scarcely noticed when the dancing came to a halt and people began to make their way to the supper room. Until Viscount Havelock brushed the fronds of the potted palm to one side, smiling down at her as he offered her his hand.

'Are you ready for a bite to eat? I must confess, all this dancing has given me quite an appetite.'

'Oh. Um…' He wasn't out of breath, though. Her

cousins were fanning their flushed faces, Mr Morgan was mopping his brow with a handkerchief, but Lord Havelock wasn't displaying the slightest sign of fatigue. He was obviously very fit.

Not that she ought to notice such things about a man.

Flustered by the turn of her thoughts, she took the viscount's hand and allowed him to place her hand on his sleeve.

It must just be that something about him reminded her of her brother's friends. Several of them had been of his class and had about them the same air of…vitality. Of vigour. And the same self-assurance that came with knowing they were born to command.

She regarded her hand, where it lay on his sleeve. The arm encased in the soft material of his evening coat felt like a plank of oak. Just like her brother's had. And those of his friends he'd sometimes brought home, who'd escorted her round the town. Not that this viscount actually worked for his living, like those lads who'd served in the navy. From what she knew of aristocrats, he probably maintained his fitness by boxing and fencing, and riding.

He was probably what her brother would have called a Corinthian. She darted a swift glance at his profile, taking in the firm set of his jaw and the healthy complexion. Yes, definitely a Corinthian. At least, he certainly didn't look as though he spent his days sleeping off the effects of the night before.

And, if he was one of the sporting set, that would explain why he wore clothing that looked comfortable, rather than fitted tightly to show off his physique. He might not be on the catch for an heiress at all.

Her cheeks flushed. She couldn't believe she was speculating about his reasons for being here. Or the body underneath his clothing. Not that she'd ever spent so much time thinking about a man's choice of clothing, either. Just because he seemed better turned out than any other man present, in some indefinable way, she had no business making so much of it.

'I hope the crowd of people we are following *are* heading to the supper room,' he said, breaking into her thoughts.

'I…I suppose they must be,' she replied, but only after casting about desperately for an interesting reply and coming up empty.

'You are not a regular visitor to this house?'

She shook her head. 'I have only been in London a few days,' she admitted. 'I don't know anyone.'

'Apart from the lady you are with. Your…aunt?'

Mary shook her head again. 'I had never even met her before I turned up on her doorstep with a letter of introduction from my lawyer. And to be perfectly frank, I'm not at all sure the connection is…'

Suddenly Mary wondered why on earth she was telling this total stranger such personal information. It couldn't be simply because there was something about him that put her in mind of her brother and his fellow officers, could it? Or because he'd given her that look, earlier, that had made her feel as though he was genuinely interested?

How pathetic did that make her? One kind word, one keen look, a smile and a touch of his hand and she'd been on the verge of unburdening herself.

Good grief—she was as susceptible to a good-looking man as the cousins she'd decried as ninnies not an hour earlier. She, who'd sworn never to let a handsome face sway her judgement, had just spent a full five minutes wondering how he managed to keep so fit and speculating about the cut of his clothes, *and* what lay beneath them.

'You don't really have any family left to speak of, is that what you were about to say?'

She couldn't recall what she'd been about to say. Nor even what the question had been. Her mind kept veering off into realms it had never strayed into before and consequently got lost there.

'Your…aunt, or whatever she is,' he persisted, while her cheeks flooded with guilty heat, 'said you are in mourning. Was it…for someone very close?'

Well, that dealt with the strange effects his proximity had been wreaking in her mind and body. He might as well have doused her with a bucket of cold water.

'My mother,' she said. 'She was all I had left.'

She might be in a crowded ballroom tonight, on the arm of the most handsome and eligible man in the room, but the truth was that she was utterly alone in the world, and destitute.

'That's c…' He pulled himself up short and patted her hand. 'I mean to say, dreadful. For you.'

They'd reached the doorway now and beyond she could see tables laid out with a bewildering array of dishes that looked extremely decorative, but not at all like anything she might ever have eaten before.

Since they'd both come without an invitation, space was found for them at a table squeezed into the bay of a window.

'Don't worry,' he said when he noted her gaze darting about anxiously. 'I shall make sure we find your aunt once we have eaten and return you to her side in complete safety.'

She was amazed he'd noticed how awkward she felt. And that he'd correctly deduced it was being separated from her aunt that had caused it. Most men couldn't see further than the end of their noses.

He must have noticed the way she'd eyed the food with trepidation, too, because he took great care, when offering her dishes, to ask if she liked the principal ingredient of each. Which deftly concealed her ignorance. For he could have explained what everything was, making her feel even more awkward, whilst puffing off his own *savoir faire*. As it was, since the other men at their table were passing dishes round, and helping the ladies to slices of this, or spoonfuls of that, nobody noticed anything untoward.

Eventually, her plate, like that of everyone else at the table, was piled high and conversation began to flow.

Except between Lord Havelock and her.

She supposed he'd gone to the length of his chivalry. She supposed he was waiting for her to make some kind of remark that would open up the kind of light, inconsequential conversations that were springing up all around them.

But for the life of her she couldn't dredge up a single topic she could imagine might be of interest to a man like him. Or the kind of man she suspected he was. She didn't really know a thing about him.

And though she was grateful to him for the way he'd behaved so far, she began to wish she was with her aunt and cousins. *They* would know how to entertain him, she was sure. They wouldn't let this awkward silence go on, and on, and on…

He cleared his throat, half turned towards her and said, 'Do you…?' He cleared his throat again, took a sip of wine and started over. 'That is, I wonder, do you enjoy living in town, or do you prefer the country? I suppose,' he said with a swift frown before she could answer, 'I should have enquired where you lived before you had to come to London, shouldn't I? I don't know why I assumed you had lived in the country before.'

'I lived in Portsmouth, actually,' she said, relieved to be able to have a question she could answer without having to rack her brains. 'And I haven't been here long enough to know whether I prefer it, or not.'

'But do you have any objection to living in the countryside?'

It was her turn to frown. 'I cannot tell. I have never lived anywhere but in a town.'

Oh, what a stupid, stupid thing to say. She should have made some remark about how…bustling London was in comparison to Portsmouth, or…or how she missed the sound of the sea. Or even better, asked him about *his* preferences. That was what men liked, really, wasn't it? To talk about themselves? Instead, she'd killed the potential conversation stone dead.

They resumed eating in silence for a few more minutes before he made a second, valiant attempt to breach it. 'Well, do you like children?'

'Yes, I suppose in a general way,' though she couldn't imagine why he might ask that. But at least she'd learned her lesson from last time. She would offer him the chance to talk about himself. 'Why do you ask?'

'Oh, no reason,' he said airily, though the faint blush that tinged his cheeks told her he was growing a bit uncomfortable. 'Just making conversation.' He reached for his wine glass and curled his fingers round the stem as though in need of something to hang on to. And then blurted, 'What do people talk about at events like this?'

For the first time in her life, she actually felt sorry for a man. He'd come here expecting to enjoy himself and ended up saddled with the dullest, most boring female in the room. And far from betraying his exasperation with her ignorance, and her timidity, he'd done his best to put her at ease. He'd even been making an attempt to *draw her out*. And wasn't finding it easy.

'I expect it is easier for them,' she said, indicating the other occupants of the table. 'That is…I mean…they all know each other already, I think.'

He looked round the table and she couldn't help contrasting the animated chatter of all the other females, who were universally fluttering their eyelashes at their male companions in the attempt to charm them. Then he looked back at her and smiled.

'Well, we'll just have to get to know each other then, won't we?'

Oh, dear. Did he mean to ask her a lot of highly personal questions? Or expect her to come up with some witty banter, or start flirting like the other women? That's what came of throwing a man even the tiniest conversational sop. She'd made him think she was interested in *getting to know* him.

'What,' he said abruptly, 'do you think about climbing boys?'

'I beg your pardon? Climbing boys?'

'Yes. The little chaps they send up chimneys.'

All of a sudden, the odd things he said, and the abrupt way he said them reminded her very forcibly of her own brother's behaviour, when confronted by a female to whom he was not related. He was trying his best, but this was clearly a man who was more at ease in the company of other men. Lord Havelock had no more idea how to talk to a single lady than she had as to how to amuse an eligible male.

He was staring at his plate now, a dull flush mounting his cheeks, as though he knew he'd just raised a topic that was not at all suitable for a dinner table, let alone what was supposed to be the delicate sensibilities of a female.

And once again, she felt…not sorry for him. No, not that. But willing to meet his attempts to entertain her halfway. For he was exerting himself to a considerable extent. A thing no other male she'd ever encountered had ever even *considered* doing. And though men did not usually want to hear what a woman thought, he had asked, and so she girded up her loins to express her opinion. It wasn't as if she was ever likely to see him again, so what did it matter if he *was* offended by it?

'It is a cruel practice,' she said. 'I know chimneys have to be cleaned, but surely there must be a more humane way? I hear there are devices that can produce results that are almost as good.'

'Devices,' he said, turning to her with a curious expression.

'For cleaning chimneys.'

'Really? I had no idea.'

'Oh? But then why did you ask me about them?'

His brows drew down irritably.

'I beg your pardon,' she said hastily, hanging her head meekly. Whatever had possessed her to question him? How could she have forgotten the way her father had reacted should her mother have ever dared to question his motive for saying *anything*, no matter how absurd?

There was a moment's awkward pause. She darted

him a wary glance to find he'd folded his arms across his chest and was glaring at his plate as though he was contemplating sweeping it, and its contents, from the table before storming off.

A kind of dim terror crept over her. A mist rising up from her past. Her own appetite fled. She pleated her napkin between nervous fingers, fighting to stay calm. He couldn't very well backhand her out of the chair, she reminded herself. Not even her father had taken such drastic action, when she'd angered him, not in public, at any rate.

No—Lord Havelock was more likely to return her to her chaperon in frosty silence and vow never to have anything to do with her again.

She felt him shift in his seat, next to her. 'Entirely my fault,' he growled between clenched teeth. 'No business bringing such a topic up at a dinner table. Cannot think what came over me.'

The mist shredded, blasted apart by the shock wave of his apology. She turned and stared at him.

'I dare say you can tell that I'm just not used to conversing with…ladies.'

Good grief. Not only had he apologised, but he, a *man*, had admitted to having a fault.

'I…I'm not very good at it myself. Not conversing with ladies, obviously, I can do that. I meant, conversing with members of the opposite…' She floundered on the precipice of uttering a word that would be an even worse *faux pas* than mentioning the grim reality of chimney sweeps.

And then he smiled.

A rather devilish smile that told her he knew exactly which word she'd almost said.

With an unholy light in his eyes that sent awareness of her own sex flooding from the pit of her stomach to the tips of her toes.

Chapter Three

'So you found your mouse,' remarked Morgan, as they strode out into the night.

'I've found a young lady who appears to meet many of my requirements,' Havelock testily corrected him. He hadn't been able to believe his luck when the bashful creature he'd had to coax out from behind her potted plant had admitted to being an orphan.

'The only problem is,' he said with a scowl, 'the very things I like most about her make it devilish difficult to find out what her character is really like.'

'How so?'

'Well, it was damn near impossible to pry more than a couple of words out of her at a time.' To think he'd congratulated himself on so deftly separating her from her more exuberant cousins, only to come unstuck at the dinner table.

'I made a complete cake of myself.' He sighed. She wasn't like the girls he was used to sitting with at such events. Girls who either flirted, or threw out conversational gambits intended to impress and charm. She'd left all the work to him. And he discovered he was a very poor hand at it. In his determination to delve to the heart of her, he'd asked the kind of questions that had both puzzled and alarmed her.

Climbing boys, for God's sake! Who in their right minds asked a gently reared girl about such a deplorable topic? Over a supper table?

Though in fairness to Miss Carpenter, she'd swiftly rallied and given an answer of which he could heartily approve. And shown her head wasn't stuffed with goose down. Devices for sweeping chimneys, eh? Where could she have heard about them? If they even existed.

'You know,' said Morgan as they turned in the direction of their club, 'either of her cousins would be only too glad to get an offer from you. Wouldn't be so much work, either. That's why I made them known to you. Family not that well off, eager to climb the social ladder. Have known them some time, so I can vouch for them both being good girls, at heart.'

'No, thank you,' said Havelock firmly, recalling the way they'd fluttered and preened the moment they heard he had a title. 'Miss Carpenter is the one for me.'

'Very well,' said Morgan with a shrug. 'Perhaps you will get a chance to discover more about her when we go and visit her tomorrow.'

'Perhaps,' he said gloomily. He wished now that he *had* been more in the petticoat line. Had more experience with plumbing the depths of women's natures. He'd plumbed other depths, naturally, to the satisfaction of both parties involved, but had always avoided anything that smacked of emotion. The moment a woman started to seem as though she wanted to get 'close', he'd dropped her like a hot potato.

He'd thought it was safer.

And it had been. Not one of them had ever managed to get under his skin. The trouble was, keeping himself heart whole had left him woefully unprepared for the most important task of his life.

'Good morning, my lord,' gushed Mrs Pargetter.

Havelock favoured her with his most courtly bow. If he was going to be frequenting these premises, he needed to be on good terms with the hostess.

Miss Carpenter's cousins, whose names escaped him for the moment, fluttered at him from their strategic locations on two separate sofas, indicating their willingness to have him join them. Or Morgan. The hussies didn't appear to mind which.

Miss Carpenter, on the other hand, was sitting on a straight-backed chair by the window, looking very much as though she would like to disappear behind the curtains.

Morgan made straight for the younger chit, so he went and sat beside the elder. He'd paid this kind of duty visit to dance partners, the day after a ball, before. But he'd never realised how frustrating they could be if a fellow was serious about pursuing a female. You couldn't engage in meaningful conversation with teacups and macaroons being thrust under your nose every five minutes. Not that he'd had much success in the field of conversation when he *had* got her to himself.

'We hope you will permit us to take your lovely daughters out tomorrow,' Morgan was saying. Havelock scowled. He didn't want to take either of *them* anywhere.

The girls looked at each other. Then their heads swivelled towards the window where Mary was sitting.

'And you, too, Miss Carpenter, of course,' said Havelock, taking his cue from them. Morgan had been right. Man-hungry they might be, but they weren't totally ruthless in their pursuit of prey. They were willing to offer Miss Carpenter a share in their spoils.

'Oh, no,' said Miss Carpenter, blushing. 'Really, I don't think…'

'Nonsense, Mary,' said her aunt briskly. 'It will do you the world of good to get out in the fresh air.'

Her brows rose in disbelief. Since rain was lashing at the windowpane, he could hardly blame her.

'It isn't really the season for driving in the park, now, is it,' said Morgan with just a hint of a smile. 'I was thinking more in the lines of visiting somewhere like Westminster Abbey.'

Westminster Abbey? Was the fellow mad? Walking about looking at a bunch of grisly tombs? How was he going to find out anything, except whether the girl knew her kings and queens, by taking her to Westminster Abbey?

'It is so kind of you,' said the girl he was sitting next to, with a flutter of eyelashes up at Morgan, 'to think of taking us all out to see the sights. And Mary would love that, wouldn't you, Mary? She hasn't seen anything of London at all.'

Before Miss Carpenter had the chance to voice her horror at the prospect of being dragged out on an expedition to examine a lot of mouldering tombs, the door flew open and a boy, who looked as if he was about eight or nine years old, and was covered in flour, burst in.

'Mother, Mother, you have to come see…'

'Will, how many times have I told you,' shrieked Mrs Pargetter, 'not to come barging in here when we have callers?'

At the same moment, Miss Carpenter leapt from her chair and cut off his headlong dash into the room by dint of grabbing him about the waist.

She alone of the four women in the room was smiling at him.

'You're all over flour, Will,' she pointed out as he looked up at her in bewilderment. 'You don't want to spoil your sisters' pretty clothes, do you?'

She didn't seem to care about her own clothes, though. There was a little boy-shaped smudge on her skirts and a white handprint on her sleeve.

'No, 'spose not,' he said grudgingly, rubbing his twitching nose with the back of one hand, making him twice as likely to sneeze. 'But you've just got to see…'

'Come on,' said Mary, taking his dough-encrusted hand in hers. 'You can show *me* whatever it is that's got you so fired up. And later, when these visitors have gone, I'm sure your mama will want to see, as well.'

The boy glared at him, then at Morgan, then turned his floury little nose up at his sisters, as though roundly condemning them for considering the state of their clothes more important than whatever exciting development had occurred in the kitchens.

'Oh, thank you, Mary,' said her aunt.

'Not at all,' she replied, with what looked suspiciously like heartfelt relief.

'Did you see that?' he asked Morgan later, as they were going down the front steps. 'Her reaction to the floury boy?'

'Indeed I did,' he replied. 'Another item on your list ticked off. Or two, perhaps. She's not totally selfish and appears to be kind to children. Unless…well, I suppose she could have been using the child to make her escape.'

'Blast.' He peered out from under the front porch into the teeming rain. 'She might not have been thinking of the child at all. She might have just wanted an excuse to bolt. And she might well have given him a good scolding for spoiling her gown, once she was safely out of our sight. You see, that's the trouble with women. They put on a mask in public that makes you think they have the nature of an angel, but it comes straight off when they think nobody's watching. If only there was some way I could be sure of getting a genuine reaction from her.'

'Our trip to the Abbey tomorrow would be a perfect opportunity,' said Morgan as they dashed across the pavement into his waiting carriage, 'to set up some kind of scene,' he said, wrenching open the door, 'where she will be obliged to react without thinking too much about it.'

In the time it took Lord Havelock to get into the carriage as well and slam the door on the filthy weather, he'd gone from wanting to tell Morgan he hadn't been serious—for what kind of man deliberately set a trap to expose a lady's faults?—to realising that too much was riding on his making a successful match, in the shortest possible time, for him to take the conventional route.

So when Morgan said, 'Best if you leave the details to me', he raised no objection.

'I'll stage something that will take you as much by surprise as her,' said Morgan. 'So that if she's clever enough to work out what's afoot, the blame will fall upon me, not you.'

'That's…very decent of you,' he said. And then wondered why Morgan was being so helpful. They'd only met, properly, a couple of nights ago. And Morgan had sneered, and mocked, and generally behaved as though he'd taken him in immediate dislike.

'What's your lay, Morgan?'

'I beg your pardon?'

'I mean, why are you so keen to get involved in my affairs?'

'Just what are you accusing me of?'

'Don't know. That's the thing. But it seems dashed smoky to me. When you consider that Chepstow, a man I've known all my life, skipped town rather than risk getting tangled with females intent on marriage.'

'You can't know that. He could have left town for any number of reasons.'

'He's running scared,' Havelock insisted. 'He would have bolted from the club after foisting me on to Ashe, if he'd thought he could get away with it.'

Morgan looked out of the window. Sighed. Looked back at Havelock. Lifted his chin so that when he spoke, he did so down his nose.

'I have a sister,' he said defiantly. 'Who is of an age to get married. And I would walk over hot coals rather than see her married to a man like you.'

'A man like me?' His voice came out rapier sharp. 'What, precisely, do you mean by that?' He was from one of the oldest families in the land. Everyone knew him. He was welcome everywhere. Not a scandalous word had ever been whispered about him.

Except, perhaps, about the duels he'd fought.

Though he'd fought them over matters of honour, not *dis*honour.

'A man,' said Morgan in an equally chilling tone,

'who won't love his wife. The last thing I want is for my sister to get drawn into a loveless marriage.'

'Oh.' He shrugged. 'That puts a different complexion on the matter. I have a sister myself. Well, half-sister, to be precise. But even so, I would walk over hot coals for her.' In fact, that was very nearly what he was doing.

'So you see why I'm keen to get you off the marriage mart, before she comes to town?'

'Oh, absolutely. Would do the same myself, if I thought Julia was in danger of getting tangled up with an unsuitable man. Like a shot.'

They nodded at each other with grudging respect.

'Westminster Abbey, though? Really, Morgan, could you not have thought of somewhere a little more conducive to courtship?'

Morgan's craggy face relaxed into something resembling a smile. 'You are the only one thinking in terms of courtship. I have no intention of taking a risk with either of those Pargetter girls. But it will be out of the wind and rain, at all events. And large enough that our two parties may drift apart…'

'So that I can get Miss Carpenter to myself while you play the elder off against the younger,' he said. 'Morgan, you're as cunning as a fox.'

'Not really,' he said diffidently. 'Just well versed in the ways of women. I have,' he added with a wry twist to his mouth, '*two* half-sisters, and a stepsister under my guardianship. There's not much you can tell me about tears and tantrums, scenes staged to persuade me to do something against my better judgement, campaigns designed to wear a man down…'

'I get the picture,' he said with an appreciative shudder. 'You clearly know exactly how the female mind works.' And thank God for it. And for Morgan's willingness to see him safely married before his own sister came to town for her Season.

'Come *on*, Mary,' Dotty urged. 'That's Mr Morgan and Lord Havelock knocking on the front door now and you haven't even chosen which bonnet you're going to wear.'

The girls, determined they should all look their best for this outing with the most eligible men it had ever been their good fortune to come across, had spent the previous evening, and the best part of this morning, ransacking their wardrobe for items to lend Mary.

'The brown velvet,' said Lotty firmly, ramming the bonnet on to Mary's head. 'Sober colour, to suit your sense of what you should be wearing for mourning, yet the bronze satin rose just takes the plainness off. And if you say you don't care what you look like one more time,' she said, tying the ribbons deftly under her chin, 'I shall go off into strong hysterics.'

There was no arguing with the sisters. And if she persisted, she was afraid she was going to take the shine off their own pleasure in the outing.

Resigned to her fate, Mary trailed the girls down the stairs, hanging back while they launched themselves with great gusto, this time, at *both* of the gentlemen who'd come to take them out.

For Mr Pargetter, upon hearing Lord Havelock's name, had divulged that though he was only a viscount, and never likely to be an earl, he was very well-to-do.

While that information had sent his daughters into raptures, it had just made Mary wonder, again, what on earth he'd been doing at such an unfashionable event as the Crimmers' annual Advent ball. If he was as wealthy as Mr Pargetter thought, he couldn't have been searching for an heiress. She peered up at him, perplexed, as he handed her into the carriage. Could he possibly be thinking of going into politics? Perhaps he'd decided to mingle with the kind of men whose votes he would have to canvass and find out what they thought about various issues. Climbing boys, for instance.

Only, that didn't explain why he'd wasted so much time with her, when he could have been mingling with the men, who were the ones who had the votes.

It was only when he smiled at her that she realised she'd been staring at him with a puzzled frown all the while he'd been taking his own seat opposite her.

Swiftly, she averted her gaze and peered intently out of the window. She had to stop making conjectures about what drove Lord Havelock and make the most of her first foray out of the immediate vicinity of Bloomsbury to see if she could spot an employment agency. But no matter how she strained her eyes, she simply couldn't make out what might be engraved on any of the brass door plates of the buildings they passed. And it wasn't the kind of thing she could ask.

Lotty and Dotty wouldn't understand her desire for independence. The yearning to be able to stand on her own two feet and not have to rely on a man for anything.

Though at least they weren't making any attempt to include her in the flirtatious sallies they were directing at Mr Morgan and Lord Havelock. They'd drawn the line at getting her dressed up smartly and practically bundling her into the carriage.

And so intent were they on dazzling the two gentlemen that they didn't appear to notice when she started lagging behind them the minute they got inside the Abbey.

She'd started hanging back more out of habit than anything, but before long she was craning her neck in genuine awe at the roof, wondering how the builders had managed to get stone looking like acres of starched lace. She barely noticed their chatter gradually fading into the distance.

'Miss Carpenter?'

Lord Havelock was standing watching her, a concerned expression on his face. And she realised she ought to have made an effort, for once, to stay part of the group. Loitering here, obliging him to wait for her, might have made it look as if she wanted to be alone with him. And she didn't want him thinking that!

'It has just occurred to me,' he said, preventing her from stammering any of the excuses that leapt to mind, 'that it wasn't particularly tactful of us, was it, to arrange an outing to a place like this. With you so recently bereaved?'

Goodness. It wasn't like a man to consider a woman's feelings.

'I can clearly recall how it felt to lose my own mother,' he said, when she carried on gaping at him in complete shock. 'I was only about…well, a similar age to the floury boy of yesterday…'

'You mean Will?' The mention of her favourite cousin brought a smile to her lips without her having to make any effort whatever.

Lord Havelock smiled in response, looking very relieved. It was a warning that she really ought to make more effort to conceal her thoughts, if even a stranger could tell she was blue-devilled.

'You like the boy?'

'He's a little scamp,' she said fondly. 'The hope of the family, being the only surviving male, you see, and hopelessly indulged.'

'Hmm.' He crooked his arm and she laid her hand on his sleeve for the second time. The strength of his arm wasn't as alarming this time. Perhaps because he'd shown her several kindnesses. Besides, if they walked swiftly, they could soon catch up with her cousins and Mr Morgan.

Only, how could she get him to walk faster, when he seemed set on strolling along at a snail's pace?

'But to return to your own loss,' he said. 'The one thing I would not have wanted to do, in the weeks immediately following my own mother's funeral, was spend an afternoon wandering through a lot of tombs.'

'Oh? But this is different,' she said. 'These tombs are all of very grand people. Not in the least like the simple grassy plot in the churchyard where my mother was laid to rest. No…this is…is history. I confess, I didn't really want to come here. But now we are here…'

His face brightened. 'Would you care to have a look at Shakespeare's monument, then? I believe it is this way,' he said, indicating an aisle that branched away from the direction the rest of the party were headed.

'Oh, um…' She couldn't very well object, not when she'd just claimed to have an interest in old tombs, could she?

And what could possibly happen to her in a church, anyway?

'Just a quick look, before we join the others,' she said. 'I don't expect I shall have leisure to do much sightseeing, before much longer, and I would—'

She broke off, flushed and curled into herself again. She'd almost let slip that she was only going to stay with the Pargetters until she could find a paid position. What was it about this man that kept on tempting her to share confidences? It was time she deflected attention away from herself. It shouldn't be too hard. All she'd have to do would be to ask him about himself. Once a man started talking about himself, nothing short of a riot would stop him.

'You said you lost your own mother at a very young age. That must have been very hard for you.'

'Oh, my father pretty soon made sure I had another one,' he said with evident bitterness.

She wished she hadn't said anything now. It was clearly a painful topic for him. And though she racked her brains, she couldn't think of anything to say to undo the awkwardness she'd caused. An awkwardness that resulted in them walking the entire length of the south transept in silence.

'What did you mean, Miss Carpenter,' he eventually said, once they'd reached their destination, 'about not having leisure to do much sightseeing?'

Oh, drat the man. Why did he have to keep asking such personal questions? He couldn't really be interested. Besides, she had no intention of admitting that she wasn't totally happy to reside with the Pargetters. Especially not now, when she could see Dotty and Lotty sauntering towards them. They'd been so kind to her. She couldn't possibly hurt them by broadcasting the fact she wanted to leave.

'Oh, look,' she exclaimed, to create a diversion. 'Sheridan!'

'What?'

She pointed to the nearest monument. 'Only fancy him being buried here. And Chaucer. My goodness!'

He dutifully examined the plaques to which she was pointing, though from the set of his lips, he wasn't really interested.

'Hi! You, boy! Stop!'

Mary whirled in the direction of the cry, shocked to hear anyone daring to raise their voice in the reverent atmosphere of the ancient building, and saw Mr Morgan shaking his fist at a raggedy urchin, who was running in their direction.

Lord Havelock let go of her arm and grabbed the boy by the collar when he would have darted past.

The urchin squirmed in his grip. Lashed out with a foot. Lord Havelock twisted his fingers into the material of the boy's collar and held him at arm's length, with apparent ease, so that the boy's feet, and swinging fists, couldn't land any blows on anyone.

The boy promptly let loose with a volley of words that had Lord Havelock giving him a shake.

'That's enough of that,' he said severely. 'Those aren't the kind of words you should ever utter when ladies are present, leave alone when you're in church. I beg his pardon, Miss Carpenter,' he said, darting her an apologetic look.

She was on the verge of admitting she'd heard far worse coming from her own father's lips, but Morgan was almost upon them, his beetling brows drawn down in anger. And her brief urge to confide in anyone turned tail and fled.

'What's to do, Morgan?'

'The little b—boy has lifted my purse,' Mr Morgan snarled. Reaching down, he ran his hands over the squirming boy's jacket, evading all the lad's swings from his grubby little fists.

A verger came bustling over just as Mr Morgan recovered his property. 'My apologies, my lords, ladies,' he said, dipping into something between a bow and a curtsy. 'I cannot think how a person like this managed to get in here.'

Dotty and Lotty came upon the scene, arm in arm as though needing each other for support.

'If you will permit me,' said the verger, reaching out a hand towards the boy, who had ceased struggling as though realising it was pointless when he was so vastly outnumbered. 'I will see that he is handed over to the proper authorities.'

'Yes, see that you do,' snarled Morgan as the verger clamped his pudgy hand round the boy's wrist. 'It comes to something when a man cannot even safely walk through a church without getting his pockets picked.'

'He will be suitably punished for his audacity, attacking and robbing innocent persons upon hallowed ground, never you fear, sir,' declared the verger.

Mary's heart was pounding. Could Mr Morgan really be so cruel as to have him dragged off to prison?

Lord Havelock, she suddenly noticed, hadn't relinquished his hold on the boy's collar.

'Hold on,' he said. 'Morgan, this isn't… I mean, I think this has gone far enough.'

The two men glared at each other, locked in a silent battle of wills.

The boy, sensing his fate hung in the balance, knuckled at his eyes, and wailed, 'Oh, please don't send me to gaol, sirs. For lifting a purse as fat as yours, I'd like as not get me neck stretched. And I wouldn't have lifted it if I weren't so hungry.'

'A likely tale,' said the verger, giving the boy's arm a little tug. But Lord Havelock kept his fingers stubbornly twisted into the boy's clothing.

Mary saw that Dotty and Lotty were clinging to each other, clearly appalled by the situation, but too scared of offending Mr Morgan to say what they really thought.

Well, *she* didn't care what he thought of her. She couldn't stand by and let a child suffer such a horrid fate.

'For shame,' she cried, rounding on Mr Morgan. 'How can you want to send a child to prison, when his only crime is to be hungry?'

'He lifted my purse....'

'Which he can see you can spare! You are so rich, I don't suppose you have ever known what it is to be hungry, to be desperate, to have nowhere to go.'

'Now, now, miss,' said the verger. 'We don't want raised voices in here. Please moderate your tone....'

'Moderate my tone!' She whirled on the plump, cassocked man. 'Your creed demands you *feed* the hungry, not toss them in prison. You should be offering him food and shelter, and help, not punishing him for being in want!'

Lotty and Dotty stared at her as though she had gone quite mad. Actually, everyone was staring at her. She pressed her hands to her cheeks, shocked at herself for speaking with such fervour, and disrespect, to a man of the cloth. For raising her voice at all. Whatever had come over her?

But then, the shocked silence that echoed round them was broken by Lord Havelock's crisp, biting voice.

'Quite,' he said with a decisive nod. And then turned

to the verger. 'And I really don't care for the way you just spoke to Miss Carpenter. Look, Morgan, you have your property back, can you not…let him go?'

Mary took a step that placed her next to him. Side by side they faced the rest of the group.

He really was rather a…rather a wonderful person. She'd been able to tell he hadn't liked the notion of throwing the pickpocket in gaol, from the way he'd refused to relinquish him into the verger's custody. But she'd never expected him to spring to *her* defence, as well. It was just about the most…amazing, surprising thing that had ever happened to her.

'Thank you, my lord,' she breathed, darting him a shy glance. And noting that the way the sunlight glanced off his bright bronze curls made him look like… Well, with his strong hand clamped firmly behind the little boy's scrawny neck, he could have been a model for a guardian angel. The rather fearsome kind who protected the weak and downtrodden against oppression.

'Not at all, Miss Carpenter,' he replied grimly. 'I believe you have the right of it. This boy's nothing but a bag of bones. When,' he said, turning his attention to the dirty scrap of humanity he held in one fist, 'did you last have anything to eat?'

The boy squinted up at him. 'Can't remember. Not yesterday, that's for sure. Day before, mebbe…'

At that, even Morgan looked taken aback. 'Look,' he began, 'I had no idea…'

The boy's face twisted into an expression of contempt. 'Your sort never do. She's right…' he jerked his head in Mary's direction '…got no idea what it feels like to have nuffink. Or what you'll do just to earn a penny or two….'

'If you had the means to earn an honest living, would you, though?' Havelock shook him by the coat collar. 'Or would you just keep right on thieving?'

The boy snorted in derision. 'Who'd give me a job? I ain't got no trade. No learnin' neither.'

'If you can learn to pick pockets, you can learn an honest trade,' said Lord Havelock witheringly. Then he frowned. 'Don't suppose anyone would want to take the risk, though.' He closed his eyes, drew a deep breath and sighed it out.

'My town house could probably use a boot boy,' he said. 'You'd get a bed to sleep in, meals provided and a wage, if you kept your nose clean.'

The boy promptly straightened up and wiped his nose with the back of his hand.

'I got no wiper, but I'd try and keep it clean if I got all what you said.'

'Morgan? Will you let the matter drop if I take charge of the boy?'

'I… Well, if you are prepared to attempt to rehabilitate him, I suppose I can do no less.'

Dotty and Lotty heaved a sigh, showing they were as relieved as Mary to see the boy escape the full force of the law.

'Then if you will excuse me, ladies,' he said, bowing first to her cousins, and then to her, 'I had better take him there myself. Straight away. And hope that his arrival won't induce my butler to leave,' he grumbled.

He was scowling as he led the boy down the aisle. He didn't slacken his hold on his collar, either. Which was probably wise. Who knew but if he let the lad go, he wouldn't run straight back to whatever gutter he'd sprung from, and the associates who'd probably led him into his life of crime in the first place?

Damn Morgan for foisting this guttersnipe on him. Obliging him to leave, just when he was beginning to coax Miss Carpenter out of her shell.

Still, he supposed this little test had proved that she was capable of coming out of it when sufficiently roused. She'd been shaking like a leaf, but she'd managed to speak out against what was clearly a gross injustice.

For the sake of a child.

He pulled up short, turned and glanced back at her.

To find her gazing back at him, with a rapt expression on her face.

She hid it at once, by bowing her head and turning away, but he'd caught something in her look that had been encouraging. It was approval. And warmth. And, not to put too fine a point on it, something that verged on downright hero worship.

There would be no trouble getting to speak to her next time he paid a call. He could use the pretext of telling her how the boy had settled in to his new life. And take it from there.

'I want me penny,' said the boy, the moment they emerged from the great church door into the drizzle that they'd gone inside to escape.

'Your what?'

'My penny,' said the boy. 'That other cove said as how you'd give me a penny if I lifted his purse, then ran straight into you and let you catch me.'

'I,' said Havelock firmly, 'am not going to give you a penny.'

'I might have known. You swindler…'

'I'm going to give you something better,' he interrupted.

'Oh, yeah?' The boy's face brightened.

'Yes. I'm going to give you that job I promised. A man has to keep his word, you see? Especially when he gives it to a lady.'

Chapter Four

Overnight the drizzle drifted away, leaving the sky cloudless. When the girls awoke, there was a layer of frosted ice on the inside of their bedroom window.

They shivered, red-nosed, into their clothes and rushed downstairs to the warmth of the parlour.

The moment she got downstairs though, Mary wished it wasn't quite so cold in their room, or she could have found some excuse to stay there. For her aunt was still upset with her over what the girls had told her of their outing to Westminster Abbey.

'I cannot think what came over you,' said Aunt Pargetter as she poured Mary's tea. 'To have raised your voice to Mr Morgan…'

'I am sorry, truly sorry, if my behaviour has offended you.'

'It didn't offend me,' said Lotty, wrapping her fingers round the cup that contained her own, freshly poured, steaming hot tea.

'Nor me,' added Dotty. 'I only wish I'd had the courage to speak up for the boy when that nasty verger threatened him with gaol. He couldn't have been any older than Will.'

'It wasn't a matter of *courage*,' Mary protested. She wasn't a courageous person. Not at all. 'I just…' She shook her head. To be truthful, she had no idea why she'd picked that particular moment to finally speak her mind. She just… She'd had to endure so much, in silence, for so long. She knew what it felt like to have nothing. To be at the mercy of strangers. And yesterday, it was as though a lifetime of resenting injustice, of knowing that the strong naturally oppressed the weak and trampled down the poor for being of no account, all came to a head and erupted without, for once, her giving a fig for the consequences.

'I just couldn't help myself.'

'I'm not denying you were right to *feel* as you did,' said Aunt Pargetter. 'But to risk driving away such an *eligible* suitor, by openly *challenging* him like that…'

'Mary did just as she ought,' said Mr Pargetter, folding up his newspaper and getting to his feet. 'The consequences must take care of themselves.'

A tense silence hovered over the breakfast table after he'd left the room. Until Dotty cleared her throat.

'You know,' she said, 'it didn't do Mary any harm in Lord Havelock's eyes.'

'No,' added Lotty. 'He looked at her as though he thoroughly approved of her standing up for the boy.'

'Hmmph,' said her aunt. 'Well, I suppose that is something.'

And though her aunt let the subject drop, the atmosphere remained tense throughout the rest of the morning, as they all waited to see if either of the gentlemen would call upon the house again.

Either Dotty or Lotty kept a vigil by the window,

while Mary kept close to the fire, steadily working her way through a basket of mending.

Until at length, Lotty let out a squeal of excitement.

'It's him! Them! Both of them! They've just got out of their carriage!'

Her cousins rushed to the mirror to check their appearance, before dashing to the sofa and striking relaxed poses. Which were only slightly marred by the way their chests rose and fell so rapidly.

It puzzled Mary to see the girls greet Mr Morgan with such enthusiasm, when his callous behaviour the day before had shocked them all so much.

She could have understood it if they'd flown to Lord Havelock's side, and showered *him* with praise, and pulled *him* down on to the sofa between them.

Instead, he was left standing just inside the door, watching them with a kind of amused disbelief.

Couldn't they see how…superior he was to Mr Morgan, in every way? When she thought of the way he'd lifted that boy out of the verger's reach…

Just as she was reflecting that she'd never seen a man use his physical strength to protect the defenceless before, he turned, caught her watching him and smiled at her.

Her stomach gave a funny little lurch. Her heart sped up.

She hastily lowered her head to stare at the sewing that lay in her lap.

She *wasn't* interested in him, not in the way Lotty and Dotty were interested in Mr Morgan. She just…she just couldn't deny it was flattering to have such a handsome, personable young man smile at her like that.

She hadn't been able to forget the look he'd shot her as he'd left the Abbey with the pickpocket still held firmly by his collar, either. Or the feeling that had come over her when he'd defended her from the verger's censure. It had washed over her again, several times the night before, while she'd been trying to get to sleep.

And it positively surged through her when he took a chair, carried it to her side and sat down.

'I bring good news,' declared Mr Morgan once the flurry of greetings had died down. 'The Serpentine has frozen over. Hard enough for us to go skating, if you ladies would enjoy it?'

Dotty and Lotty beamed and clapped their hands, saying what a wonderful idea it was. Just as though the incident the day before had never happened.

'You will be coming with us, won't you, Miss Carpenter?' said Lord Havelock, with a hopeful smile.

She shook her head.

'I cannot skate,' she said with what felt suspiciously like regret.

Regret? No! She didn't want to spend any more time than she had to with these two men. They both made her uncomfortable—Mr Morgan because of his harsh manner and Lord Havelock because of the tendency she had to say far more than she should when she was with him. And for feeling that she could say it to him. And most of all—she had to be honest with herself—because she found him so…attractive. Which made him downright dangerous.

'I will teach you,' said Lord Havelock, somehow turning up the warmth in his smile in such a way that she wished it wouldn't be such a terrible idea to draw closer to him and warm herself at it.

'Oh, Mary, please! You have to go,' begged Dotty.

'Yes. For we cannot go out and leave you here on your own,' pointed out Lotty.

And they both really, really wanted to go.

There was nothing for it but to surrender with good grace.

With cries of glee, the girls took her upstairs to ransack their wardrobe again, going back down only when all three of them were swathed in gloves, scarves, boots and several extra layers of petticoats.

Her cousins sat one on either side of Mr Morgan in the carriage, which meant that she and Lord Havelock were sat next to each other, with their backs to the horses.

Once they'd tucked luxurious fur rugs round their legs, they set off. Even though the carriage was very well sprung, and they had far more room than the three squeezed together on the opposite seat, every so often the jolting of the carriage meant that their legs bumped. Whenever she felt the warmth of Lord Havelock's thigh pressing against hers beneath the concealment of the fur, everything else faded into the background. The chatter of her cousins, the buildings at which she was pretending to look through the window—none of it reached her senses. Once or twice, he made an attempt to speak to her, but she wasn't able to give a coherent reply. It was a relief when they arrived, and the gentlemen got out so they could help the ladies down.

Lotty and Dotty stuck close to Mr Morgan, which meant Lord Havelock was left to escort Mary.

She laid her gloved hand on his outstretched arm and let him lead her to the frozen expanse of water, besides which several enterprising people had set up various stalls to earn what money they could from this unexpected cold spell.

The men hired skates from a booth where a ruddy-cheeked woman helped to fit them over their boots.

Dotty and Lotty rushed on to the ice, shrieking with laughter and clutching at each other for support as they almost fell over. Mr Morgan went to their rescue, offering them one arm each. Clinging to him, the trio set out, wobbling and giggling, across the frozen lake.

Which left her alone with Lord Havelock.

'Come, you need not be afraid,' he said with a sincerity that made her wish she could trust him. Made her wish she could let go of her habitual distrust of the entire male sex, just once.

'I won't let you fall.'

It wasn't falling she was worried about. It was the increasing frequency with which she was having foolish, feminine thoughts about him. Foolish, feminine reactions, too.

She gave Lotty and Dotty a wistful look. They weren't tying themselves up in knots about the wisdom of plastering themselves to a man and relying on his strength and balance to keep them from falling over. They were just enjoying themselves.

There were skaters of all ages, shapes and sizes twirling about on the ice. All looking as though they were having a splendid time. Life didn't offer many opportunities like this, to try something new and exciting. And the ice probably wouldn't last all that long. She might never get another chance to have a go at skating.

When had she last let herself go, the way they were doing? Living in the moment?

Having fun?

When had she got into the habit of being too afraid to reach out and attempt to take hold of the slightest chance at happiness?

She reached out and took the hand Lord Havelock was patiently holding out to her, vowing that today, at least, she would leave fear on the bank, launch out on to the ice and see what happened.

What happened was that the moment she set her feet on to the slippery surface, she very nearly fell over.

With a shriek that sounded remarkably similar to the ones erupting from her cousins' lips, she grabbed at Lord Havelock, who was maintaining his own stance with what looked like total ease.

'I hadn't thought it would be so hard to just stand upright,' she said. 'How do you manage to make it look so effortless?'

He shrugged. 'I've skated a few times before. But I had my share of falls the first time I tried it, I can tell you. If you have any sense of balance, you'll get the hang of it in no time.'

Mary made a tentative effort to let go of his arm. Each of her legs promptly attempted to go in opposite directions. How vexing. It was only by clinging to Lord Havelock that she could even manage to stay upright.

'Perhaps you will fare better once we get going,' he suggested. And then, without waiting for her agreement, made a move that somehow set them both gliding away from the shore.

'See? That's better, is it not?'

'Not,' she gasped, clinging to his arm for dear life. She had no control over the situation at all. Whenever she attempted to wrest it back, her feet went skittering off all over the place, resulting in her having to clutch at him with increasing desperation.

Though neither Lotty nor Dotty looked any more accomplished. They were both clinging to Mr Morgan with what looked like the same desperation she felt, though being far more vocal about their slips, shrieking and laughing with an abandon that she almost envied.

'Oh! Oh, dear,' she gasped as, once again, her outside leg shot off on a course she hadn't expected.

'This will never do,' said Lord Havelock. 'You'll fare a lot better if you let me put my arm round your waist, see, like this.'

He did so, tucking her into his side, and then pushing off with the leg that was nearest her own. She felt the power of it propelling them forward as he reached across her front and took hold of her other hand.

'My lord, I'm not at all sure this is quite proper,' she squeaked in something very close to panic.

'It's only like a sort of dance hold.'

That was true. But in a dance they'd only be as close as this for a moment or two, whilst turning into a new figure. Not plastered to each other from hip to shoulder for as long as he chose to keep them like that.

'Please,' she begged him. 'This is making me feel…' warm. Yearning. Excited '…most uncomfortable.'

He glanced down at her. She was sure her cheeks must be bright red.

'I beg your pardon,' he said, with a sigh of what sounded like regret. 'I did not mean… That is, I do not want you to feel I'm taking advantage. Let me just steer us both across to the side, there, and you can catch hold of that tree and see if you can manage to stand up on your own, now you've had a bit of a go.'

'Thank you,' she managed to say, since it was the polite response to the gentlemanly way he'd reacted to her protest. But it wasn't easy to thank him for finding it so easy to let go of her. It meant he wasn't all that keen on having her hang on to his arm. Though why she should find that so disappointing she couldn't think. What on earth was the matter with her?

'Thank you,' she gasped, again, when he'd delivered her to the promised tree, untangled their arms and helped her to get a good hold on a low branch. 'Oh, dear, this is most awkward.' Her legs were shaking so much, she felt sure he must be able to see it. She glanced his way, expecting to encounter a look of masculine scorn, only to find that he'd taken up the kind of stance she'd seen fielders take on a cricket pitch. As though he was braced to catch…her. Should she fall.

He had very strong, very capable hands. She'd thought so the day before, when he'd had hold of the little boy.

'How did he go on? The little boy you took home with you yesterday?'

He blinked.

'It was very good of you to offer him work, instead of letting Mr—' She broke off as the branch she'd been holding showed signs of giving way. With a wobble, and a lunge, she got hold of another one.

'I couldn't bear to think of him being thrown in prison. It's been on my mind all night. I'm glad,' she said, lifting her chin, 'that we are a little apart from the others so I can ask you about it.'

He didn't reply straight away. In fact, he looked a touch…uncomfortable.

'You don't mind me asking you about him, do you?' Oh, dear. Perhaps she shouldn't have said anything. But it felt so very strange being alone with him like this, under the shelter of the tree. Not that they were alone, exactly. There were dozens of other people whizzing about on the ice. Yet there was a certain intimacy about the way there was nobody else within hearing distance. An intimacy that she'd instinctively tried to dispel.

'First of all,' he said, squaring his shoulders, 'I have to confess that I didn't exactly take him home. I live in a cosy little set of rooms, y'see, which are too small to take in stray boys. Besides, I wouldn't know what to do with a lad like that. And nor would my valet.'

'Oh, never say you abandoned him?'

'Absolutely not!'

He looked so affronted she immediately wanted to beg his pardon. But before she could do so, he went on, 'I have another property in town. Durant House. Huge great barn of a place. I took him there.'

'Then why…?'

'If you must know, I feel a bit of a fraud accepting any praise for my actions when the task of reforming the wretch will fall to the staff of Durant House. I really did very little.'

'Oh.'

'Please don't be too disappointed in me.'

Her gaze flew to his face. The words were apologetic, but his tone was confrontational.

'I could have made up some tale that would have made you look at me the way you did yesterday,' he pointed out a touch belligerently. 'As though I were some kind of hero. Instead I've chosen to tell you the truth. Because I never want there to be any misunderstanding between us.'

Well, how was she supposed to respond to that? Given

the choice, she would have mumbled something vapid and moved away. But she couldn't go anywhere. All she could do was cling to the tree, study his boots and tell herself he couldn't possibly be implying he was planning to prolong their acquaintance.

And yet, the way he kept looking at her…

'And while we're about it, I have something else to confess, too. I deliberately got you alone, so that I could talk to you freely. For I have something I particularly wanted to ask you.'

'Oh?' She winced. How many times had she said that this afternoon? He must be starting to think she was a complete ninny.

'Yes. You said something about not being in London long and having plans. I know you do not want your cousins to know about these plans. But perhaps you might feel you could confide in me?'

'Why would I want to do that?'

'I may be able to help you.'

'I doubt that very much.'

'You won't know unless you tell me.'

'Why would you even want to help me? I am a complete stranger to you.'

'And yet something about you calls to me,' he said, giving her a look that was unlike anything she'd ever seen in a man's eyes before.

'You do not appear to have anyone to help you. You need…a friend.'

Suddenly everything fell into place with sickening disappointment. She couldn't bear to think Lord Havelock was the kind of man who preyed on defenceless females. When he'd taken that robber boy under his wing, she even started to think that…to think that…

Oh, how could she have been so naïve?

'I do not want the kind of friendship you are offering me,' she snapped. 'Poor I may be, but I would never, ever...'

His brows snapped down. 'Nor would I, ever, make a gently bred girl the kind of offer you seem to think I'm about to make. What kind of man do you think I am?'

She flushed. Felt her insides skid about as much as when she'd tried to walk a straight path on the ice. 'I...I don't know what kind of man you are, that's just the point. I just cannot see why you should concern yourself over someone like me. I'm nobody. And it's not as if I'm even pretty. And you're so handsome and dashing you could have any girl you want at the snap of your fingers.'

In mortification, her hand flew to her mouth, though it was too late to stop the words that had tumbled out.

And letting go of the branch proved to be as reckless as speaking her mind. For her left leg promptly shot off to the right while her right leg went straight forward. She had no choice but to grab hold of the front of Lord Havelock's coat, which had the effect of spinning them both right round, then landing her flush up against the tree trunk, with her wedged between it and the solid bulk of his body.

'So. You think I'm so handsome I could have any girl I wanted, do you?'

'I didn't mean it!' She uncurled her fingers and gave his coat a firm shove. It only had the effect of propelling her harder against the tree. 'At least,' her honesty compelled her to admit, 'I didn't mean to say it out loud.'

'But you did say it,' he replied with a grin, closing the small gap she'd opened up between them. 'Which gives me hope. I was beginning to think I'd never break through your defences.'

'B-break through my defences? Why would you want to do that? And as for saying never…why, we only met a handful of days ago.'

'And yet the attraction was instant. And powerful. You feel it, too. Though you are trying to resist it.'

She hadn't thought it possible to feel more embarrassed, but hearing him lay her innermost soul bare in that way, when she hadn't even worked it all out for herself, was utterly mortifying.

'You don't need to resist it, Miss Carpenter. For I want you, too. Very much. And just so there is no misunderstanding about it, I mean, as my wife.'

It was just as well she was wedged between the tree, and his body, because the shock of hearing him propose took all the strength from her legs.

'Your wife? But you cannot!'

'Why not?'

'Because we know nothing about each other.'

'We know enough,' he said, giving her another one of those melting looks. She was suddenly very aware of how close they were. And how their breath, rising on the air in two plumes of white vapour, mingled and merged not very far up into one cloud.

'Let me prove it to you.'

He began to lower his head. Her breath hitched in her throat. He was going to attempt to kiss her. And there was no way to escape. If he let go of her, she would fall over.

That was the moment she realised he wasn't actually holding her. No, she was the one who was clinging to him, or at least, to his coat. But it was only so that she wouldn't fall over. Not because…

Not because…

And anyway, if she really, really didn't want him to kiss her, all she would have to do was turn her head away and his lips would land relatively harmlessly on her cheek.

But she couldn't move her head. She stayed frozen in place while his mouth came closer and closer to hers. Until his lips touched hers. Pressed, and caressed, and coaxed her own apart. And then their breath was mingling not five feet up in the air, but in her very mouth. And the swirling sensation went right down through her stomach, getting hotter, and hotter, until she wondered that the ice beneath their feet did not melt and suck them down into a vortex that would drown them both.

She'd never felt anything like it in her life. So powerfully all-consuming. So compelling that she didn't care if carrying on experiencing it did melt the ice and she drowned.

With a whimper, she pressed up against him and slid her arms round his waist. His own went round hers, so that she was no longer the one clinging to him, but they were clinging to each other.

'So,' he breathed, ending the most wonderful encounter she'd ever had in her life, 'you will marry me, then?'

'What?' Hearing him persist in talking of marriage felt like plunging right through the ice into the black void beneath. 'No!'

She tried to pull out of his arms, skidded and had no choice but to grab hold of him again.

'What do you mean no?' He frowned down at her. 'You enjoyed that kiss as much as I did.'

'That is not the point.'

'Then what is the point? What can you possibly want from life, if you can turn up your nose at a proposal from a *dashing*, *handsome*, and I'll have you know, solvent peer of the realm? Who could have any other woman for the snapping of my fingers?'

She sucked in a short, shocked breath. How cruel of him to fling her very own words back in her face.

And his face was hard now, harder than she'd ever seen it. Gone was the mask of affability he'd worn when he'd been trying to win her round. Gone the charming smile and the warmth in his eyes. It had been replaced by something with which she was far more familiar.

Cold, hard anger.

Oh, but it was just as well she'd seen this side of him, before it was too late. Before she'd forgotten just how miserable her father had made her mother, within the cage that their marriage had become. She would never, ever, let a man bully her and break her down. Nor coerce her with…with deceitfully delightful kisses!

This time when she tried to break from his hold, he let her go. As though he'd recognised the determination in her eyes and realised it was over.

'The only sort of man I would even consider marrying,' she retorted, 'not that I have any intention of doing anything so stupid, would be…would be…a sailor!'

'A what?'

'You heard me. A sailor.'

'Why the deuce would you prefer a sailor to me?'

'Because a sailor,' she snapped, almost beside herself with fury at the way she was having to hang on to a tree merely to maintain her upright position, while he was standing there, hands on his hips, looking down his nose at her with the kind of disdain only an aristocrat could ever muster, 'would hand over his money, and go off to sea for months, perhaps even years, and leave me in peace to live exactly as I wished!'

There. That had done it. He'd stalk away now—or rather skate away—without a backward glance. And never deign to so much as recognise her if he saw her in the street.

But to her astonishment, he did no such thing. On the contrary, the anger that had seemed to consume him vanished as he flung back his head and burst out laughing.

'You are perfect,' he cried, taking hold of her by the elbows and restoring her to a more upright stance. 'Absolutely perfect. You no more want to get married than I do!'

'But…if you don't want to get married, then why…?'

'Look, there are reasons why I need to have a wife. Which I won't go into just yet. But I am definitely willing to hand over a deal of my money, and leave you alone, if that's what you want. We can live virtually separate lives, if, after an initial period, you find you really can't stand the sight of me. I shan't cut up rough. You'll still have a generous allowance.'

'An allowance?' She couldn't quite get her breath. She shook her head. 'I don't understand….'

'Come, Miss Carpenter, I can see you are tempted, if not by my kisses, then at least by my money.'

'That sounds… You're making me sound horrible. Mercenary….'

'Then what can I offer you, that would make you agree to take my hand? Name it. Whatever it is you've always craved, and feared you could never have, I will give it to you.'

'You can't want to marry me that much….'

'So there is something? I knew it. Tell me and it shall be yours.'

'It isn't anything…really.'

'It's something.'

'Well, it's just that of late…' She stopped and shook her head.

'Yes? Come on, tell me. If it is in my power to give it, I will.'

'It will probably sound silly to you. But…oh, I so wish I could have a room of my own. A room I can do whatever I want in. Where people have to knock before they come in. A room that nobody can ever turn me out of…' She faltered to a halt as tears stung her eyes. She hadn't realised how precious privacy was, until she'd been forced out of her childhood home, and had to rely on the grudging charity of others. Even here, in London, she had to share not only a room, but a bed, with two other girls. They'd made space for her, but it was just a corner. And she was sick of having to make do with just claiming a corner of other people's rooms.

'You want security,' he said, once more hitting the nail on the head. 'I can give you that. And as for privacy, well, I have several properties. And you may have your very own room in each one of them.'

'Really?' It sounded too good to be true. 'But I still don't understand why…'

'Never you mind about why,' he grated. 'Just think about this.' And without further ado, he pulled her into his arms, and kissed her again. And this time, there was nothing gentle, or tentative, about it. This kiss was one that claimed her, body and soul. She had no more chance of escaping him than a snowball did of surviving in the kitchen fire.

She melted into him, swept away by his ardour, her own body's clamouring and the joyous thought that if she agreed to his proposal, she would have a place of her own. Money to spend as she wanted.

And kisses like this.

She came out of her blissful haze to the sound of Dotty and Lotty, shrieking.

And opened her eyes to see them speeding across the ice towards her.

Lord Havelock spun round to face them, his arm snaking round her waist as they offered their congratulations on a betrothal she hadn't actually voiced her agreement to.

But she couldn't very well say so. Why else would she have been kissing a man, in broad daylight, unless it was because they'd just become engaged?

Then something struck her. 'You can both skate. You don't need Mr Morgan to stop you falling over at all!'

Dotty and Lotty, completely unabashed, giggled, took her by an arm each and towed her away from her…well, she supposed she had to call him her fiancé.

'If he'd known we could skate, do you think he would have let us hang on to him like that? He's the most hardened case in town. Girls have been trying to get him to the altar since…oh, for ever, and nobody has yet got as far as either of us did today.'

She blinked at them in shock. They'd been pretending they couldn't skate, just so they could get close to him?

She'd never heard of anything so…unscrupulous!

Unless it was letting everyone think she'd just accepted a proposal, when she had no intention of doing any such thing.

Chapter Five

He held her hand, in the carriage, all the way home.

She could have tugged it free, she supposed, but then she would have to explain herself.

And she had no excuse. None. She couldn't very well claim Lord Havelock had forced those kisses on her. She'd put her arms round him and kissed him back. With some enthusiasm.

And Dotty and Lotty looked so pleased for her. Even Mr Morgan had a twinkle in his eye, and a smile that softened that stern mouth whenever he glanced at their clasped hands.

Her stomach clenched into a cold, hard knot. If she made any attempt, now, to tell them they'd all made a terrible mistake, then…well, she wasn't sure quite what would happen, but there was bound to be a dreadful scene. She'd upset everyone badly enough by shouting at a man in public. What would they make of her *kissing* one?

It would be better to wait till they got home. She'd beg a few moments alone with her aunt, and try to explain what had happened. And then…

And then the carriage stopped, and Lotty and Dotty leapt out and went bounding up the front steps, shrieking out the news of her betrothal.

And when Aunt Pargetter came to the front door, it was to Lord Havelock she held out her hands. Even when Mary made frantic signals, behind his back, to try to convey her need to speak with her, she paid no heed.

'In a moment, Mary,' she said. 'His lordship wants to have a private word with me first. Since Mr Pargetter is not at home just now. Though I can guess what you want to say,' she finished, shooting him an arch look.

'No, no, I don't think you could possibly…' she said, though her voice was drowned out by Lord Havelock saying, 'My behaviour has been a little unconventional. I should have approached you, that is to say, Mr Pargetter, first, and asked your permission to pay my addresses.'

'Not at all,' said Aunt Pargetter, ushering him into her husband's study. 'We aren't legally Mary's guardians, you know. She is free to make her own choices.'

'Nevertheless…'

And then the study door closed on whatever he'd been about to say, leaving Mary on the wrong side of it.

Free to make her own choices! If only that were true.

And then Dotty and Lotty were shooing her into the front parlour and divesting her of her coat.

'She's in a complete daze,' said Dotty, untying the ribbons of her bonnet.

'No wonder,' said Lotty, pushing her into a chair. 'His lordship swept her completely off her feet.'

'No, he didn't, it was the opposite. He stopped her slipping over,' quipped Dotty with a giggle. 'Got his arm round her waist and held her so tight she couldn't possibly have lost her footing.'

'Oh, I've never seen anything so romantic.'

'Romantic? No! I...'

'Oh, but it was,' sighed Dotty, pressing her hands to her heart and flinging herself backwards on to the sofa as though in a swoon.

'Aren't you cross with me? Why aren't you cross with me? When the whole purpose of going skating at all was to try and...and... Well, you were both trying so hard to attract Mr Morgan....'

Who was nowhere in sight, she suddenly realised. The moment they'd gone into the house, he'd slipped away, unnoticed in all the excitement.

'Oh, that's so sweet,' said Lotty. 'And so like you, to think of us, rather than yourself.'

Dotty bounced off the sofa, and flung her arms round her neck. 'You mustn't feel bad because you got a proposal, today, and not us. And as for Mr Morgan...' She made an airy gesture with one hand. 'When a man as wealthy as that, and single, comes your way you simply have to make a push to get him interested. But it's not as if either of us developed a *tendre* for him, did we, Lotty?'

Lotty shook her head so hard her ringlets bounced.

'Yes, but...' As she floundered to a halt against the impenetrable barrier of her own behaviour, Lotty and Dotty both collapsed in giggles again.

And then they heard the front door slam, and Aunt Pargetter came in, beaming all over her face.

'Mary, I'm so proud of you,' she said, enveloping her in a lavender-scented hug.

'No...you shouldn't be. I didn't mean to...'

'Well, I dare say that is what won him round. You are so very...modest. And...and, oh, everything a lady ought to be, I'm sure. A viscountess,' she exclaimed, sinking on to the sofa next to Dotty, gazing at her with starry eyes. 'You will be presented at court…'

The girls both squealed with an excitement that passed Mary by completely.

'And you will go to all the most *tonnish* events.'

'But…' Mary attempted to protest.

'And then,' she carried on, regardless, 'once you are established, you will be able to invite all those *tonnish* people to parties you throw.'

Mary blinked, completely unable to envision herself ever throwing any kind of party.

'And I just know you are too kind-hearted to forget my girls. This will be a foot in the door to a world they'd had no hope of entering otherwise. And with both of them being so pretty—no offence to you, my dear, but if you managed to land yourself a viscount, without even trying, only think what my girls could accomplish. I shouldn't wonder at it if this means an earl, or perhaps even a marquis.…'

No wonder they'd let Mr Morgan escape without a twinge of regret. The girls now had visions of getting themselves a title apiece.

'Aunt Pargetter, please! You don't understand. I never actually wanted to get married. I thought I would…find work as a housekeeper, or a governess, or something.…'

'Well, that is because you lived in such an out-of-the-way spot, and didn't have any prospects,' said her aunt complacently.

'And she feels a touch guilty,' explained Dotty. 'For stealing a march on us.'

'Oh, we don't begrudge you your good fortune,' said her aunt kindly.

'No, but…'

'Well, I can see this sudden reversal in your prospects has overwhelmed you,' she said, tilting her head to one side. 'And no wonder, if all you ever hoped for was to obtain some menial position. A good strong cup of tea is what you need.' She flicked her hand to Lotty, who went to the fireplace and pulled the bell to summon the maid.

'And you are so shy,' she added with a knowing nod, 'that having such a very…masculine man as Lord Havelock positively…bowl you over…'

'Yes, he did, Mama. He kissed her quite passionately.'

'Twice!'

Oh, if only the chair cushions would open up and swallow her whole.

'Oh,' said her aunt with a sympathetic look as Mary's face heated to what felt like boiling point. 'I see what this is. But, my dear,' she said, reaching across to pat her hand, 'Lord Havelock must be very taken with you, to propose so quickly. You know, I saw there was something, that very first night at the Crimmers'. Why, he started at the sight of you as though…as though his ship had come in, as you would probably say. It is clearly a case of love at first sight.'

As though that made it all right.

Except that it was most definitely *not* love at first sight. The things he'd said made that crystal clear. Like, going their separate ways, for instance. And being glad she was no more keen to marry than he was. Immediately after he'd proposed.

She shook her head in complete frustration. There was no way she was going to be able to get Aunt Pargetter to understand her reluctance to marry. Or the girls, not now their heads were full of eligible titled men.

There was only one thing for it. She would have to tell

Lord Havelock, to his face, that she couldn't go through with it.

And then—she glanced at the happy, glowing faces of her aunt and cousins—she'd have to endure their disappointment.

Lord Havelock was coming to call on Mary the very next day, Aunt Pargetter informed her husband over dinner that night. To talk about arrangements.

So Mary had all night to marshal her arguments. And the longer she thought, the more convinced she became that he wouldn't be all that bothered to have it all come to nothing. Hadn't he said he was no keener to get married than she was? He'd probably just thought he *had* to propose, after kissing her in such a public place. Especially as she'd made it crystal clear she wouldn't be his mistress.

It was the only reason that could possibly account for it.

Satisfied she'd reached the nub of the matter, and that Lord Havelock would be positively grateful when she let him off the hook, Mary finally drifted off to sleep. And if a few tears leaked from under her tightly closed eyelids, they were only a symptom of the extreme stress she'd been under all day. She was relieved, truly she was. And quite calm, now that the terrifying prospect of being shoehorned into a marriage she really, really didn't want was over.

It was strange, therefore, that the next morning she felt as though her limbs were weighted with lead.

It was worry, that was what was making it so hard to dress, or eat breakfast. Worry that she might not be able to persuade her aunt to let her have a few moments alone with Lord Havelock. The fear she might have to continue with the charade one moment longer.

So why did her heart sink still further when Lord Havelock was the one to ask if he could have some private speech with her? He was giving her the very opportunity she sought, to speak freely.

'Won't you sit down?' It was the only thing Mary could think of to say. She'd never been on her own in a room with a man and this one seemed to fill it with his presence. It wasn't as if he was particularly tall, but he was so full of energy. She could still feel the strength of him as he'd guided her round the ice the day before, his arm effortlessly pinning her to his side. How immovable he'd been when she'd tried to push him away after the kiss.

The kiss. She shouldn't have thought about the kiss. It made every single inch of her feel far too…feminine.

He took a seat as close to hers as he could find, which didn't help. Now he could reach out and take her hand, if he wanted. Or she could reach out and take his.

Not that she wanted to. Absolutely not!

'Thank you for agreeing to speak with me alone,' he said. 'I know it is a little unconventional, but there are things we do need to talk about.'

'Yes, there are,' she agreed. 'I understand that you felt obliged to make me an offer of marriage, yesterday, after kissing me.' She couldn't look at his face. Not with his mouth right there, close enough that if she leaned forward, and he leaned forward, just the tiniest bit, they could be kissing again. She looked hard at her hands instead, which she was clasping tightly on her lap. 'And

I'm also aware that you do not truly wish to marry me. And so I release you—'

'You jolly well don't!' He leapt to his feet again. 'No wriggling out of this. You gave me your word....'

'Actually, I didn't. You said a lot of things, and everyone congratulated us, but I never, not once, said I would marry you.'

'Well, you are going to marry me and that's that.'

'No.' She got to her feet, as well. She wasn't going to risk backing down simply because she felt intimidated with him looming over her like that. 'It is better to end this engagement now than to take a step we will both regret for the rest of our lives.'

She'd seen, at close quarters, just how miserable two people could become when bound together by chains of matrimony that neither of them wished for any longer.

'Our engagement will only end one way,' he growled, jabbing his forefinger at her. 'In marriage.'

She flinched at the first physical expression of his anger, but held her ground.

'I've already purchased the licence,' he rapped out. 'And spoken to your uncle, and taken a light-fingered guttersnipe into my employ all on your account. We. Are. Getting. Married.'

As the volume of his voice increased, the memories of raised voices that led to clenched fists, and thence to bruised ribs, made her recall how dangerous it was to be some man's wife, some man's property to deal with as he saw fit. And she began to tremble.

'If this is an indication of the way you mean to go on, whenever your will is crossed, then...'

His eyes widened. He shook his head and ran his fingers through his hair.

'I didn't mean to scare you. Please…' he waved a hand at the chair '…sit down again and I will try to talk this over calmly.'

'Only if you sit down, too.'

He frowned, then nodded.

Gingerly, she sat in the chair he'd indicated and he sat down, too.

'Look, Miss Carpenter. I have a terrible, hasty temper. Bane of my life, actually, but I do try not to let it govern my actions, the way it once did. I am sorry I let it get the better of me this morning. Ungentlemanly of me.' He lowered his head for an instant, the picture of contrition, before lifting it, looking directly into her eyes, and saying, 'Do you think you could find it in your heart to forgive my…outburst and start this interview again?'

She could hardly believe it. He didn't appear to believe, the way her father had, that it was his God-given right to harangue a female, when he had her behind closed doors. On the contrary, he'd said it was 'ungentlemanly' behaviour. And had asked her to forgive him.

How could she do anything *but* forgive him? When she nodded, mutely, he heaved a sigh of relief.

'Thank you. It is just that…this means so much to me. And I was so certain you felt the same way I did. That the fact you were a touch reluctant to get married would make us…allies. Then the cool way you talked about pulling the rug from under my feet just made me—' He broke off, shaking his head as though he didn't have the words to describe what he felt.

She felt every bit as confused as he looked.

'But if you don't truly want to get married, then…'

He heaved another sigh and ran his fingers through his unruly curls again.

'I don't truly *want* to get married, no,' he admitted. 'But I cannot see any other way out. But it's not because I'm in debt, or anything of that nature. My trustees have done a sterling job of managing my capital, up till now. Of course the trust will wind up when I get married,' he said gloomily. 'So I'm going to have to learn all that side of things myself now.'

'And you don't want to.'

He shrugged. 'In some ways it will be good to take up the reins myself instead of letting others drive the team. But I'm going to be far busier with that sort of thing than I'd like.' He slouched back into his seat, his expression mulish.

'Well, then, why? If it isn't money? And you aren't really ready to…take up the reins…' And it certainly wasn't because he'd fallen in love with her. There was nothing lover-like in the way he'd reacted to her rejection. Besides, men only fell for beautiful girls.

'I suppose I should blame Ashe for suggesting I court a girl with brains,' he said cryptically. 'You aren't going to be fobbed off with the usual nonsense, are you?'

'Nonsense?'

He tilted his head to one side and made a wry attempt at a smile.

'Nothing of nonsense about you at all, is there? Very well,' he said, leaning forward and clasping his hands between his knees. 'I will take you into my confidence. I hadn't meant to until after we were married, but I can see you're unlikely to marry me at all unless I give you a very good reason for me acting in a way that must make you think I've taken leave of my senses. I have a sister, you see.'

She didn't see, but before she could say so he leapt

to his feet and, clearly in some agitation, paced away from her. 'Or, to be more precise, a half-sister.' He had to stop when he got to the window, but instead of turning round, he stayed just where he was, his shoulders hunched, and started fiddling with the curtain tie-backs.

'My mother died when I was eight, as I told you before, and then my father remarried pretty swiftly. Before another year was out, she presented him with a daughter. The marriage lasted a few more years before he died. And then my stepmother—' He started in surprise as an ornamental tassel came off in his hand. He laid it down on the windowsill and, taking a step back from further temptation, turned towards Mary and kept his eyes fixed firmly on her as he took up his tale again.

'My stepmother remarried. She…she was only the daughter of our village grocer. But she was beautiful. Her parents, I found out some years later, were so thrilled to have her elevated to the ranks of the peerage, that they pushed her into accepting my father's proposal. She tried to make the best of it, but she was never very happy with him. Anyway, the minute Father died, she took up with the man she'd loved all along. A pretty decent fellow, actually. At least, he was good to me. Paid me more attention than my own father ever had, to tell you the truth, but that's beside the point. He was a nobody, that's what my own father's family said. And they were correct. He hadn't a title. Little money. No land, nothing of that sort, but…'

He turned and paced up and down, raking his fingers through his curls yet again.

'It's all such a tangle it's hard to know how to explain it. You see, my legal guardians didn't actually want me to live with them, but they didn't want me contaminated by the man they called a commoner, either. So they sent me away to school. But you know what? My stepmother, my half-sister and her new stepfather were the only ones to show a real interest in me. Their letters kept me from… Well, school can be a pretty harsh sort of place. I got through because I knew how to defend myself. Thanks to the very man my guardians said I shouldn't go near. He taught me to box.' He glanced down at his fists, which he'd clenched the moment he'd mentioned his school.

'It was to his home I went during school vacations. With him, and my stepmother and Julia I felt I had the nearest thing to a home. I was…very cut up when he died. And for his sake, I kept in contact with his sons. The sons my half-sister's mother bore him.'

She blinked. He caught the bewildered expression in her eyes, at the end of one of his circuits of the room, and pulled a wry face.

'I warned you my family ties are complicated. But that is only the start. You see, after he died, she—that is my stepmother—was left in slightly tricky circumstances. There was talk of taking Julia away from her and having her brought up by her father's—*my* father's family. Only she hadn't been all that impressed by the way they'd treated me up to then. So when she got an offer of marriage from yet another titled man, she agreed, in an attempt to keep them all, Julia and her two sons, together as a family. Following it so far?'

'Yes, I think so.'

'Well, although financially she did well, she was even more miserable with her third husband than she was with my father. Died giving him his heir. And then… well, for the next few years it felt as though every long vacation I went back to a different marital home as either the husband or the wife died and remarried. It was like living through some bizarre form of farce, with a different infant squalling in a crib, being introduced to me as my new brother or sister, by an adult I was supposed to call Mother or Father.'

'Hold on,' said Mary. 'Why were you calling all these strangers Mother? I don't quite understand.'

'Well, nobody really wanted to take on Julia's brothers, because of who their father was.'

'The decent, but common man.'

'That's him. But they all wanted to keep Julia under their wing, because she has a great deal of money settled on her, and whoever has wardship gets to control it. And wherever she went, I went, too. Because—well, I didn't have anywhere else to call home. And by that time I'd gained a bit of a reputation for being a hellion. Not the trustees or any of my father's extended family thought it worth the bother of attempting to discipline me, or cross my will. If I wanted to take myself off to the wilds of Wiltshire, or Yorkshire or Devon so I could be with my half-sister, they were only too glad to see the back of me.'

Mary's heart went out to him, or rather, the abandoned, unloved little boy he'd been. No wonder he went a bit wild. No wonder he made a point of going where he truly was wanted. Where he would be loved.

'I...I see....'

'No, you don't.' He shook his head and grinned at her. 'My family connections are so incredibly complicated that even I cannot keep track of all the people who claim kinship with me these days. Suffice it to say that Julia is the only one of them I give a rat's a— I mean, care very much about.'

She ought to have been offended by the way he'd almost slipped into vulgarity. But she was beginning to find his very clumsiness of speech rather endearing. In a way, he was treating her with a unique form of respect by saying whatever came into his head, rather than trying to bamboozle her with glib speeches. As was the way he pulled himself up, without her having to so much as lift a brow in reproof, either.

'Very well,' she said. 'Go on.'

'Thank you.' He sat down in the chair he'd used before, leaned his elbows on his knees and clasped his hands.

'Now, the thing is, the woman who is currently standing in the place of Julia's stepmother is about to get married again. And the man she's marrying is…' He scowled. 'Well, put it this way. I wouldn't want *any* innocent girl to have to live under the same roof as him. Julia's fifteen now and pretty as a picture. And Lord… Perhaps I shouldn't tell you his name.' He frowned, rubbing his thumb across his nose. 'Although, if people didn't gossip about him, I never would have found out that he's assuming nobody cares what becomes of Julia, given the way she's been passed round like a parcel up till now.'

'Oh, I see.' Mary leaned forward, clasping her own hands. 'By marrying, you are launching a rescue. You plan to provide a stable, safe environment for her to live in. That's…' she smiled at him a little mistily '…that is truly noble of you.'

He sat up straight again. 'Is it? I hadn't thought of it like that.' He shook his head. 'I just couldn't think what else to do. I spent hours discussing Julia's future with my lawyers, and hers. My first thought was to make an attempt to be declared her legal guardian. I'm pretty nearly old enough now, you see. But found out that would take too much time. Couldn't very well drag her out of the house and take her back to live in my bachelor lodgings either, while the lawyers worked through all the red tape. It would look damned peculiar. Probably cause the very kind of talk I don't want her exposed to. But if I got married, they said, and moved back to Mayfield, it would seem perfectly natural to invite her to live with us. Reunite the Durant family in the ancestral home, sort of thing.'

And if she didn't marry him now, he'd have to abandon that plan. Start all over again trying to find someone else to become his convenient wife. For that was what he wanted, she finally saw. Just a woman to make his rescue of his sister appear respectable and above board.

Could she really let him down, this way, after he'd confided the delicacy of his sister's plight to her? Could she let the girl, Julia, down, for that matter? She knew what it felt like to be all alone in the world, a burden to everyone, yet nobody's responsibility. Though she'd never been in the kind of peril that faced Julia. She simply wasn't pretty enough.

And then there were the Pargetters, who'd been so kind to her when she was just about at the end of her tether. They were banking on her to launch Dotty and Lotty into society. Give them the chance their beauty and vivacity deserved.

Could she trust him though, to keep his word? To grant her an allowance and treat her with respect?

From the way this interview had gone so far she thought, yes, perhaps she could.

And as for his temper, which seemed to flare out of

nowhere—well, at least he regarded it as the bane of his life and tried to keep it in check.

And apologised when he couldn't.

'Very well,' she said. 'I will help you. Of course I will, now I understand what is at stake.'

'Thank you.' He heaved a sigh of relief. Reached across the small gap that divided them, took both her hands in his and gave them a little squeeze.

'I have been at my wit's end. I couldn't tell anyone of my fears for her, in case it started the very kind of gossip that would be almost as bad as the fate I was afraid would await her if she ever got into Lord Wakefield's clutches. Now we can nip any schemes he might have been hatching in the bud. But…you must understand, time is of the essence. I want a place made ready for her to come to, a place she can feel safe, before her current stepmother marries him.'

'Which is why our wedding must take place so soon.'

'That's it. In fact, I was hoping we could get the knot tied tomorrow, then travel straight down to Mayfield and look the place over.'

'Mayfield? Why, is there something wrong with it?'

'I shouldn't think so. But I do want to just make sure before I tell Julia she can move in. You see, when my father died, I was too young to live there alone, so, as I mentioned, my guardians packed me off to school and let the place out to tenants. Better than letting it stand empty, they reckoned, and renting it out paid for its upkeep.'

'Oh, dear. Are you going to have to evict the current tenants? It's so near to Christmas….'

'And it may very well snow, too.' He chuckled. 'No, I'm not going to play the part of an evil landlord, don't worry about that,' he said, chucking her chin. 'Fortunately, a couple of years ago, when it fell vacant, I told the letting agent I didn't want them to find another tenant. Don't need the money and have never liked the thought of strangers living there. Good country round about, too. Had some thoughts of doing a bit of entertaining, having some fellows down for the hunting, that sort of thing, though I never got round to it. And just as I told you before, the trustees never bother arguing when they can see I've made up my mind. For some reason, they stopped letting out Durant House, too.'

'Oh, hang it! I suppose I shall have to reside there once I'm married and have Julia in tow.'

'You don't like the place?'

'It's like a cross between a barn and a mausoleum,' he said gloomily.

'Can you not make it more comfortable?'

'I don't see how.'

'W-well, I've never lived anywhere that cannot be made more…cheerful, by the strategic placement of furniture and a lick of paint.'

'If you can make Durant House anything like approaching cheerful,' he said fervently, 'I will consider myself for ever in your debt.'

'R-really?'

He pounced on the hopeful note she couldn't help trembling through her voice.

'I'll give you a completely free hand. In fact, I would prefer it if you didn't bother me with any of the details of the refurbishment at all.'

'You are willing to give me a totally free hand in the redecoration of your town house?'

'Mayfield, too, if you think you'd enjoy it. The only

stipulation I will make is that I want it to feel like somewhere Julia can really feel at home.'

'A…a home.' She pressed her hands to her cheeks. 'You want me to turn your ancestral seat into a home?'

'Actually,' he said, as though it had just occurred to him, 'it's *traditional* for the new bride to make some changes.'

'Oh,' she breathed, her hands clasped at her bosom now. She'd asked him for one room to call her own and he was presenting her with two whole houses.

'You'd *really* enjoy doing that?'

'Yes. Very much.'

'Good. Told you I wanted you to be happy! And if buying new carpets and wallpaper will do it, then so much the better. Though…' He rubbed his nose with his thumb as though a thought had just struck him. 'If your taste really runs counter to mine, I might just have to reserve a room or two for myself.'

'I wouldn't dream of making you uncomfortable anywhere in your own homes,' she protested.

'You won't,' he said firmly. 'This will be a very… That is, I've already told you I don't want us to be in each other's pockets all the time. You can go your way and I'll go mine. Within limits.' He frowned. Then shook his head. 'No, no, never mind. I trust you to set a good example for Julia to follow. You won't go creating any sort of scandal, will you?'

'I…I don't think I'd know how to,' she said, a little stung by his warning, even though he had retracted it almost at once.

He smiled at her again. A smile so warm and full of approval that she quite forgave his blunt speaking yet again. It was just the way he was and she was going to have to get used to it.

'So, you have no objection to marrying tomorrow and heading straight down there, then?'

'What?' She wasn't sure how they'd moved from living separate, but parallel lives, the way she'd heard many *tonnish* people did, to rushing into the wedding itself.

'Your aunt tried to make some objection about not having time to get a trousseau together, but do you really need one?'

'N-no, of course not.' She hadn't even thought about it. All that had exercised her mind since the day before had been how to avoid marriage altogether.

He frowned. 'You do mind. I can tell. Your aunt is right. It is downright selfish of me to deny you all the folderol most brides have. You'll want a new gown at the least, and shoes.'

'I...I think I could contrive to get something you won't be ashamed to see me in, by tomorrow,' she said.

His face lit up. 'I'll pay for it, of course. Send whatever bills you run up to me. Well, I think that's all settled, then.'

He reached into his pocket and pulled out a sheet of paper. Having scanned it swiftly, he thrust it back, his face flushing. 'You wouldn't believe how many things a chap has to remember,' he said, fishing around in another pocket, from which he produced a second list.

'No wonder most women insist on having several weeks to organise a wedding. Ah. Yes, thought so,' he said, thrusting the list back into his pocket. 'There is just one more thing I do need to discuss with you, before we tie the knot.'

He cleared his throat.

'This may be a businesslike arrangement, but it won't be a paper marriage.'

'I don't follow.'

'To be blunt, I need an heir. I've thought about this a lot, since…well, since I decided on marriage. And I've come to the conclusion we should get that side of things started straight away. I can tell you're quite a bashful sort of girl and that you might think I ought to give you time to become accustomed to the idea of being married, before I make any demands of that nature. But it's like this…'

He leaned forward and took hold of both her hands in his. 'At the moment, we both like each other. Don't we?'

When she nodded, shyly, he smiled. 'Now, the sad fact is marriages can turn sour remarkably quickly. I've seen it time and time again. If we get to the point where we cannot stand even being in the same room as one another…well, let's just say attempting to get an heir in those conditions won't be pleasant. Not for either of us. But at the moment, when we kiss…'

He looked at her mouth. Her lips tingled in remembrance of the kisses they'd shared the day before. And then every other part of her began to tingle, as well.

He was probably right. She'd grown up in a house where husband and wife could barely stand to be in the same room as each other. Whereas now…

Well, it really sounded as though he wouldn't try to suffocate her. He had at least two houses that she knew of. So they needn't ever be cooped up in a cramped little cottage, resenting the very air that each breathed. And they weren't marrying for love, so they couldn't fall out of it and grow bitter and resentful.

But, oh, she did like kissing him. And now that he'd

mentioned it, and was looking at her mouth that way, she wanted him to take her in his arms again, the way he'd done yesterday. And…she blushed, and the rest.

As if he knew the direction of her thoughts, he dropped to his knees in front of her, never letting go of her hands, leaned forward and touched his lips to hers. Just lightly.

Her eyes fluttered shut. She gripped his hands tightly. And she leaned forward, too, this time pressing her lips to his.

In a heartbeat, he'd got his arms round her, she'd put her arms round him and each was kissing the other for all they were worth.

'Mmnhh…stop,' he mumbled, pulling away. 'We have to stop,' he said, staggering to his feet and backing across the room. 'Or I won't be able to. You…' He drew in a great, ragged breath.

'My God,' he said unsteadily. 'I would never have believed it, but do you know, I'm actually looking forward to my wedding day.'

'Me, too,' she admitted, stunned. 'And I wouldn't have believed it, either.'

'See?' He grinned. 'We're perfect for each other.'

To her amusement he then sidled round the edge of the room to the door, as though avoiding a dangerous precipice.

As though she was utterly irresistible.

Just for a moment, she almost believed it herself.

Chapter Six

Wedding fever swept through the household. Aunt Pargetter took Mary to a street where there was a whole parade of shops where you could buy clothing ready-made. And not all of it used. And by dint of sitting up well into the night, with as many lamps as they could gather, the four women, working together, had both her gown, and the coat they'd bought to wear over it, altered to fit as though it had been made for her, then trimmings added so that the whole ensemble looked as though it had been designed from the outset instead of bought piecemeal and cobbled together.

She slept surprisingly well considering she was about to take a step she'd once vowed she would never take at all. Even though she'd only met Lord Havelock a matter of days before, the prospect of marrying him didn't fill her with dread. Every time either Dotty or Lotty rolled over, kicking her in the shins in their sleep, it reminded her of their willingness to make room for her when they had so little of it themselves. And she got a warm glow of satisfaction, knowing that she would soon be in a position to help this family, the only ones who'd shown her any compassion when she'd been at her most desperate.

And help Lord Havelock's sister, too.

How many men, she sighed, would make the supreme sacrifice of surrendering their bachelor freedom for the sake of a sister? Not her own brother, that was certain. He'd escaped their unhappy household as soon as he could and never looked back. Oh, he'd visited when on shore leave, but during those brief visits their father had been on his best behaviour and Kit had never once looked beneath the surface....

Not that she had begrudged him his career. Not in the light of how it ended....

She turned on to her side, resting her cheek on the palm of her hand. No point dwelling on the failings of a brother who was no more. Besides, she'd much rather dream about her husband-to-be. She smiled into the darkness as she recalled his insistence they get the business of providing an heir to his estates settled quickly, *before they went off each other.* Some women might have taken his attitude as an insult. She preferred to regard it as eminently practical. And a touch flattering that though he assumed his ardour would cool, he really felt some now. Quite a lot, if that last kiss in the parlour was anything to go by. And the difficulty he had in breaking it off.

Which meant that very soon she would have a baby to hold. Possibly even a couple before he went back to his... Well, a man as energetic and healthy as he was bound to have some arrangement to satisfy *that* form of appetite. Though even when it got to that stage in their marriage, she was not afraid he would become a cruel, or even an indifferent, parent. The lengths to which he was prepared to go for his sister assured her of that.

The next morning, when she stood before the mirror, she couldn't help exclaim in thanks for the Pargetters' hard work and inventiveness. She'd never looked better dressed.

Oh, if only her mother could see her now. Or her brother…though it wasn't likely he would have been on leave to walk her down the aisle even if his ship hadn't gone down with all hands.

For a moment, stark loneliness had tears welling in her eyes. Resolutely she dashed them away. She didn't want to appear in church with red eyes, as though she was going to the altar like some…sacrificial lamb. Besides, she was gaining a new family today, a husband who didn't seem as though he had the slightest inclination to browbeat and control her, a sister who would need her and eventually children of her very own to love her.

It was with a pale, but determined face that she left the room she'd shared with her cousins and made her way downstairs and to the carriage waiting to carry her, her aunt, uncle and cousins to church.

Her uncle Pargetter had taken leave from his place of work so that he could walk her down the aisle. The gesture should have made her feel less alone, but somehow the fact that she knew him as little as the man who was waiting for her at the altar merely lent the proceedings an air of unreality.

It had all happened so fast. And before she knew it, the vicar declared they were man and wife, and Lord Havelock was bundling her into a carriage, which whisked them off to the Clarendon, where Lord Have-lock treated them all to a splendid breakfast.

'You've landed on your feet and no mistake,' her uncle commented as he shook her hand before leaving. 'Very open-handed, this new husband of yours.'

'Yes, and so handsome,' added Aunt Pargetter, giving her a kiss on the cheek. She added a hug to the parting kiss, so that she could whisper into her ear.

'But please, don't think of this as a permanent part-ing. You must feel free to come and talk to me, or write, if you have any little problems. Getting used to the mar-ried state can be a touch tricky and I know you have no other female relative in whom you can confide.'

She didn't know how her aunt had guessed, but she did feel rather as though she was sailing into uncharted waters without a compass. And also now she'd boarded this ship called matrimony, it wouldn't be possible to return to the shore from which she'd embarked. Her aunt's willingness to give her the benefit of her advice, should she reach troubled waters, made her feel not quite so alone.

She hugged her aunt back, fiercely.

'Thank you' was all Mary managed to say, with a voice thickened with emotion. She was going to miss them, all the Pargetters. They were good people. They didn't have much, yet they'd been far more generous than closer relations who were far better off.

'Our rooms are this way,' said Lord Havelock, the moment the last of the Pargetters had exited the hotel and she'd dabbed her eyes dry with a darned handker-chief. He offered her his arm, and she laid her hand on his sleeve.

They mounted the stairs in silence, in the wake of a

smartly liveried hotel porter. The man opened a door with a flourish and bowed them into what looked like some wealthy person's best parlour.

'I took a suite of rooms,' said Lord Havelock once he'd dismissed the porter. 'I hope they meet with your approval.'

'In all honesty,' she said, hands clasped to her bosom, 'I have never seen such a magnificent room in all my life.' The thickness of the carpet alone made her yearn to take off her shoes and stockings so she could sink her toes into it. A fire blazed heartily from an ornate marble fireplace and all the furniture looked as though it had been specially selected to match not only every other piece in the room, but also the wallpaper and curtains.

He had casually mentioned having both a country estate and a town house, as well as his more comfortable bachelor rooms, but it hadn't really struck her, until this moment, what it meant. A man who could afford to buy a marriage licence and get a ceremony organised within a couple of days, splash out for a wedding breakfast in a hotel notorious for the expense of its meals and hire a whole suite of rooms like this, must be very, very wealthy indeed.

In a daze, she let him lead her across the room.

'This is your bedchamber,' he said, throwing open the door to the right of the fireplace. 'I did promise that you would always have your own room, a room that nobody could enter without your permission.'

'You did,' she said, hovering tensely on the threshold, looking in. The room was as tastefully opulent as the sitting room. But what caught her eye, and held her rooted to the spot, was the enormous four-poster bed it contained.

He came to stand very close behind her.

'I shall be knocking on this door later on,' he said, his breath rushing over the back of her neck and giving her goosebumps in the most remarkable places. 'I hope very much you will let me in, but if you really don't want me…bothering you in that way, tonight, then of course you only have to say so.'

Well, that was very considerate of him. And perhaps she ought to feel reluctant to welcome him into that bed when she scarcely knew him. Except that the heat of his kisses would keep searing into her mind at the most unlikely moments, making her squirm and melt inside. And she wasn't ever likely to get any less shy of him than she felt now. And they were married. Making a baby was one of the reasons he'd given for marrying her. And it was his right…

'I won't *demand* my husbandly rights, if that is what is making you blush,' he murmured into her ear. 'Not until you are ready. Though I do want you. Badly.' He leaned down and brushed a tantalisingly barely there kiss on her neck, just below her ear. 'And I really do think,' he growled, 'it would be better to jump this hurdle before too long.'

Was she blushing? She pressed her hands to her cheeks, which did indeed feel as if they were on fire. Because she was ready right now. And rather ashamed that what he was taking for maidenly modesty was a complete inability to know what to do with her reaction to the nearness of his body. The seductive pull of his mouth on her skin…

'Beg pardon,' he said, stepping away just as she was on the point of turning and flinging her arms round his neck. 'I'm being a bit too blunt for you. But, look, you may as well know that I'm not a man given to fancy speeches and wrapping things up in metaphors. I hope you will soon get used to me and learn not to take offence, because I won't change.'

There was a touch of belligerence to his voice that made her turn to look warily up into his face. Was he angry with her? He probably thought he had a right to be, having spent so much money, only to have her appear to…shy at the first fence.

He was frowning, but before she could stammer out the confession that he'd got it all wrong, that not only did she agree that it was better to get on with the physical side of their marriage, but was actually rather looking forward to it, he'd turned away, and was striding across the room to a door on the other side of the fireplace.

'This is my chamber,' he said gruffly, 'where all my things are stowed.' He whirled round, his frown deepening.

'Was that luggage I saw, next to your bed, all you have with you?'

She nodded. 'It's all I have.'

'All you have?' The frown altered in tone. He came to her and took her hands. 'We really ought to be spending a few days in town putting that right, but… Look, I'm sorry, I've already made arrangements to travel down to Mayfield and get the place ready for Julia to come. Still, there's bound to be a dressmaker in Corleywood— that's the nearest sizeable town—who can fit you out with some new gear.'

'I don't mind about clothes,' she said. 'I know it is more important to ensure Julia's safety.'

His handsome face broke into a grin. 'I don't know another woman who'd look at it like that.' He lifted her hands to his mouth and kissed them. 'But you must have some decent things to wear, before the local gentry all turn out to have a look at you. Once word gets out in the neighbourhood that I've married and brought my bride to Mayfield, they'll all be coming to call. And you will want to be able to look 'em in the eye.'

Meaning, she wasn't able to now? In the outfit she'd been so proud of that very morning?

'Well, that's another thing to add to my list.' He gave her a rueful smile. 'Every time I think I've got everything organised, something else crops up that I've entirely overlooked.'

'I'm quite capable of buying my own clothes,' she began indignantly, only to founder on the rock of her completely penniless state.

'You just get whatever you want and have the dressmakers send the bills to me,' he said. 'You'll have an allowance, too. That's one of the things… Damn!' He let go of her hands and thrust his fingers through his hair. 'I've an appointment with my lawyers in…' he glanced at the clock on the mantelshelf '…about half an hour's time. I've a deal of stuff to discuss with them, documents to sign and so forth, which couldn't be done until I'd got the marriage lines. I know it's not the thing to leave a bride alone, so soon after the ceremony, but…'

'I understand.' He'd married her for necessity, not inclination. And if she took offence every time he reminded her of that fact, she was going to end up being badly hurt a dozen times a day. 'Go. Do what you have to do. I shall be quite content here, in this beautiful room.'

In a way it would be good practice for her. She was going to have to get used to spending large amounts of time on her own while he went off doing whatever it was he spent his days doing.

'Thank you,' he said, his look of relief being the only indication that, up till that point, he had been concerned about her reaction.

'I will return as soon as possible, I promise you.' With a heartbreakingly compelling smile, he leaned forward and gave her a peck on the cheek. Then he turned and left her, and she pressed one palm to her face as though to cling on to it, on to him, as long as she could.

For a few moments after the door closed behind him, Mary just stood there, in the stately isolation of the sitting room, marooned on her desert island of Axminster.

But there was no point in moping. Better to keep herself busy. She might as well use the spare time to unpack. Only…they would be setting off for his country estate the next morning, so it hardly seemed worthwhile. She'd only have to pack all over again.

She wandered over to the window, from where she had a good view over Blackheath, if she'd *wanted* to look at it. She shook her head reproachfully over her spurt of pique. Lord Havelock had warned her that he didn't want them to live in each other's pockets and she'd agreed it sounded much better than having a jealous, vengeful sort of husband who'd be breathing down her neck the whole time. She was going to have to cultivate the habit of finding things to do, when she was on her own. And not dwell on what it had made her feel like when he *had* been breathing on her neck, brushing that kiss on it…

She shook herself. What did married ladies do when their husbands were out on business, that was what she should be thinking about. Drank tea, probably. There.

That was something she could do. She would definitely feel better for a cup.

She rang for a servant, and before much longer she had not only tea, but also a selection of cakes and sandwiches brought up. As the waiter set them out on one of the many small tables scattered about the sitting room, she had to suppress a wild urge to giggle. It was like being a little girl, play-acting at being a princess, clapping her hands only to have invisible servants magic up food and drink out of thin air.

She couldn't look at him as he bowed himself out of the room, lest she really did burst out laughing. And so, when the door slammed, she was looking in exactly the right direction to see a sheet of paper, lodged under her husband's bedroom door, flutter in the draught.

Even from where she was sitting she could see it was some kind of list. And the moment she registered what it was, she recalled him saying how many things he had to remember, how he'd frowningly pulled not just one, but two lists out of his coat pocket the day he'd called to discuss arrangements.

Oh, dear, she hoped this one wasn't important. But if it was, perhaps she could summon up one of the hotel genies to whisk it to the meeting he was having. That would prove what a good and useful wife he'd married.

She bent down and pulled it out from under the door, her eyes snagging on the first item.

Compliant, it said, in an elegant copperplate script. And then next to it, in heavier, darker letters, another hand had added, *A Mouse*.

What kind of list was this?

Needn't have any dowry.

Oh. Oh! She clapped one hand to her mouth as she read the next item: *Won't demand a society wedding.*

This wasn't a list of things he needed to remember at all, but a list of what he was looking for in a wife.

A Mouse, the heavier hand had scrawled next to the bit about the ceremony, and underlined it.

Not of the upper ten thousand, her shocked eyes discovered next.

Orphan.

Her stomach roiled as she recalled the look on Lord Havelock's face when she'd told him, that fateful night at the Crimmers', that she'd just lost her mother. She'd thought he couldn't possibly have looked pleased to hear she was all alone in the world, that surely she must have been mistaken.

But she hadn't been.

She tottered back to the tea table and sank on to the chair the waiter had so helpfully drawn up to it. And carried on reading.

Not completely hen-witted, the sloppier of the two writers had added. And she suddenly understood that cryptic comment he'd made about finding a wife with brains. Suggested by someone called…Ashe, that was it. How she could remember a name tossed out just the once, in such an offhand way, she could not think.

Unless it was because she felt as though the beautiful little dainties set out on their fine china plates might as well have been so many piles of ash, for all the desire she had now to put one in her mouth.

Good with children, *Not selfish*, the darker hand had scrawled. Then it was back to the neater hand again. It had written, *Modest*, *Honest* and *Not looking for affection from matrimony.* And then the untidier, what she'd come to think of as the more sarcastic, compiler of wifely qualities had written the word *Mouse* again, and this time underlined it twice.

But what made a small whimper of distress finally escape her lips was the last item on the list.

Need not be pretty.

Need not be pretty. Well, that was her, all right! Plain, dowdy, mouse that she was. No wonder he'd looked at her as though—what was it Aunt Pargetter had said—as though his ship had come in?

But which of the men who'd compiled that list had harped on about the need to find a mouse, that was the question that now burned in her brain like a fever. Had Havelock's been the hand to scrawl that word, not once, but three times?

Getting to her feet, she strode to his bedroom door and flung it open. Somehow she had to find a sample of his handwriting to see if he'd been the one to…to mock her this way, before he'd even met her. And then she would… She came to an abrupt halt by his desk, across the surface of which was scattered a veritable raft of papers. What would she do? She'd already married him.

With shaking hands she began to sift through what looked like a heap of bills, some of them on the hotel's headed notepaper. Until she came to what was unmistakably a letter. *Dear Lady Peverell*, it began. There was another underneath, in the same bold scrawl, which started, *Dear Chepstow*. She flipped to the bottom of the page. The one to Lady Peverell was signed *Havelock*. And she couldn't help noticing, on her way to the end of the sheet, that he was informing her of his marriage. He hadn't got very far with the other letter, so there was no signature, but it began in the same vein. Except…

Oh! He'd informed his friend that *She meets all the requirements we fixed on, bar one.*

The room seemed to swim as several facts all jostled rudely into her mind at once. This Chepstow person had taken part in compiling the wife list. Ashe was another. Were theirs the two sets of handwriting? And then there was Morgan. She'd wondered why Lord Havelock had come to such an unfashionable place as the Crimmers', but now she understood perfectly. He had been looking for a wife who didn't come from the upper ten thousand and Mr Morgan had made it possible to meet one, by taking him there.

So, Mr Morgan, too, must know about the infamous list.

And how many others?

She had a sickening vision of half a dozen drunken bucks sitting round a table in some crowded tavern, suggesting what Lord Havelock should look for in a wife who would be so grateful to receive a proposal at all, that she'd never dare lift her voice in complaint about any treatment he might decide to mete out.

With an expression of disgust, she dropped the list on to the rest of his papers and hurried from his room.

Which didn't look like a palace out of a fairy tale any longer, but a gilded cage.

A cage she'd walked into with her eyes wide open.

Or so she'd thought. But that was before she'd discovered he'd made out a list of what he wanted from a wife. Just as though he was going shopping for groceries!

She stood quite still, eyes closed, head bowed against the tide of humiliation that washed over her.

She was such a fool.

He'd been honest with her from the start. He'd told

her he was looking for a convenient wife. That he'd been in a hurry to get one, so that he could get on with the far more important business of rescuing Julia.

At what point had she forgotten that? When had she started hoping there might be a glimmer of truth in what Aunt Pargetter said about him falling for her? Men didn't need to even *like* a woman to want to get her naked and in a bed. She knew that. She'd been brought up in a coastal town swarming with lusty sailors, for heaven's sake!

She clasped her hands to her waist as her middle lurched almost painfully. How on earth could she possibly have thought that such a handsome, wealthy, titled man would suddenly become enamoured of a penniless, plain little…*mouse* of a creature like her? She'd mistaken his relief at finding a compliant, orphaned, modest woman to be his convenient wife so quickly for delight in *her*.

She shook her head. It had been useless flinging the list back amongst his other papers. The words of it were scored into her brain as though carved with a knife.

The sound of footsteps striding along the corridor had her opening her eyes and gazing in horror at the door. She couldn't face him, in all his good humour, not now, not while she felt so…wounded!

To her relief, the feet kept on walking. It must just have been another guest returning to his room, or one of the hotel staff bustling about their business.

Still, it had been a warning. With fingers that shook, she poured some tea into her cup, selected a pastry at random and put it on to a plate. If he walked in now, he would simply see a woman taking tea. She would make her face show nothing of what she felt.

And she would *not* weep.

* * *

When Lord Havelock eventually returned, she was still doggedly dry-eyed. Sitting stock-still at the table with her cup of tea, untouched, in front of her.

'Sitting in the dark?' He frowned at her as she started, then stared at him as though she wasn't quite sure who he was.

'You should have rung for candles.' He strode across and tugged on the bell pull. 'And the fire has almost gone out, too.'

She turned, slowly, to look at it.

'At least you've had something to eat…' He frowned as he noted that nothing appeared to have been touched. Even her teacup was full.

Though her eyes were empty.

'I've been a perfect beast, haven't I,' he said, pulling up the other chair to the table and grasping her hands. 'To leave you alone for such a long time.' He raised each hand in turn, kissing it penitently.

She looked at him in confusion. No wonder she'd started to think he was developing some real affection for her. But this was just…gallantry. If she'd had any experience of suitors, in the past, she would have known that this was how men behaved with women. That it meant nothing.

He should have picked either Dotty or Lotty. Either of them would have coped with him far, far better than she was doing.

'Well,' he said, starting to chafe her hands between his own. 'I've achieved everything I needed to get done today, so now I'm all yours.' He gave an uneasy laugh. 'Though from the look you're giving me that information doesn't exactly please you. Dash it, where's that waiter? Your hands are like ice. Your feet, too, I dare say.'

She thought she'd kept her face impassive, but something must have shown, for he shook his head and said ruefully, 'Ah, Mary. You don't have anything to worry about. On my word of honour, I'll do better from now on. To start with, we'll have a slap-up meal, and…and talk to each other. Yes? Not downstairs in one of the public rooms, but up here, since you are looking a little…'

Plain? Mousy? Not smartly dressed enough to be able to look the well-heeled clientele in the eye?

'Uncomfortable,' he finished.

'I…I don't feel very hungry,' she said. 'Today has been…just a bit…rather…'

'Hasn't it, though? Not two weeks ago I thought I'd *never* get married. Now here I am in a hotel room with my bride, on my wedding night. Takes your breath away, don't it?'

She nodded.

'Do you know what I think?'

She shook her head. That was the trouble. She kept imagining he was thinking things he'd told her point-blank he wasn't going to think.

'I think by leaving you hanging all afternoon, you've ended up feeling like a game bird ready for plucking. And that I ought to set about making you feel like a bride, instead.'

'What do you mean?'

'I think you know very well what I mean,' he growled, pulling her to her feet.

She uttered a squeak of surprise when he hefted her into his arms.

A woman with more pride, she expected, would have put up some form of protest.

Mary put her arms round his neck, buried her face in his shoulder and clung to his solid warmth as he strode with her over to his bedroom.

Chapter Seven

He tumbled them both on to the bed and kissed her with an ardour that left her breathless. And strangely comforted.

Even though he'd only chosen her with his head, not his heart, he had chosen *her*. There must be dozens of poor, plain, penniless orphans in London, yet he hadn't looked any further once he'd met her.

And, yes, maybe that was only because he was in such a hurry to get married, but...

With a moan that was half distress, half desperation, she curled her fingers into the luxuriant softness of his hair and kissed him back for all she was worth.

They were married now. Did it really matter how it had come about? No. It was what they made of their future that mattered.

Her response brought a feral growl of appreciation from his throat. And then, for a few moments, it was as though he had been let off some invisible leash. His hands were all over her while his body strained against hers in a way that thrilled her to the soles of her boots.

His excitement called to something buried deep in

the heart of her. Something wild and wanton that came roaring to life and swept aside her every inhibition. Her hands were every bit as greedy as his, seeking and stroking and learning. She couldn't get close enough to him. She wanted to wrap herself round him. Press every single inch of her against every marvellously thrilling inch of him.

Until, quite without warning, he reared back.

'This is going too fast,' he panted, frowning.

'What do you mean?' It all felt perfectly wonderful to her.

'This is your first time,' he gritted out between clenched teeth. 'I should be taking it far more slowly. Making it good for you.'

Well, she couldn't argue with that. After all the horrible things she'd read on that list, the dreadful afternoon she'd spent sitting alone, cold and brutally wounded, the least he could do was make *this* part of their marriage good.

He'd closed his eyes on a grimace. When he opened them again, only a few seconds later, he'd calmed down considerably.

'I didn't even pause to get our shoes off.' He sighed, with a shake of his head.

He sat up, scooted down the bed and rapidly unlaced her rather worn leather half-boots. Aunt Pargetter had wanted to get her some dainty footwear to go with her wedding finery, but there hadn't been time. And she'd thought her own comfortable boots would stand her in better stead, considering the coldness of the season. Only now did she wish she'd taken them off herself, during the hours he'd been away seeing his lawyers.

He didn't say anything about the patched soles, or

the worn-down heels, but his frown did deepen once his fingers encountered her stockinged feet.

'Your feet are like ice! Well, that won't do.' Taking her left foot between both hands, he first chafed it, then raised it to his mouth to plant a hot kiss on the sole. The action sent her skirts slithering up her legs.

His hot eyes followed their movement. Swiftly followed by his hands.

'I need to get these stockings off,' he said, as though warning her of his intent.

She shivered with pleasure when he deftly undid her garter, then slid one stocking down.

'Cold?'

She shook her head. Far from it. It felt as though a bolt of lightning streaked from the heat of his hands against her bared skin, right to her very core. She subsided into the pillows again, luxuriating in the sensations he evoked whilst removing her other stocking—with slow deliberation.

Her eyes half-closed, she watched with growing interest as he got up, shrugged off his jacket, undid his shirt and yanked it impatiently off over his head.

He had, without doubt, the most impressive masculine torso she'd ever seen. And she had seen many. Sailors often worked in just their ragged breeches, when loading and unloading ships during the hottest months of the year.

But she'd always averted her gaze and hurried past. She'd never been even remotely tempted to pause and drink her fill of any single one of them. She hadn't struggled to keep her hands neatly placed at her sides, rather than reaching out and running her fingers over each clearly delineated muscle. Or thought about letting her tongue follow in the wake of her fingers. Or got a mad urge to lick her way up that strong column of a masculine throat to the stubbled texture of his chin.

Not that she was bold enough to do any such thing. Besides, he'd just said he was going to make it good for her. And part of her, the part that was still smarting over the things she'd read on the list, wanted him to exert himself to make it up to her. Not that he would be aware he was doing any such thing, but still, she would know.

Anyway, he inadvertently helped her to resist the temptation by sitting down on the edge of the bed to remove his boots, which gave her eyes an entirely new view to appreciate. His back. The broad shoulders, the ridges of muscle down either side of his spine, which disappeared into the narrow waistband of his breeches.

She was a little disappointed when he drew the line at removing them. Although perhaps it was only fair. After all, she was still in her gown. Not that it took him long to take it off her once he set to it. My, but he certainly knew his way round lacings, and corsets.

Her heart was beating nineteen to the dozen by the time he lay down beside her and put his arm about her shoulders. The dexterity he'd just displayed with her clothing convinced her that he truly could make this experience good for her.

Even though he wasn't all that proficient at flirting and charming his way into a woman's bed, it didn't mean he hadn't had encounters of an…earthy nature, with willing women.

Willing? Oh, what an inadequate word. If any of them had guessed what kind of body he concealed beneath his casually comfortable clothing, plenty of them would have ripped them off just to get their greedy hands on it.

Just as she wanted to get her own hands on it.

She was so glad he didn't wear the kind of clothing that showed his stunning physique to better advantage. If he'd needed a couple of valets to peel a tightly fitted coat from those bulging biceps, she would have missed the enthralling spectacle of him gradually revealing more and more of his masculinity for her eyes alone.

He wouldn't have been able to just take her to bed because he felt it was time, either. She liked that they could be spontaneous about this, rather than having to involve servants.

She reached for him as he ran his fingers through her hair—hair that had come out of its fastenings during their first bout of kissing on this bed.

As she ran her hands down his back, glorying in the fact that there were no longer any clothes to impede her exploration, it occurred to her that a 'modest' woman wouldn't be doing this. Wouldn't have clawed her way under his waistcoat and writhed up against him like some kind of snake when he'd tumbled her on to the bed earlier, either. Nor would a 'modest' woman let her husband strip her naked at four in the afternoon—even if daylight was fading—and be glad of the way firelight bathed the room in a warm glow, so she could feast her eyes on her new husband's magnificent masculine nakedness.

But then, nor would a man who truly wanted a modest wife be looking at her like that—as if he wanted to devour her.

Which was pretty much what he did next, tasting and nibbling her all over as though she was some rare delicacy. He didn't leave an inch of her unexplored. And everywhere he put his mouth, he left behind such glorious feelings she didn't know how to describe them.

She bit down on her lower lip when he finally stroked her legs apart and began trailing kisses up the inside of her thighs.

Her aunt Pargetter had warned her, during a private little talk the night before, that the things her husband might wish to do to her, once in the marriage bed, might seem strange and perhaps a little frightening at first. She had advised her against resisting, or protesting, because nine times out of ten he would have more of an idea what would end up making it lovely.

It was all she could do not to laugh out loud. Resist him? Protest about this? Oh, no. The slow slide of his tongue, the little nips of his teeth, combined with the firm caresses of those strong hands, those knowing fingers, were exactly what she wanted.

Oh, very well, so her aunt had got part of it right. He did know more than her about this.

And he was taking the time to make it lovely for her, too. Which was somewhat surprising, considering he'd so far given the impression of always being in a hurry to get things done.

There was just one awkward little interlude, after he'd shucked off his breeches, where what he did hurt quite a bit, but then he brought the lovely feelings back, with skill, with patience, until…until…oh, utter rapture. It was as if she had completely left her body behind. She was floating somewhere—somewhere he'd taken her. And he was there, too. She could tell. His whole body was quivering with it. Pulsing with it.

'Mary.' He sighed, as she began to drift back to reality. A reality that had somehow been transformed, though she couldn't have explained how. And anyway, she felt too peaceful to rack her brains over what had changed between them, or within her, or…

He shifted his weight to one side and dropped a kiss on her forehead. Though how he found the energy to move so much as one eyelid, she couldn't imagine. She felt as though all her bones had melted. And as for muscles— there was not one left, in her entire body, that wasn't completely and utterly drained.

'Thank you for being so generous,' she heard him murmur, as he tucked her into his side.

Just before she drifted into sated oblivion.

There was no need to panic. He'd managed to bite back his urge to tell her that the way they'd reached the pinnacle of rapture together had been just about the most blissful experience of his life. He'd turned it into a far more temperate expression of gratitude, thank God.

And he was grateful. Grateful that they were so compatible, sexually. He'd specifically sought a woman he could enjoy taking to bed, hadn't he? So that getting an heir wouldn't be a hardship. She'd just ticked off another item on the list, that was all. His heart wasn't going to be at risk, just because he'd had a momentary, overwhelming feeling of rightness. Of belonging.

No. It just meant he'd made a very sensible choice of bride.

The next time Mary opened her eyes, it was because someone was insistently shaking her shoulder, pulling her up from a dream that featured her new husband, shirtless, skilfully skating away from her and disap-

pearing into a thick swirling fog while her own useless
legs melted away from under her.

'I am a little sorry to have to wake you,' said Lord
Havelock gruffly.

She blinked up at him sleepily. Last thing she knew
he'd been wrapped round her like a living blanket. Now
there was a real blanket tucked up to her chin, and he
was... She frowned. He was dressed and standing over
her looking a touch reproachful.

'Lying there like that you look...'

He paused, searching no doubt for a polite way to
tell her she looked a mess, with not a single pin remain-
ing in her hair, which was more than half over her face.
Still, at least that would be concealing the sleep creases
she'd no doubt have from the embroidered pillow slip.

'Absolutely edible,' he finished with a wicked grin.
'And speaking of edible, while you slept I ordered that
supper I promised you earlier. And it's arrived. I'm having them set it out in the sitting room, if you'd care to
join me?'

He indicated the foot of the bed, where, to her astonishment, she saw the nightgown and wrap her cousins
had given her, because, they'd said, her much darned and
patched nightgown and a woollen shawl would simply
not do for her wedding night.

The nightgown was of the sheerest lawn she'd ever
seen. Even when she'd folded it into her portmanteau
she'd been able to see the outline of her hand through
it. And the wrap was of scarlet silk, patterned all over
with lush oriental flowers of some sort.

But he was indicating he wanted her to wear them
and join him for supper in the sitting room.

'I thought you'd prefer a private supper, up here,

rather than go through all the bother of getting fully
dressed and dining in one of the public rooms.'

Well, there was that.

And also, she'd like to see how he reacted when she
walked around wearing a nightgown that revealed as
much as it covered. With her hair loose, she suddenly
decided, and flowing unbound all the way down her back
to her waist. She'd wager he wouldn't reprove her for not
being modest. Given the way he was watching the blankets now, which were only just covering her breasts, he
was more likely to enjoy the show.

But all she said was 'That was very thoughtful of
you.' Because, to be fair, it did sound as if he'd actually
thought about how she might feel. This once.

'I will join you in a moment.'

After catching a glimpse of herself in the mirror,
she had to steel herself to walk into the next room. It
wasn't as easy to walk about wearing attire that was
outrageously seductive as it had been to roll about on
the bed stark naked.

But she wasn't, most definitely wasn't, going to let
him get away with claiming he wanted a modest bride,
when his behaviour earlier had shown it was the exact
opposite.

She made it to the threshold, and paused, certain that
her face had gone the same shade of scarlet as the silken
wrap. For it wasn't only her husband who could see her
in her scanty nightclothes. But also the two waiters who
were setting out their supper.

'Ah, here she is now,' he said, drawing the eyes of the
two male staff in her direction. Her face went a shade
hotter as they looked her up and down before swiftly
bending their heads to concentrate on their tasks.

As if that wasn't bad enough, she now noticed that he wasn't fully dressed at all, but only wearing his breeches and the shirt he'd earlier tossed on to the floor.

'You can be off,' he said to the waiters, without the slightest hint of self-consciousness. 'I will serve my wife.'

She supposed people who worked in hotels must be used to having guests who wandered around half-dressed, at all hours of the day. Who'd very clearly spent most of the afternoon in bed. But she couldn't bring herself to look their way as they melted out of the room, dreading what she might see written in their faces.

'You certainly look like a bride now,' said Lord Havelock, in a tone that had her lifting her head again. Just as she'd hoped, his eyes were gleaming with appreciation as they roamed her diaphanous gown.

'How do you feel?'

Embarrassed. Rather foolish. Out of her depth, for trying to play the wanton, only to run aground on the shoals of slippery-eyed waiters.

He crossed the room to her, tilted her chin up with one finger and planted a brief kiss on her flaming cheek. And she no longer felt anything but aware of him, standing so close. His warm breath on her face. And the way he'd made her feel in the bed that was only a few faltering footsteps away.

But before she could summon up the words to express even a tithe of what she was feeling, her stomach rumbled. Rather loudly.

He grinned. 'Hungry! Good. So am I. I hope you like what I've ordered,' he said, taking her hand and leading her across to the table the waiters had been so busy over just moments before.

'It…it certainly all looks lovely,' she managed to stammer. The table had been set for two, with fine linen and sparkling crystal, delicate china and fresh flowers. The fire, she also noted, had been stoked up again so that the room was warm enough for them to sit about in a state of undress.

She was excruciatingly aware of his body now. Of exactly where it was and how it all felt. Whenever his legs so much as brushed against the hem of her nightgown, under the table, it brought back how they'd felt, pushing her own sleeker, softer legs apart. The muscles bunching and flexing as he'd…

He'd apparently lost the ability to talk, as well. In fact, the atmosphere reminded her very much of the time they'd striven in vain to make some sort of conversation over the supper table at the Crimmers'. Except that now it was charged with sexual awareness.

His as well as hers, she would stake her life on it.

He might be frowning as he spooned a helping of fricassee on to her plate, but it wasn't the frown of an angry man. She'd spent years studying her father, learning his moods in the faint hope she could avoid the worst of them. And that frown wasn't one of displeasure.

If anything, she would say he felt awkward. Though that was absurd! He'd wandered around earlier, ordering the waiters about as though it meant nothing.…

But now they were alone.

And he'd readily admitted, that night at the Crimmers', that he didn't know how to converse freely with ladies.

Particularly not to ones he'd just married, apparently.

Perhaps it wasn't so surprising he'd got friends to

help him compile a list when he'd decided he had to get married.

Perhaps she'd overreacted when she'd found and read it. He hadn't intended her to know he'd resorted to such lengths, after all.

And hadn't she already decided that she ought not to dwell on how this marriage had come about? But to just make the most of what they had?

And when it came right down to it, wouldn't she rather be married to him, with all his faults, than a glib-tongued man whose charm marked him down as a seasoned womaniser?

So she met his eye and gave him a tentative smile.

He smiled back, his shoulders dropping a good inch as some of his tension melted away.

I did that. I put him at ease.

Her aunt Pargetter had hinted that if their marriage was to be a happy one, it would be up to her. She hadn't seen how that could possibly be true, but already, today, she'd made a start. She could have flung the list at him when he returned from the lawyers and demanded an explanation, and an apology. She wouldn't have received one. Instead of making such wondrous love together, they would have had a fight. They wouldn't be sitting here, remembering how good it had been, and wondering when they could do it again, either. They would be at daggers drawn.

Not that she would ever let him treat her with such disrespect in future. She was *not* a mouse. And she had no intention of letting him turn her into one. The thought she might ever end up like her mother, too scared to draw a breath without the permission of her tyrannical husband, had almost made her cry off altogether.

Except that she'd seen Lord Havelock was nothing like her father. And they weren't eloping, in the face of opposition from both their families. They'd come together for very practical reasons.

Not that she felt very practical about him at this moment. Her mind was a whirling jumble of emotions and desire and, above all, hope.

All of a sudden, Lord Havelock broke into her musings by uttering an oath and throwing the serving spoon back into the dish with a clatter.

'I should have taken you out to the theatre, or something, shouldn't I? Not kept you cooped up indoors all evening, with only me for company.'

And that was the nub of the matter. He wasn't an unkind man. Only a touch thoughtless.

And apparently willing to learn to do better.

'It was just,' he said, seizing her hand across the table, his face screwed up with contrition, 'that I'd planned on getting an early night.'

When she flushed, and dropped her head to gaze at her plate, she heard him chuckle.

'Not because of *that*. Well, not only that. You see…' he gave her hand a slight squeeze '…we need to get on the road as early as we can, with the days being so short. I don't want you to have to put up at any of the inns on our way. And if we make an early enough start, providing we don't encounter any problems, we should be able to make it in one stage.'

'Yes, I see. Well…um…' Her heart was pounding so hard she was amazed he couldn't hear it.

'I…I don't mind having an early night,' she finally managed to confess, shooting him a coy look from under her eyelashes.

'Well, yes, but that was before my patience ran out and I swept you off to bed the minute I got back from the lawyers. And...' He cleared his throat. 'It probably isn't such a good idea to attempt... I mean...' He coughed. 'You are probably a bit... That is, I've heard...' he flushed '...that the first time can leave a lady feeling a bit, um, sore.'

'I don't feel sore.' What she did feel, had started to feel from the moment he'd hinted he wanted to take her again, was an ache. An ache that she knew only he could assuage. 'You were so careful with me that I...'

'I will be careful again,' he vowed, cutting her hesitant response off so swiftly, and with such fervour, that she could tell he wanted her as much as she wanted him.

It was the greatest compliment he could have paid her.

Holding both her hands in his, he looked straight into her eyes.

'That is, if you want to... I mean, I don't expect you to...only hope that you...'

He pulled himself up straight, giving his head a little shake, then laughing ruefully.

'Here's the thing. Lady Havelock, I would like to invite you to come to my room now, for an evening of... exploration, let's call it that. I'd like to find out what gives you pleasure. So if, at any time, anything I do causes you discomfort, you have only to tell me, and I will stop. And move on until we find something that you do enjoy. Will you...will you come with me?'

He wanted to spend the evening discovering what gave her pleasure?

How could she possibly refuse?

For one thing, he was only inviting her to do exactly

what she'd wanted from the moment she'd woken up, naked, to find him standing over her.

For another, he'd warned her that this stage of their married life might not last long. One of them might take the other in dislike and then all this ardour would cool.

But most of all, only an idiot wouldn't make the most of having a man like Lord Havelock take her to bed.

And she most certainly wasn't an idiot.

It was still dark when the porter came next morning with hot water for her husband to wash. She slid as far beneath the blankets as she could, until he'd gone, then flung back the covers with grim determination and sashayed across the room to pick up her robe, which was lying in a scarlet puddle by the door.

'I will go to my own room to wash and dress,' she said as she plunged her arms into the sleeves and fumbled for the sash. It was all very well, she'd discovered, attempting to flout his hope she would behave modestly, but she really didn't have the stomach for it.

From his bank of pillows, her husband stretched and gave her a lazy smile.

'I will meet you back in the sitting room. They'll be setting out breakfast in there, so you might want to, um…' He indicated the neckline of the robe, which was revealing rather more of her than she'd like.

She gripped the edges close over her throat, leaving the room to the sound of her husband's throaty chuckle.

It didn't take her long to wash and dress.

'You'd better make the most of this,' he said, indicating the array of dishes set out on the table when she joined him. 'I won't be making long stops on the way, if I can avoid it. Besides, none of the inns I've ever tried on the way to Mayfield can offer anything half so good.'

Mary dipped her head as she sat down. How could he be talking in such a matter-of-fact way when she was feeling so…so awkward? So vulnerable? Didn't he care?

Or hadn't he noticed how hard this was for her?

Though perhaps that was for the best. After all, she'd vowed he would never have cause to think of her as a mouse.

And anyway, he was at least explaining his reasons for making the travelling arrangements the way he had. Which sounded as though he was looking out for her, in his own way.

She sat up a little straighter and began to nibble at a slice of toast while he demolished a vast quantity of steak and eggs, and ale and coffee. Lord, but he had a healthy appetite.

In more ways than one. She flushed as her mind flew back to the boundless energy he'd displayed the night before. The inventiveness, and the patience, and the amazing stamina…

He looked up and caught her looking at him in a sort of sexual haze. His fork faltered halfway to his mouth.

'Eat up,' he said gruffly. 'You need to keep your strength up. It will be a long and arduous day, and after such a long and…energetic night…'

She lowered her head and slid a mound of fluffy scrambled egg on to her fork. It wasn't easy to sit at table with a man who'd had his hands and mouth all over her. She knew this was what married people did—and quite a few people who weren't married, too—but how did they hold conversations, as though they hadn't done the most shocking things to each other under cover of darkness?

She raised the fork to her mouth. As she parted her lips, her husband gave a strange, choking sort of sigh. When she raised her eyes to his in enquiry, she saw him looking at her lips. His fingers were clenched tightly round his own fork, which hadn't travelled any nearer to his own mouth.

So he wasn't as unaffected by their night of intimacy as she'd at first thought. With a little inward smile, she reached for her cup and took a delicate sip of tea, shooting him what she hoped was a saucy look over the rim as she drank. The look he sent her back was heated enough to make her toes curl.

It kept her warm for the rest of the morning. As did his constant care for her comfort. Though he'd warned her that the journey was likely to be arduous, she found it the least unpleasant she'd ever undertaken. For one thing, she was sitting in a comfortable post-chaise, swathed in travelling furs with a hot brick at her feet, next to a man she…really liked. A man who kept her entertained with a fund of anecdotes about adventures he'd had whilst travelling this route before. It was a far cry from being cooped up inside the common stage with a bunch of malodorous strangers. Then again, wherever they stopped, the landlords gave him swift and respectful service. No waiting around in draughty public rooms, suffering rude stares and coarse remarks. They made good speed and dusk was only just descending into true night by the time their carriage swept through the gates of what he told her was to be her new home.

'I am sorry you cannot see very much of it,' he said as they bounced up a lengthy drive. 'I will show you around tomorrow. The horses should have settled in by then. I had them sent on ahead, by easy stages, the minute I knew we'd be coming down.'

She turned, slowly, and looked at him. He'd sent his horses by easy stages, but pushed her to make the journey in one day?

Just when she'd made allowances for him writing that dreadful list, he…he…

She drew in a deep breath, grappling with the wave of hurt that had almost made her lash out at him. She would *not* take his casual remark about his horses as a sign he didn't care about her. Hadn't he proved that, in his own way, he did? As he'd related all those tales about adventures he'd had in the posting inns on the way here, she'd seen *exactly* why he hadn't wanted her staying at any of them.

She'd got to stop looking for signs that he was going to turn out to be just like her father.

'There are some decent rides on the estate itself, but we can hack across country if you like, see a bit of the surrounding area, too. You'll want to know where the nearest town is, get the lie of the land, and so forth….'

'Oh, no,' she said, lifting her chin. 'I cannot ride.'

'You cannot ride?' He looked thunderstruck. And then crestfallen. And then resigned.

Funny, but she'd never noticed what an expressive face he had before. He'd warned her he was blunt, but not that he was incapable of hiding his feelings.

Which gave her food for thought. He might be thoughtless, even inconsiderate, but she would always know exactly where she was with him. And he would never be able to lie to her.

And though she hadn't known she'd been carrying it, she certainly felt it when a layer of tension slithered off her shoulders. She hadn't been able to help worrying about what kind of husband he was going to be.

But so far he'd shown her more courtesy than any other man ever had.

Eventually they drew up in front of a large, and completely dark, bulk of masonry. He muttered an oath and sprang from the carriage with a ferocious scowl. 'Where is everyone?' He strode away and pounded on the front door with one fist while she clambered out of the vehicle unaided.

It was so very like the way her father would have behaved, after a long and tiring journey, that it resurrected a few bad memories that made her feel, just for a moment, the way she had as a girl. That there was always something more important, more interesting, for a man to do than care for his wife and child.

'I wrote to the Brownlows, the couple who act as caretakers, warning them I would be coming down and bringing my bride with me.'

With a determined effort, she shook off the shadow of past experience as Lord Havelock took a step back, craning his neck up to the upper storeys of his house. 'I can't see any lights anywhere,' he said. 'Did you see any lights, perchance, as we were driving up?'

'No.'

'What the devil,' he said, planting his fists on his hips and glaring at her, 'is going on, that's what I want to know?'

'I have no idea.' He *wasn't* like her father. He *wasn't* yelling at her because he blamed her for whatever was going wrong. He was just…baffled, and frustrated, that was all. For all she knew, he might really be asking her what she thought was *going on*.

Well, there was only one way to find out.

'Well, perhaps…'

'Yes? What?'

'Perhaps they didn't get your letter.'

'Nonsense! Why shouldn't they get it? Never had any trouble with the post before.'

It wasn't nonsense. He'd arranged their marriage really quickly. And written dozens of letters, to judge from the state of his desk at the hotel.

'Are you quite sure you wrote to them?'

'Of course I did,' he said, snatching off his hat and running his fingers through his hair.

'Well, then, perhaps, if they were not expecting you… not in the habit of expecting you to call unexpectedly, that is, they may have gone away.'

'Gone away? Why on earth should they want to do any such thing? I pay them to live here and take care of the place.'

'Because it is almost Christmas? Don't you permit your staff to take holidays?'

She had his full attention now. But from the way his eyes had narrowed at her dry tone, she was about to find out how far his temper might stretch before snapping.

'Begging your pardon, my lord,' said one of the post-boys, as he deposited the last of their luggage on the step. 'But since you seem not to be expected here, will you be wanting us to take you to the inn where we'll be racking up for the night?'

Lord Havelock rounded on the poor man, his eyes really spitting fire now.

'I'm not taking my wife to the Dog and Ferret!'

'No, my lord, of course not, my lord,' said the hapless individual, shooting Mary a pitying look.

She supposed she ought not to despise them for turning tail and fleeing. But, really! What kind of men abandoned a woman, outside a deserted house, in the sole charge of a husband whose temper was verging on volcanic?

And then, just when she'd thought things couldn't get any worse, an eddy of wind tugged at her bonnet, sprinkling her cheeks with light, yet distinct drops of rain.

Chapter Eight

'That's all we need,' he said, ramming his hat back on his head. Things had been going so well until they'd reached Mayfield. She'd been warming towards him throughout the day. It hadn't even been all that difficult. She had a generous nature and seemed disposed to try to like him.

But now her face had changed. It put him in mind of the way his great-aunt had looked at him when he'd turned up to one of her ridottos in riding boots. No credit for remembering the insipid event and tearing himself away from a far more convivial gathering to get there. And more or less on time, as well. No. Only disapproval for being incorrectly dressed.

Not that the cases were a bit the same. He couldn't really blame Mary for being cross with him.

He scowled at the carriage as it disappeared round a curve in the drive, wishing now that he hadn't dismissed the post-boys with such haste.

'The Dog and Ferret really is no place for you,' he said aloud, as much to remind himself why he'd had all the luggage unloaded, as to explain himself to her.

'But,' he said, turning to her at last, bracing himself to meet another frosty stare, 'at least it would have got you out of the weather. And now,' he said, shooting the back of their post-chaise one last glare, 'we are stuck here. Can't expect you to walk to the village at this hour, in this weather.' If it had been just him, he could have cut across the fields. But he'd seen the state of her boots the night before. They wouldn't keep her feet dry. Nor was that fancy coat and bonnet of hers cut out for hiking through the countryside in the rain.

'Only one thing for it,' he said, and before she could raise a single objection at leaving the shelter of the porch, he seized her arm and set off round the side of the house.

She shivered when the rain struck them both with full force. When she stumbled over some unseen obstacle, he put his arm round her waist and half carried, half dragged her through what was starting to become something of a storm, under the gated archway that led to the back of the house.

It was much darker in the enclosed courtyard, so that even he had trouble navigating his way to the servants' entrance. But at least it was sheltered from the wind that was getting up.

He rattled the door handle, cursing at finding it locked.

Not that it would be all that hard to get inside.

Couldn't expect Mary to climb in through a window, though. Which meant he'd have to leave her out here while he groped his way along the darkened passages and got a door open for her.

He shucked off his coat.

'Here,' he said, tucking it round her shoulders, 'this should keep the worst of the wet off you while I break in.'

'B-break in?'

He couldn't see her face, it was so dark, but he could hear the shock and disapproval in her voice.

'There's a window, just along here,' he said, feeling his way along the wall, with Mary following close on his heels. 'Ah, here it is.'

He reached into his pocket and found a penknife. 'Never used to fasten properly,' he explained, flicking open the knife blade. 'The footmen used to use it to get in after lock-up, when they'd sneaked off to the Dog and Ferret.'

'That's…'

'Dreadful, I know.' He worked the knife blade under the sash. 'As a boy, I shouldn't have known anything about it. But nobody paid me much mind in those days.' The lock sprang free and he heaved the window up. 'Never thought knowing how to break into my own house would come in so handy,' he said, getting one leg over the sill. 'You just wait there,' he said firmly. He didn't want her stumbling about in the dark and hurting herself. 'I'll come and let you in, in just a jiffy.'

If it had been dark in the courtyard, it was black as a coalhole in the scullery. And yet he had little trouble finding his way past the sinks and along the wall, round to the kitchen door. This place was deeply embedded in his memory. Even the smell in here flung him back to his boyhood and all the hours he'd spent below stairs in the company of servants, rather than wherever it was he was meant to have been.

In no time at all he'd laid his hands on a lamp, which was on a shelf just beside the back door, where it had always been kept.

As he lit it, he pictured Mary, huddled up under the

eaves in a futile attempt to find shelter from the wind and rain, and no doubt counting the minutes he was making her wait. And wondering what the hell he'd dragged her into. All of a sudden he got a sudden, vivid memory of the day his stepmother had first come to Mayfield. How she'd stood—not in the rear courtyard, shivering with cold, but in the imposing entrance hall, nervously watching the servants, who'd all lined up to greet her. She'd attempted a timid smile for him and he'd returned it with a scowl, seeing her as an interloper. A woman who had no right to take the place of his mother.

He couldn't recall her ever smiling again, not while she'd lived here.

He paused, the lighted lantern in his hand, recalling how he'd complained to his friends about how a woman changed a man when she got him leg-shackled. But the truth was that it wasn't just a man who took a huge risk when he got married. When a woman chose the wrong partner, she could be just as miserable. He knew, because he'd seen it with Julia's mother. She'd blossomed when she'd finally married her childhood sweetheart. Only to shrivel to a husk of her former self when shackled to her third husband. Who'd been a brute.

It was all very well protecting himself from hurt, but not at Mary's expense. Theirs might not be a love match, but there was no reason why he shouldn't do whatever he could to make her happy.

He set the lamp back on its shelf by the back door before he unbolted it. And when Mary saw him, and came scurrying over, he caught her round the waist, then swept her up off her feet and into his arms.

'Nothing else has gone right so far,' he said. 'But at least I can carry my bride over the threshold.'

To his immense relief, she flung her arms round his neck and burrowed her face into his chest.

She must be freezing, poor lamb. Else she wouldn't be clinging to him like this.

He set her down gently and shut the door. Turned, and took both her hands in his.

'I haven't made a very good start as a husband, have I,' he said ruefully. 'I must have written a dozen letters yesterday. Thought I'd organised it all so brilliantly. But never took into account the possibility the Brownlows might have already made their plans for Christmas. And…' he squeezed her hands '…I fear you are right. There's nobody here but us. And there's no telling how long they'll be away. I dare say you must be really cross with me, but…'

'No!' She stunned him by placing one hand on his cheek. 'Not at all. There are far worse things for a man to be, than a bit disorganised.'

'Well, it's good of you to say so,' he said gruffly, raising his own hand to cover hers where it rested on his cheek, 'but you do realise we've no option but to rack up here for the night? And that there are no servants, no beds made up for us…'

She gave him a brave smile. 'It will seem better once we can get a fire going,' she said bracingly. Clearly determined to make the best of a bad job. 'And if the Brownlows normally live here, then there's bound to be some provisions in the larder. We can manage.'

'Come on, then,' he said, kissing her hand in gratitude at her forbearance. 'Let's raid the kitchen.'

Pausing only to pick up the lantern, he led Mary along the stone-flagged corridor, his brow knotted in thought. His father had never really appreciated Julia's mother.

He'd treated her as though she ought to have been grateful he'd given her his name and title. He hadn't seen it as a boy, but his father had treated his dogs and horses better than his own wife.

The minute he thought of horses, he recalled the hurt look that had flickered across Mary's face when he'd told her how he'd sent his own horses down by easy stages.

Lord, he'd started out as badly as his own father had done! Pampering his horses and pitching his wife headlong into hardship.

'You ought by rights to be ripping up at me for making such a botch of things,' he growled as he opened the door to the kitchen for her.

She gazed up at him, wide-eyed. Then gave a little sniff and shook her head.

'You were just in a hurry to get things ready for your sister,' she said. 'You were concentrating on getting her to a place of safety. It would have been a miracle if, somewhere along the line, your plans *hadn't* hit a snag.'

'That's very generous of you—to take that attitude,' he said, setting the lantern on the shelf just inside the door, which had always been used for that very purpose.

'Let's just hope this is the worst snag we hit,' she said, untying the ribbons of her bonnet and setting it on the massive table that stood in the very centre of the room. Then she walked across to the closed stove and knelt in front of it.

'Good, dry kindling laid ready,' she said, opening the door and peeking inside. 'And plenty of logs in the basket.' She stood up, and scanned the shelf over the fireplace. 'And here's the tinderbox, just where any sensible housewife would keep it.'

Thank goodness she wasn't one of those useless, helpless females whose sole aim in life was to be decorative. It would be an absolute nightmare to be stuck in this huge, empty house with one of those.

Fortunately, he managed to keep his thoughts to himself rather than blurting them out and provoking an argument. For what woman liked to hear a man think she was useful rather than decorative?

'I'll go and take a look around, then,' he said, going to light another lamp. 'See what I can discover. So long as you will be all right here for a while?'

She glanced at him over her shoulder and nodded, with a look that told him he was an idiot for even asking.

He gave a wry smile as he set out to explore the house. He'd contracted a practical marriage, with a practical, no-nonsense sort of woman. Of course she wasn't going to have a fit of the vapours because he was leaving her alone to get a fire lit.

By the time he returned to the kitchen, it was noticeably warmer. And there were plates and bowls and things out on the sides, which had previously been bare.

'While you were gone I had a good look round the larder, found some tea and made a pot,' said Mary, pouring some into two cups. 'There's no milk to go in it, but we can sweeten it with some sugar.'

'I didn't expect you to have to act like a servant,' he said glumly as he set the lamp on its shelf.

She put the teapot down rather hard.

'Would you rather sit all night in the gloom, with an empty stomach, and wait for someone else to turn up and wait on you?'

'No. I didn't mean that! It's just—I promised you a life of luxury. And on the first day, you're already reduced to this.' He waved his arm round the big, empty kitchen.

'Oh.' Her anger dissipated as swiftly as his own ever did. She shot him a rueful glance as she dumped two full spoons of sugar into both cups. 'I don't mind, you know. It's the biggest house I've ever had to call my own. And I'm sure, come the morning, you will be able to find out what has become of the couple who should be taking care of the place. The state of the larder leads me to believe they have not been away all that long.'

'It looks as though there's been a horse in the stables very recently, too,' he said, taking a seat at the table next to the place settings he noted she'd laid. Then he picked up his cup and braced himself to swallow the sickly concoction without grimacing. She'd been looking through the larder and preparing a meal, when she could have been sitting in front of the fire sulking. Her temper was frayed—the way she'd slammed down the teapot and ladled sugar into his drink without asking whether he liked it or not told him that much. So he'd be an ungrateful oaf to provoke her again, by complaining about such a small thing, when she was clearly doing her utmost to make the best of things.

'Though no sign of any of my own. Nor my groom,' he finished gloomily. Dammit, where was everyone?

'Well, at least we have plenty to eat. Would you like something now? I can make an omelette, if you'd like it.'

'I am starving,' he admitted with a wry smile. 'I suppose we ought to do something about finding somewhere to sleep really, but I could do with fortifying before I can face going upstairs again. The whole place is like an icehouse.'

'We…we could sleep in the kitchen,' she suggested, taking a sip of her own tea. 'It is, at least, warm.'

'Absolutely not,' he said, setting his own cup down firmly on the table—with some relief that he had a valid excuse for doing so without having to endure any more of the noxiously syrupy drink. 'There are a dozen perfectly serviceable bedrooms above stairs. And just because you've put on an apron and have to act like a cook doesn't mean you need to sleep below stairs, as well.'

'I've slept in worse places,' she admitted.

'Yes, maybe you have, but you're married to me now and it is my job to take care of you.' He was going to do better than his own father had done with Julia's mother. He wasn't going to assume Mary should be grateful for the privilege of bearing his name, and his title, no matter what the circumstances.

'Of course,' she said meekly, before rising and going across to a sort of preparation area near the stove and cracking several eggs into a bowl.

She didn't utter a word of reproof, but the set of her back as she grated some cheese into the egg mixture told him he really shouldn't have raised his voice to her just now.

He cleared his throat.

'It's very clever of you to know how to do all this sort of thing.'

'It was necessary,' she said, pouring the egg mixture into a pan where she'd already started some butter melting. 'If I hadn't learned how to cook, once Papa died, we would have gone hungry. We'd never been all that well off, but after he went, we had to move into a much smaller place and let all the servants go.' She frowned as she kept pulling the slowly setting mixture from the edges into the middle. 'Mama did the purchasing and tried to learn how to keep the household accounts in order, while I did the actual physical work of keeping house.'

'Well, I'm glad of it,' he said, and then, realising how heartless that sounded, added hastily, 'I mean, glad you can turn your hand to cooking. That smells wonderful,' he said, desperately hoping to make up lost ground. 'Anything I can do to help?'

She stirred the egg mixture several more times before making her reply.

'It might go down better with some wine,' she suggested as she added some ham to the egg mixture. 'But only if you can fetch it quickly. This won't take but a minute more.'

He didn't need telling twice. Lord, but he needed to get out of the kitchen before he said something even more tactless and shattered the tentative hold she must be keeping on her temper with him. He returned, with a dusty bottle and two wine glasses, just as she was sliding the omelette on to a plate.

'Not the best crystal,' he said, putting the bottle down beside his place setting and pulling a corkscrew from his pocket. 'But you did specify haste, so I got these from the butler's pantry.'

'I'm not used to the best crystal, anyway.'

She startled him then, by looking up at him and smiling ruefully. That she could still muster a smile, any kind of smile, and turn it his way, felt nothing short of miraculous. He dropped into his chair with relief, picked up his fork, swearing to himself he'd praise her cooking to the skies no matter what it tasted like.

But in the event, there was no need to feign appreciation.

'This has got to be,' he said, 'one of the tastiest omelettes I've ever eaten.'

She flushed and smiled again, this time with what looked like real pleasure.

'The…the wine is very good, too,' she reciprocated, having taken a sip.

'Don't go heaping coals of fire on my head. Coming here has been a disaster. All my fault. And you haven't uttered a single word of complaint. You're the only woman I know who wouldn't be ringing a peal over my head.'

'This really isn't so very bad,' she replied, lowering her gaze to her plate, 'compared to some of the things that have happened to me.'

'What do you mean?' He hadn't really learned all that much about her past, now he came to think of it. He'd been in such a hurry to get her to the altar he hadn't taken the time to talk.

'Oh, just…well, it was bad enough after Papa died, but at least Mama and I managed to maintain our independence. Even if it did mean moving frequently, to keep one step ahead of our creditors.' She flushed, and moved the omelette round and round on her plate, before taking a deep breath and plunging on.

'But when she died, her annuity died with her. I really did have absolutely nothing, for a while. Fortunately, I managed to track down the lawyer who'd dealt with Papa's affairs, hoping he would have some solution. But all he did was refer me to Papa's relations. None of whom wanted the added burden of an indigent female. I really was at my wit's end by the time I reached London and my aunt Pargetter. I thought…' She looked up and flashed him a tight smile. 'Well, you can see why all this…' she waved her hand round the kitchen, much as he'd done earlier '…doesn't seem so very dreadful. At least nobody can turn me out into that storm, can they? And we have food and a fire.' She shrugged and popped another forkful of omelette into her mouth.

He didn't know what to say. She'd been through so much. So bravely. And all on her own. And here he'd been, half expecting her to throw a tantrum like some spoiled society miss.

He pushed his empty plate to one side.

'Come on, let's go and see about somewhere to sleep.'

'But I need to wash the dishes.…'

'Leave 'em. Plenty more about the place, I'm sure. So we can have clean ones in the morning. The staff can do the washing up when they get back. That's what I pay 'em for.' He went round the table and pulled her to her feet. 'I'm glad you've pitched in and put a meal together, but I draw the line at you washing dishes.'

'I'll just stack them in the scullery, then.'

'Very well.'

'I think,' she said, with a shy smile, 'that I'm going to like being Lady Havelock.'

'What! After this?'

'I have always hated washing up,' she said, wiping her hands and tossing her apron aside. 'It's wonderful to just do the things I enjoy and leave the unpleasant tasks to others.'

Wonderful? From his point of view, it was wonderful she could describe *any* part of this evening in positive terms. 'Glad to hear it,' he said, tucking her arm into his and leading her up the stairs.

'This way,' he said, tugging her to the left and pulling a bunch of keys from his pocket.

He proudly flung open the double doors at the head of the stairs.

'The master bedroom,' he said. Then reeled back, coughing, at the musty smell that wafted out to greet him.

'It doesn't look as if anyone has used this room for years,' she said, wrinkling her nose.

'About a dozen, I suspect,' he groaned. 'I seem to recall the trustees saying something about only letting the tenants use certain rooms. I should have realised this one would be one of the ones out of bounds.' He ran his fingers through his hair. The Dog and Ferret was looking more appealing by the minute.

'Well, let us find a room that has been in use more recently and is a bit better aired,' she said, stepping smartly back into the corridor.

'What a good job you thought of coming down to look the place over before telling your sister she could come to live here,' she said brightly, after they'd inspected several more rooms and found them in a similar state to the master suite. 'I'm going to have my work cut out, getting it ready for her return.'

Not if he could help it. He'd hire an army of servants to scrub and clean this place from top to bottom. Hang the expense. He wasn't going to have her working her fingers to the bone on his account.

Mary was just beginning to think they would have to go back to the kitchen, after all, when Lord Havelock opened the door to a room that didn't reek of damp and mice.

'It doesn't strike so cold in here, does it?' he said, stepping over the threshold. 'I'll tell you what it is,' he said sagely, as she lifted the corner of a cover that shrouded an item of furniture that turned out to be a bed. 'Right at the end of the corridor, here, the room faces south. It must get the sun all day. Bound to keep it drier than the others, which face west or east.'

'Even so, I'm not too sure we can use this bed,' she said, lifting the cover higher to reveal a rolled-up mattress at the end of the frame.

He sighed. 'The bedding at the Dog and Ferret may have been dirty and damp, but at least there would have been some.'

'We could air the mattress for a while in front of the fire, once we get it lit,' she suggested. 'And we can use our coats, and what have you, for bedding. Just for one night. If…if you wouldn't mind fetching our luggage.'

'I'll do that,' he said. Then, as he passed her, he swept her into his arms and gave her a swift, hard kiss. 'You think of everything.'

Well, in the past, she'd had to. She wouldn't have got as far as Aunt Pargetter, if she hadn't had the sense to track down the lawyer who'd dealt with her father's affairs.

But, only fancy, now she was telling her husband, a peer of the realm no less, how to deal with the situation in which they found themselves. And sending him off on an errand.

She wouldn't have believed it, if someone had told her, even a few weeks ago, that she'd have the courage.

But it came easily to her, with Lord Havelock, she mused, kneeling on the hearth to see if she could get the fire going. In fact, as she set a taper to the wadded-up paper in the grate, she decided she was going to ask him to fetch some more coal, when he came back with their luggage. For there were only a few dusty coals sitting on top of the kindling, and only a handful more in the scuttle. And she really didn't think he'd mind.

Thanks heavens she'd decided to make the best of things, rather than nursing her grievances. What was the point, after all, of dwelling on past mistakes, when he was clearly making such an effort with her now? He'd been an attentive companion during the journey, apologised profusely for the state of the house and even carried her over the threshold—a romantic gesture that had taken her completely by surprise. Not that she was going to read too much into it.

She didn't care that circumstances were far from ideal. They were making a much better job of being married than her parents ever had, with each blaming the other for everything that went wrong and neither of them lifting a finger to do anything about it.

She put her hand to her lips, which were still tingling from his last kiss, a great surge of hope rising up in her heart.

'How are you getting on?' said Lord Havelock as he came back to the room with one of her cases and one of his.

She opened her mouth to thank him for being so even-handed, rather than just bringing up his own cases first. But the moment he'd opened the door a cloud of smoke came billowing into the room instead of going up the chimney, making her cough and wipe at her streaming eyes.

'Now I can see,' he said, shutting the door hastily, 'why this room was never occupied by the family, in spite of the view. It looks as though it has one of those fires that sends more smoke into the room than up the chimney.'

'It doesn't seem to be drawing very well,' she said. 'I just thought the chimney was probably a bit damp.'

'No. I've just remembered something. I never understood it before, but it was so odd, that it stuck in my mind,' he said, striding to the window. 'Nobody ever lit the fire in here without shutting that door and opening this window first.'

He turned the handle and pushed at the casement. It didn't budge.

'Stuck,' he said gloomily. 'Frame is probably warped with damp. Will probably need to get a lot of the frames shaved,' he said, giving it another, harder shove, 'or replaced.'

Suddenly, the window gave. Only not just the casement, but the hinges, too. His entire top half disappeared through the opening for a moment while a gust of wind whooshed in.

The smoke curled in on itself and got sucked up the chimney while flames finally started dancing across the sluggish kindling.

Lord Havelock hauled himself upright and staggered away from the window. He was sopping wet. And swearing fluently at the segment of window frame he was still clutching in his hand.

'You…you…' She pressed her hand to her mouth. But it was no use. She couldn't suppress the torrent of giggles fizzing up inside.

'You are quite…' she managed shakily. 'Quite right, the fire d-does draw better with the window…the window…'

Finally rendered speechless with laughter, she pointed at the frame dangling from his hand.

'You think this is funny?'

She nodded, completely unable to frame any words for the laughter bubbling over.

With a low growl, he spun away from her, wedged the window frame back in place and thumped it home with several strategic blows from his large, powerful fists.

Strange, but she wasn't the least bit intimidated by the demonstration of raw masculine frustration. If that had been her father, now, she would have been crouching lower, keeping her eyes down, her head bowed. Anything and everything to render herself small and invisible.

But Lord Havelock wasn't cast from the same mould as her father. He might be hot-tempered, but he wasn't bad-tempered. And that made all the difference.

As if to prove the point, the second he'd mended the window as well as he could, he strode across the room, dropped to his knees beside her and draped one arm about her shoulders.

'You're a good sport,' he said brusquely, before planting a kiss on her temple. 'I know I've said it before, but you must be the only woman alive who would see the funny side, rather than ripping up at me.'

He took the poker from the set of fire irons and started pushing the coals into more strategic positions.

'So far today you've had to skivvy like a kitchen maid and now you're going to have to sleep in conditions that are tantamount to camping out.'

Whatever must the women in his past have been like, to carp over such trifles as that? No wonder he'd been so reluctant to get married, if that was his expectation of female behaviour.

'All I really asked of you was a room of my own, in whichever of your properties I happened to be,' she countered. 'We never specified it should have fully f-functioning, w-windows…' And suddenly she couldn't quite stifle another bout of giggles as she recalled the look on his face when the whole thing had come away in his hands. 'Or f-furniture of any kind, come to that.'

'Like I said, a good sport,' he said, smiling at her with approval.

'What would be the point of ripping up at you, over something as silly as this? You didn't mean me any harm. It's just…' She reached up and cupped his cheek.

'Oh—you are so cold. You must get out of those wet things at once.'

His smile turned a shade wicked.

'Now that's what a man likes to hear from his bride. An invitation to get out of his clothing and into—' He stopped short. 'Only, hang it, we haven't actually got a bed to get into.'

'It won't take long,' she said, a touch breathlessly, 'to make one up.'

He tossed the poker aside and gave her a look that made her heart leap behind her breastbone.

'In fact, all we need to do…'

'Yes?'

'Is to bring the mattress over here and unroll it in front of the fire.'

'Brilliant notion,' he said, dropping a swift kiss on her cheek.

As she went to open their cases, he ripped off his damp jacket and shirt and tossed them into a corner. Her mouth dried at the sight of his naked torso. Though she was supposed to be selecting the items of clothing most suited to form bedding, she just grabbed handfuls at random, unable to keep her eyes straying from the sight of him wrestling the mattress into submission. In the end, it happened to be a couple of his shirts and her spare petticoat that she spread over the mattress, and heaven alone knew what she had wadded up into makeshift pillows.

They fell to the mattress together, lips meeting and locking in a heated kiss.

She ran her hands up and down the smooth, sleek muscles of his back as he rolled her beneath him. And moaned with pleasure when he grabbed a handful of her skirts and pushed them up out of the way.

'Lord,' he groaned, 'we should slow this down, somehow. You are so new at this.'

No! He couldn't stop now. Not when she needed him so badly.

'We can go slow next time, if you like. But please…' She shifted her hips impatiently.

'Next time, she says,' he growled into her neck. 'Do you know what it does to a man, hearing the woman he's taking, promising him there will be a next time?'

'No….'

'Of course you don't, my little innocent. That's what makes you so adorable.'

Adorable? He thought she was adorable? Well, she thought he was adorable, too. She hugged him hard, on a wave of tenderness.

'And I don't want to wait any longer than I have to, believe me,' he assured her.

'Good.' She half sighed, half moaned, as he slid his hand, and with it her skirts, all the way up to her waist.

'Oh, God,' he moaned, exploring her with his fingers. 'You are so ready for me. I can't believe it. I don't deserve you.' He raised himself up to claw open the fall of his breeches. 'I don't deserve,' he said, thrusting home, 'this.'

It was heavenly. She knew the pleasure he could bring this time, and instead of lying back and letting him do all the work, she became an equal participant, striving to reach the finishing line alongside him. And this time, instead of a soft, gentle burst of pleasure, it was like a thousand rockets going off inside her, all at once. Shattering. Sparkling. Satisfying. So satisfying. She clutched at him, stroking his back as he settled over her, his face buried in her neck.

'Mary,' he growled after a moment or two. 'Mary?'

'Hmm?'

'I know I said you could always have a room of your own,' he said plaintively. 'But I hope you're not going to insist I find somewhere else tonight.'

'You must be joking,' she said. 'I will need you to keep me warm.'

When he would have rolled off her, she clung on.

'Not so fast.'

He half rose up to look down into her face.

'You mean, now I can take it slowly?'

'I didn't mean that,' she protested.

But with a wicked grin, he reached down between them and began to toy with her, just where their bodies were still joined.

She gasped. 'I didn't know... Can you do it all over again?'

'It seems that with you, I can. You are an astonishing woman.'

'Me?' She looked up at him, perplexed. Though she couldn't meet his eye for very long, not when he was doing what he was doing.

'Oohh,' she groaned.

'Oh, indeed,' he agreed. And wrapped her legs round his waist.

Chapter Nine

She didn't know what woke her, but the moment she did so, she knew she was alone. And the place where her husband had been was cold.

She could hear windows rattling somewhere, chimneys moaning as the wind protested its inability to get in. The fire had died down considerably, but it still cast a dim glow over the room. She snuggled down further into the pile of clothing that had become her bed, marvelling that she could feel so calm, that the sounds of the storm raging outside only made her feel more secure.

She'd never known this. This complete faith that she was safe. There'd always been a feeling of dread hanging over her, as far back as she could remember. But it had gone now.

She rather thought it had started to lift the moment Lord Havelock had slid his ring on to her finger.

She heard the sounds of footsteps in the corridor, then, as she turned her head towards the door, she saw her husband, wearing nothing but his breeches and boots.

'D-didn't mean to w-wake you,' he stammered through chattering teeth. 'Had to f-fetch more c-coal.'

He dumped the bucket he'd been carrying and tossed several shovelfuls of coal on to the fire.

'You must be frozen,' she said, noting the goose-bumps all over his back.

'That's p-putting it m-mildly.'

'Why on earth didn't you put your coat on?'

'What, and rob you of your b-blank-kets?' He shook his head, a scowl darkening his features.

It might be cold in the house, but her heart felt as if it was melting. What a perfectly wonderful thing for him to do. She sniffed back a welling tear. He was such a *chivalrous* man.

'B-besides,' he added as he came back to the bed, 'you'll soon warm me up.'

With a growl, he burrowed under the mound of clothing, then wrapped his arms and legs round her as though she was his own personal hot-water bottle.

She couldn't help shrieking as an ice-cold hand slid inside the bodice of her chemise.

'Mmmhh.' He half sighed, half groaned. 'You feel wonderful.'

'Ow! You don't,' she yelped as he ran a cold foot up her calf.

'Is that any way to thank me for going all that way to fetch coal? Come on, Mary,' he murmured, burying a cold nose into her neck. 'Don't you think I've earned a reward?'

He had. He definitely had. But just as she started to tell him so, his cold hands had her dissolving into giggles. He kept on searching for particularly sensitive places, tormenting her until she was begging for mercy.

He ignored her pleas, ruthlessly turning her giggles into moans of pleasure, her wriggling to escape into writhing to get closer. Pretty soon, neither of them felt the slightest bit cold. Together, they stoked up the fires of passion until it consumed them both in a blaze of wonderful completion.

It was daylight stuttering in through the broken window that brought Mary awake the next morning. With a contented sigh, she snuggled into her husband's side and put an arm round his waist.

'Thank God you're awake at last,' he said. 'For the past half hour, at least, I've been so hungry I've even started to wonder what coal tastes like.'

'You are awake?' But he'd been so still. 'You should have woken me.'

He traced one finger over her creased brow. 'You looked so peaceful lying there. So…lovely, with the fire-light flickering over your hair. I could quite happily have stayed here all day, admiring you.…'

Why was he saying that, when they both knew she wasn't the slightest bit pretty? He'd even made a point of saying it didn't matter.

Need not be pretty.

She'd been lying there, feeling warm and contented, and grateful that marrying him had brought her into a cosy shelter from the storms of life, and with one careless remark he'd brought that horrid list to the forefront of her mind.

'If only we had someone to bring us breakfast up here,' he finished ruefully.

That was more like it. She preferred honest, even mundane, conversation, as long as he didn't try to…to soft-soap her with the kind of meaningless, insincere flattery that was an insult to her intelligence.

'Since we don't,' she said with a stiff smile, 'we will just have to go down and make it ourselves.'

'By which you mean you will conjure up something, while I am obliged to watch from the sidelines,' he grumbled, sitting up and rummaging through their bedding until he came across a shirt. 'You shouldn't have to do it all,' he said, pulling the shirt over his head, while she reached for the least crumpled item of clothing she could find. 'I may not know my way round a kitchen, but surely I could spare you some of the heavy work? Heaving coal, or hauling water, or something?'

Once again, she was glad she'd kept her brief spurt of annoyance to herself. He might have his faults, but at least he was willing to pitch in and help, rather than leaving her to struggle alone.

And he'd certainly got the muscles for it, she reflected, watching his beautiful back flex and stretch as he thrust his arms into the sleeves.

'If you are sure, then…thank you.'

The smile that blazed across his face had the strange effect of making her want to pull him straight back down on to the mattress.

Just because he'd smiled at her? How…weak and pathetic did that make her? Rather shaken by the strength of the feelings he could rouse, without, apparently, even trying, she pulled on her dress.

Only to feel her insides turn to mush when he took her hand as they ventured out of their room into a corridor that was so cold their breath misted in the air in great clouds. He kept it clasped firmly in his all the way to the kitchen. If she'd wanted to retrieve it, she would have had a struggle. And there didn't seem much point in taking objection to such a harmless demonstration of affection.

Affection! No, it couldn't be that. He'd specifically warned her not to go looking for affection.

'What would you like me to do first?' he asked when they reached the kitchen. 'Fetch more coal? Or wood?'

She'd rather he stopped being so amazing, she thought crossly. So she wouldn't be tempted to forget this was supposed to be a practical arrangement. Or start thinking that gestures such as carrying her over the threshold, or holding her hand, or saying she was adorable, were just the sort of things that went on in a love match.

'Whichever you prefer.' She sighed, going to the stove and kneeling to rake out the ashes. 'The log basket does need filling,' she admitted. The sooner she set him to work, the sooner she'd get back into a sensible frame of mind. Rather than wondering what it would be like if they were really lovers, stranded here alone. Or how romantic it would seem to have a lord chopping wood and hauling water while she sat indoors in the warm...

She shook her head. She needed to stay focused on practicalities, not drift off into stupid daydreams.

'We will need quite a lot of water. This stove has a place where you can pour it, to heat, and then we can draw it off from this tap here, see, whenever we want some.'

'Ingenious,' he said. And then his stomach rumbled.

And she recalled him lying quietly, so as not to disturb her, even though he'd jested he was hungry enough to try the coal.

'There is no rush,' she said, ashamed of constantly getting annoyed with him when, in his own way, he was clearly doing his best. 'There is enough wood to get the fire hot enough to put the breakfast rolls in. Why don't you help yourself to some of that ham we had last night while I fetch them?'

'You're sure?'

'Yes.' She got up, dusted her knees and smiled at him. 'No point in setting you to work on an empty stomach.'

He didn't need telling twice before he'd got the ham out of the larder and carved himself a huge slice.

'I had no idea,' he said, much later, once breakfast was ready and they could both sit down together, 'that so much work was involved in just throwing a bit of breakfast together. And do you know, I don't think I'll be half so impatient about getting served in inns, after this. When I think of some of the insults I've heaped on waiters, when I've come in, sharp set...' He shook his head ruefully, before breaking open a roll and slathering it with butter.

He groaned, half closing his eyes as if in ecstasy.

'That has to be the most delicious thing I've ever tasted. You're a marvel.'

She shook her head. 'I'm no marvel. You are simply very, very hungry. I don't suppose you would think a simple bread roll would be all that delicious if you weren't.'

'That may be part of it,' he agreed, reaching for another roll, a faint frown furrowing his forehead. 'Perhaps I have fallen into the habit of taking such simple things for granted. But I shan't any longer. And as for—'

He'd just reached across the table to take her hand when there came a knock at the back door.

Muttering under his breath, Lord Havelock strode

across the room to answer the knock while she stood up and whipped off her apron.

'Mornin',' said a short, wiry man who was knuckling his forehead.

'Gilbey! Where the devil,' snapped her husband, 'have you been?'

He then, belatedly, seemed to recall she was there. 'Pardon my language,' he said perfunctorily, over his shoulder at her, before waving his arm in her direction.

'My wife, Lady Havelock,' he said to the wiry man, who'd sidled in out of the cold.

Out of habit, Mary dropped a curtsy, causing the wiry man's shaggy eyebrows to shoot up his forehead.

'This is my *groom*,' said her husband with a touch of impatience. 'You don't need to curtsy to such as him. Now, you, explain yourself,' he snapped, turning his attention back to the wiry man too quickly to notice Mary flinch.

How could he reprove her like that? In the man's hearing?

'I expected to find you, and, more important, Lady and Lightning, in the stables when I got here last night,' snapped Lord Havelock.

'Well, when I got here yesterday, me lord, seeing as how there was nobody about, and the stables deserted, I thought it best to take them, and your chestnuts, to the nearest inn, make sure they was taken proper care of, like. And see if I could find out what was afoot here. Brought 'em back as soon as I'd made sure there would be proper provisions for them and knew as you'd arrived yourself.'

'Hmmph,' said Lord Havelock and stalked out into the yard, the groom trotting behind in his wake.

Mary stood looking at the door for a moment or two, her mouth hanging open. Where had his appetite gone? He'd been complaining of hunger ever since they awoke. So hungry he'd even joked about trying the coal. But the moment he heard his horses had arrived they'd driven every other thought from his mind.

He must care about them a lot, she decided, closing first her mouth, then the kitchen door through which he'd just vanished without a backward glance. She should have picked up on the clues the day before, when he admitted he'd had them travel by stages so as not to tire them, though he'd pushed her into making the entire journey in one go. And the way his face had fallen when she'd admitted she couldn't ride.

Which told her two things. First, he must have thought about going out riding with her. Not only thought about it, but looked forward to it, or he wouldn't have looked so disappointed.

And second, that she'd been right about his character. Even though Lord Havelock had looked as angry as she'd ever seen him, the groom hadn't seemed the slightest bit scared of the way he'd shouted. He'd just stood there letting her husband rant a bit, then stated his case clearly.

And her husband had listened.

Just as he'd listened to her, when she'd stood up to him over the matter of their betrothal. He'd scared her a bit, back then, the way his anger had blown up seemingly out of nowhere. But it had blown out just as swiftly.

Not that it excused him rebuking her in front of a third party. Her father had exercised that particular form of cruelty towards her mother, whittling her sense of worth down, insult by insult, until there had been nothing left but splinters.

Well, she wasn't going to let her husband do the same to her. Not that she really thought he was doing it deliberately.

Nevertheless, she needed to take a stand, now, so that he would learn she wouldn't tolerate such treatment.

She strode to the dresser and took down another cup to set on the table. Outside staff generally came into the kitchen for their meals. Since there was nobody else to provide them, she would have to take on the task of feeding the groom.

Even if her husband disapproved of her sitting at table with him.

Well, she didn't care if he did think she was committing yet another social *faux pas* by extending common humanity to the poor wretch, the way he'd done when she'd dropped that curtsy.

Lifting her chin, she strode to the table and placed the cup down firmly before one of the empty chairs. She half hoped he *did* disapprove of her willingness to hobnob with a lowly groom. She went back to the dresser and picked up a plate, a knife and a fork with a toss of her head. For then he'd discover that he had most definitely not married *a mouse*.

She set about preparing such a substantial meal that it was bound to earn his forgiveness, once she'd shown him that he couldn't get away with trying to browbeat her in front of servants.

'You were right,' said Lord Havelock, the moment he came back into the kitchen. She glanced up from the stove to assess his mood, before reaching for the kettle.

'Was I?' She poured water into the pot, noting that

her hands were shaking as she braced herself to stand up for herself for the first time in her life. 'What about?'

She couldn't see any sign of the anger that had driven him out to the stables, which must mean he was pleased with the condition of his horses, and had forgiven the groom for not being on hand the night before. She just hoped he'd be as quick to forgive her.

'About the caretaker and his wife. Gilbey found out— Stop loitering there in the doorway, man,' he barked at the groom over his shoulder. 'Come in and shut it before you let all the heat out,' he said, depriving her of the opportunity of inviting him in herself.

The groom snatched off his hat, shuffled forward and closed the door behind him, while Lord Havelock sauntered over to the stove, holding out his hands to warm them.

'Gilbey put up at the Dog and Ferret last night,' he said. 'The landlord told him that the Brownlows have gone away to visit relatives of some sort for the season. They don't plan to come back until the twenty-eighth. It was a shock to everyone in the taproom to hear I'd come back, expecting to take up residence. God only knows where my letter to them has gone. Still at the receiving office, I shouldn't wonder. Is that a fresh pot of tea? Capital.'

To her intense irritation, he then pulled up a chair at the table and indicated the groom should do so, as well. Where had his insistence on keeping the groom in his place, and she in hers, gone? She was torn between wanting to hug him for being so affable, or slap him for depriving her of the opportunity to take a stand. In the end, all she did was pour both men a cup of tea.

She'd have to find some other way of showing him

he couldn't speak to her like that. Only…if she launched into that kind of speech right now, wouldn't she look a bit shrewish?

'Looks as though my wife has cooked enough to feed an army,' he said. Cheerfully.

He clearly had no idea what he'd done to her.

'And even if you've had something at the Dog and Ferret, you should at least have a couple of these rolls,' he said, putting some on a plate and pushing them over, with what looked suspiciously like…pride. 'They're first-rate.'

No, she definitely couldn't start complaining about the way he'd talked to her when he'd been in a temper, not when he was being so complimentary about her cooking. Lips pressed tightly together, she served both men with eggs and ham, then sank, deflated, on to her own seat.

'Which leads me to the next question,' said her husband, in between mouthfuls. 'What are we going to do until the Brownlows return, my Lady Havelock?'

'I don't understand.'

He wasn't asking her opinion, was he? Men didn't do that. So what was he about now? And why was he addressing her so formally? When all through the night he'd used her given name. Over and over again.

Mary, he'd whispered into her ear.

Mary… he'd growled.

Oh, Mary… he'd moaned.

Oh, it was all so confusing. *He* was confusing!

'Well,' he said very slowly, as though explaining to a child, 'we could go and rack up at the Dog and Ferret. We'll have plenty of food and a proper bed.'

'If'n you don't mind damp sheets and bedbugs,' muttered Gilbey.

'It doesn't sound very…appealing,' Mary agreed.

'Trouble is,' said her husband, 'the only alternative is to remain here. And you've already discovered how uncomfortable this place is, too, without servants.'

He laid down his knife and fork, and gave her a straight look.

Both her husband and groom were watching her intently, she realised after a moment or two.

Heavens, they really were waiting to hear what she thought. Her husband hadn't just told her what the choices were, before telling her what he was going to do. He really was going to let her decide. Well, she'd wanted the chance to take a stand. And though it wasn't exactly the topic she'd wanted to confront him about, it was better than nothing.

'This is my home now,' she therefore stated firmly. 'I would much rather stay here and try to make the place a bit more comfortable, than throw myself on the mercy of a landlord who sounds as though he doesn't care about the welfare of his guests one bit.'

'Capital,' he said, beaming at her as though she'd just said the very thing he was waiting to hear. 'I didn't really want you to have to put up with the rabble that frequent the Dog and Ferret. No offence to you, Gilbey.'

'None taken. I've got no wish to go back there meself,' he said, scratching his neck. 'There's the makings of decent quarters over the stables. Just want a bit of sorting, like.'

'It's the same with this house, I'm sure,' said Mary.

Lord Havelock frowned. 'But you are going to have to do it single-handed. Da—dash it, this isn't the Christmas I'd planned to give you,' he said, slamming his half-emptied cup down on to the table. 'But I will make it up to you, I swear. I'll tell you what I'll do,' he said, his face brightening. 'I'll go into the village and see if I can purchase the makings of Christmas dinner.'

'That's a very...' she'd been going to say, a good idea. But he'd already reached the back door and was striding out into the yard.

'That's his lordship all over,' said the groom, eyeing her astonishment with amusement. 'Get's a notion in his cockloft and don't stop to consider if it's even possible, never mind sensible.'

'R-really?' She hadn't known him long, but, yes, she could well believe that he was the type of man to act on impulse, rather than planning anything in great detail. He was so full of energy. And with the kind of confidence that came from being both wealthy and having a secure position in society. Yes, he could very easily set off into the unknown, assuming that everything would work out well for him.

Except when it had come to marriage. When he'd contemplated marriage, he'd sat down with a group of friends and got them to help him plan it all out down to the last detail.

Which only went to show how hard it must have been for a man who was used to doing as he pleased, whenever he pleased, to shackle himself to just one woman.

She supposed she ought to look upon his making of that list as a symptom of his determination to get it right. She'd seen several examples of that determination. That drive to do his best. Though it still hurt to read herself, the wife, described in such terms.

'I'd best get back to the stables, if you will excuse

me,' said Gilbey, getting to his feet. 'Unless there's anything you want helping with, in the way of heavy work?'

'That's very good of you, but I won't know until I've taken a good look about the place, to see what wants doing.'

'Ah, you're just what his lordship needs,' observed the groom with a knowing air. 'Sensible. And calm. Begging yer pardon for speaking so free, but...' He twisted his hat between his rather grubby fingers. 'You oughtn't to listen to those who will tell you he's wild. Or worry about his temper,' he said knowingly.

'I don't,' she replied firmly. She hadn't been afraid of him since...since...

Actually, she hadn't ever been really afraid of him. Nervous, yes, of the pull he exerted over her. Scared of her reactions to him. But of him, not really ever.

'Sure, he's fought his duels,' Gilbey added. 'But he's a good lad, at heart.'

'Duels? He's fought duels?'

'He didn't mean no harm by them,' hastily put in the groom. 'It's just, he ain't never had nobody, not since his mother passed, to care what he did, one way or another, y'see. 'Twill make all the difference to him, to have someone steady, to be his...well, his anchor, like,' he finished gruffly, before slapping the hat on his head and scuttling off out of the door.

She reached for her cup of tea and took a long, sustaining drink. Now that the initial shock had worn off, she could see exactly how her husband could have stumbled into fighting a duel or two. Not only did he have a hair-trigger temper, but he also had a highly developed sense of his own honour. Only look at the way he'd reacted when she'd assumed he'd been making her an insulting proposition.

He'd calmed down as soon as she'd explained herself, though. Which only went to prove that whoever he'd fought hadn't attempted to apologise. So if he had shot them, it was entirely their own fault.

He was good at heart, the groom had insisted. And gone on to talk about Lord Havelock's mother. Which showed he'd stayed with the family for years, as well as sort of proving his point. Servants didn't stay with cruel masters. She should know. They'd gone through dozens of servants during the time they'd been able to afford to pay their wages.

Besides, she'd seen many instances of his deep-down goodness. Only look at the way he'd set to work hauling water for her. Or going to fetch coal in the middle of the night, shirtless, and come back shivering rather than deprive her of the warmth of his coat. Or let her sleep as long as she wanted, even though he wanted his breakfast.

She drained the cup and set it down on the table.

But what impressed her most of all was the way he'd apologised. And tried to make amends for all that had gone wrong. He'd even gone charging off, just now, to buy food in an attempt to *make it up to her*.

A smile played about her lips as she recalled the look on his face when he'd set off to the village as if he could purchase the answer to all his problems there. It was sweet of him, but she could think of far better ways he could make it up to her, if his conscience was troubling him.

None of which involved him *buying* anything at all.

Chapter Ten

'Duck,' he announced, some hours later, as he came in the door.

'Why, are you going to throw something?'

'Ha ha,' he said. 'Very droll. Though I just might, if you provoke me like that, you minx. Anyway, what I meant is, I've got a duck for Christmas dinner,' announced her husband with pride as Gilbey followed him into the kitchen, carrying a game bag. 'And a meat pie for tonight. There is cake, and fruit, too.'

'All…all in that sack?' Oh, dear.

Gilbey solemnly laid the bag on the kitchen table and opened the tie at the neck. The first thing to come out of it was the pie. The crust was a little the worse for wear, but it was definitely still edible. As were the apples that had done most of the damage, to judge from the amount of gravy coating them.

'Apples in gravy, how…novel,' she said diplomatically. 'Is there gravy on the cake, too? No. Oh, well…' she sighed as she lifted it out and set it to one side '…I suppose I can bear to eat it without.'

'Now look here,' snapped her husband. 'I had the

devil of a job to get hold of this little lot. You wouldn't believe the haggling I had to do.'

'I'm very grateful,' she said soothingly. 'This is the makings of a true feast.' It really was. She'd been worrying, ever since he'd set off in such a hurry, that he'd come back with all sorts of ridiculously inappropriate things. But in the event, the only thing he hadn't got quite right was the method of bringing everything home.

'I shall have no qualms about sending you shopping in future.' Although she might hand him a shopping basket rather than let him snatch up a game bag, as if he was going out shooting.

'Shopping,' he cried indignantly, planting his fists on his hips. 'That was not shopping. That was…foraging.'

'I see. Well, in that case, I have to say I am impressed by your foraging skills. In fact, I think you would make a good soldier.'

He would certainly look good in a uniform. All that scarlet cloth stretched across his broad shoulders, with a sword dangling from his slender hips to complete the very picture of masculine perfection.…

'A soldier, eh?'

'Yes.' She sighed, dragging herself out of a brief vision of him pulling a pistol from his belt and shooting some random marauder. 'Actually,' she said with one part of her mind while another was seeing him metamorphosed into the captain of a ship, his hair tousled by an Atlantic gale rather than his restless fingers, 'I think you could be anything you set your mind to.'

Anything he set his mind to? No, surely she didn't mean *anything*. Oh, he had total confidence he could rise to any form of physical challenge. He was a crack shot, a bruising rider and a long-standing member of the Four-in-Hand club. But nobody, in his entire life, had ever expressed any faith in his ability to put his *mind* to work. And so far, surely, he'd demonstrated he was a total dunce when it came to organising anything. Even with the help of his lists, he'd overlooked several important issues that any man who exercised his brain occasionally would have thought of before he set off into the winter weather with a brand-new bride in tow.

Yet she was looking at him as though he'd just done something remarkable. As though he really did have it in him to accomplish…*anything.*

He stood quite still, basking in the completely novel sensation of having a female look at him with whole-hearted admiration.

Totally unwarranted admiration, as far as he was concerned. If he hadn't made such a mull of opening up Mayfield, he wouldn't have had to go out on the foraging expedition in the first place.

She'd come to her senses before long. End up wishing him elsewhere, the way everybody always did, eventually.

She lowered her eyes to the spread on the table. Just as though she'd sensed him bracing himself against the day it happened.

'I think—that is, I hope,' she said, darting him the kind of look from under those dark lashes that made him catch his breath, 'that you will be pleased with what I have been about today, as well.'

'I'm sure I shall,' he said. As far as he was concerned she could have been sitting in front of a fire toasting her toes all day, after looking at him the way she'd just done, merely because he'd managed to rectify *one* of the blunders he'd made.

But he couldn't help wondering what kind of treatment she must have been used to, if it took so little effort to get her to look at him as though he was some kind of…hero…stepped straight out of the pages of a romance novel.

Not that he'd ever read any, but a lot of girls seemed to do so, then spent hours sighing over characters with odd names and complaining he wasn't a bit like any of 'em.

'I went exploring,' she said. 'And I discovered that all the rooms in the part of the house that used to be let out are in very good order. It looks as if those caretakers of yours have kept them in readiness for tenants to come in at a moment's notice. So I lit a fire and aired the mattress in the one I liked best,' she said with a slightly defiant tilt to her chin, as though expecting him to object. 'And I ironed the damp out of some sheets I found in a linen closet and made up a bed.'

'That's wonderful news.'

'Oh. I am so glad you don't mind which room we have tonight,' she said with evident relief. 'Indeed, there are so many in a state of near readiness that if you don't like it you can soon choose another.…'

'No, no, I shall be glad to sleep in a real bed tonight, thank you.' He went to her, seized her hand and kissed it. She really was a treasure. 'And I don't care which room you picked. I told you this is your home as much as mine. You must do whatever you like in it. But,' he added, 'don't you see what this means? After the window came away in my hand last night I was beginning to think the whole place had fallen into ruin while I wasn't paying attention. But now I can write to Lady

Peverell and tell her that Julia can come here as soon as she likes. I can get her safely out of that man's reach before he has a chance to—'

He shot a look at Gilbey, who was folding up the sack, with the wooden expression of a servant who was listening to a conversation not meant for his ears.

'In fact, I think I shall go and write immediately. Gilbey, instead of hanging around in the kitchen, you can make yourself useful by riding down to the post with it as soon as I've written it.'

'Yes, m'lord.'

Mary sat blinking at the swirl of dust that eddied across the kitchen floor after he'd slammed the door on his way out.

He'd been a bit like a whirlwind himself. Breezing in, delivering his mound of booty, then dashing off to his next task. She couldn't stop smiling as she pottered about the kitchen. The more she learned about her husband, the better she liked him.

She liked him even more when he turned up for supper on time, praised her cooking to the skies and then tried to prevent her from doing the dishes.

'I thought I'd made my views on that sort of thing plain,' he growled when she started to carry a stack of plates to the scullery.

'Yes, you did,' she said. 'But if the Brownlows aren't going to return until the twenty-eighth, every useful surface will be covered with dirty dishes by then. It wouldn't be fair to them to have to come back to that sort of mess.'

'It would serve 'em right for sloping off just when I

particularly wanted 'em here.' He scowled. 'And if you don't want the working surfaces cluttered, why don't you stack the dishes on the floor?'

'I could do that, I suppose,' she said with a shudder. 'If you want the house invaded by rats.'

'Point taken,' he said. 'Dishes need to be done. But I won't have you doing them. I made you a vow.'

For one moment she thought he was going to order Gilbey to do the dishes for her. But then, to her amazement, he stood up, removed his jacket and rolled up his shirtsleeves.

'I shall need instruction,' he said, as he strode into the scullery.

He meant to do the dishes himself?

Well—she'd always thought that it was a man's actions that revealed his true nature. And after seeing him literally roll up his sleeves to perform such a lowly task, she would never make the mistake of suspecting he was anything like her father, ever again.

'Not that it can possibly be all that hard,' he said airily. 'I've never met a scullery maid yet with anything approaching half a brain.'

'Have you met many scullery maids?' she heard herself say, inanely, as she tipped a bucket of hot water into one of the sinks. Still, it was better than blurting out any of the other thoughts swarming round her head. Or simply gazing at him, wide-eyed and slack-jawed in wholly feminine appreciation.

For heaven's sakes! All he'd done was roll up his sleeves and she was practically dribbling at the sight of his forearms.

'I'm sure I must have done,' he said, as she handed him a scrubbing brush. And only just managed to stop herself from running her hand up that enticing expanse of sinewy, hair-roughened flesh.

'On their days off. At fairs and such,' he added, seizing the nearest plate and manfully dunking it into the soapy water. 'And there was definitely one who used to prowl around the stables after the head groom at…well, never mind where. She couldn't have had much in her cockloft to throw herself at him the way she did. Without the slightest sign of encouragement, I might add. Remember her, Gilbey? I can see you loitering in the doorway, so don't bother trying to pretend you aren't listening to every word. Don't you have work to do?'

'Yes, m'lord,' said the groom, before disappearing out into the night to do whatever it was he did for the horses.

Thank heaven she hadn't started stroking her husband's arms. She hadn't been aware the groom was there, so rapt had she been by the sight of a man, her man, cheerfully engaging in what her father would have scathingly described as woman's work.

'The tale of me up to my elbows in soapsuds will spread like wildfire through the taverns,' Lord Havelock grumbled, holding out the plate he'd scrubbed for her inspection.

'Perfect,' she said with a sigh. Then blushed. 'The plate, I mean,' she added hastily. 'At least it will be once you rinse it. Or perhaps I should rinse it.' She went to take it from him.

'Oh, no, you don't,' he said, dunking the plate into the clean water in the next sink over and clasping her about the waist. 'I am quite capable of doing this, you know.'

'Yes, but if you don't want people to talk—'

'I don't care what people might say about me,' he declared, before dipping his head to kiss her. 'They can go hang for all I care.'

She totally lost the thread of what they'd been discussing as he kissed her over and over again, walking her backwards across the room until she fetched up against a wall. The slide of his wet hands up her legs as he impatiently thrust her skirts out of the way, and the thrill of complying as he murmured heated, explicit instructions into her ear.

The joy of having this man want her so much that he couldn't even wait to find a horizontal surface to lay her down on thrilled her.

And the gratitude that came from discovering that for all his impatience to have her, he possessed the self-control to wait until he'd satisfied her, before taking his own pleasure.

It got better every time, with Mary. He'd thought nothing could surpass their wedding night, yet sharing that mattress in front of the fire, the next night, had somehow been even better.

And as for last night…even when they'd eventually finished 'doing the dishes', the fire between them hadn't gone out. They'd raced up the stairs to the room she'd prepared and torn each other's clothes off with such haste they hadn't bothered using the warming pan she'd insisted on filling with embers from the kitchen fire.

He raised himself on one elbow to look at her. Just look at her. How had he ever thought her plain? Not that she had one of those faces that attracted notice at first glance. No, what she had was an attraction that shone from the intelligence in her eyes, or the warmth of her smile.

He couldn't help just sifting her soft, silken hair through his fingers, then fanning it out across his pillow. He liked the fact she didn't wear it in bunches of fussy ringlets. In fact, he wouldn't be surprised if she found it hard to make it take a curl. It was so straight—like her.

He wasn't a fanciful sort of man, not normally, but when it came to her hair, he'd surprised himself by comparing it to all sorts of things that another man, the kind of man who was bookish, might work up into a poem. It put him in mind of hot summer nights when, as a boy, he'd stolen away from this house to go swimming in the lake. Naked, he would float on his back in water that had felt like silk against his skin and gaze up at the stars. Stars whose reflection shimmered in the water that bore him up. There seemed hardly any distance between water and sky. He'd got the notion that if he stretched his hands up, he could have touched them, made them shiver the way their reflections all around him shivered. As though he was floating in sky, and stars, and water, all at the same time.

And when he plunged his fingers into her hair while he was plunging himself inside her, he got the feeling that what he was doing was not just slaking a physical urge, but something more…something almost mystical.

Her eyes fluttered open, fixed on him and…warmed. Welcomed his presence.

There was no pretence about it. There hadn't been a moment of hesitation, followed by the calculated smile he was used to getting from the women he'd taken to bed in the past. She was genuinely pleased to see him when she woke up.

A strange feeling stirred inside. A feeling of acceptance he hadn't felt since… Well, he wasn't sure he'd ever had anyone show such fondness for him, not once they'd got to know him as well as she'd done, over the past few days. He couldn't remember his mother all that well. He'd been too young when she'd died to work out whether those vague feelings of acceptance had truly come from her, or whether he'd just dreamed them up in his childish need for...for something he certainly never got from his father. His father had definitely never been *fond* of him. He'd seen him pet his hounds and horses, but never, not once, had he been anything but brusque with his own offspring.

Things changed a bit when Julia was born. As soon as she could walk she toddled around after him. Wanting him to notice her. Believing he could do no wrong in spite of all evidence to the contrary. Even when she got old enough to develop some discernment, her face would still light up when she first saw him after sufficient time apart.

Which was one of the reasons why he'd been determined to move heaven and earth to keep her safe.

Although, what had it cost him, really? Marriage hadn't turned out to be anything like the irksome chore he'd imagined. By some miracle, he'd found the only woman on earth who could have made becoming a husband a positive pleasure.

And it wasn't just because she matched practically every item on the list his friends had helped him make. It was because, in spite of all the ways he'd gone wrong, she appeared to genuinely like him.

So he kissed her. Well, what else was a man to do when a woman looked at him like that?

'You were looking very serious, just now,' she said

when he broke off to take a very necessary breath. 'What were you thinking?'

He was damned if he was going to upset her by telling her she met every criterion on his list of what constituted an acceptable wife. Or admitting that he'd dreaded the prospect of marriage so much he'd actually sought the moral support and guidance of his friends in compiling it.

And he certainly wasn't ever going to share, with *anyone*, that he'd had that moment of…metaphysical madness…diving into star-studded lakes of black silk to find the road to…some spiritual realm where souls could entwine, or some such rot, indeed!

He'd tell her the first thing he'd thought on waking, instead. Haul his mind back to the arena in which he felt far more at home.

'I was thinking,' he admitted with a rakish smile, 'that every time we change the venue for our…conjugal activities, it gets more enjoyable. Do you know,' he said, shifting over her, 'I have this…craving to…' he nudged her legs apart with his own '…enjoy you in every single room in this house.' He nuzzled her neck. 'Just to see if I'm right.'

For a moment it looked as though she was going to yield. But then her sinuous, responsive movements turned into unmistakable attempts to wriggle out from under him.

'We can't…not now,' she said apologetically. 'There's so much to do this morning. If you want to eat Christmas dinner at a decent hour…'

'Hang dinner,' he said, catching her round the waist just as she was about to leave the bed and pulling her back. 'And hang decency. We'll eat whenever what you make *is* ready.'

'But Gilbey will expect—'

'And hang Gilbey, too. He'll eat when we do.'

'But—'

He stopped her mouth with a kiss. And smiled against her lips when, with a sigh, she wrapped her arms round his neck and kissed him back.

It was the happiest Christmas she'd ever known. And it wasn't just because, at last, she had a secure home, plenty of food to eat and no need to worry about how to pay for it.

It was because of Lord Havelock.

He made Christmas Day pass in a whirl of merriment and lovemaking. Which he topped off by declaring it had been the best Christmas of his own life, too.

'Don't look as though you don't believe me,' he said, a touch belligerently, when she gaped at him in surprise. 'You may as well know, right now, that I *never* lie. Have never seen the point,' he finished loftily.

'I didn't mean to imply you would,' she said, going to the oven and kneeling down to rake embers into the warming pan. 'It is just, well, it was all so… I mean, you must have had far more grand food and all sorts of entertainments, other years.'

'Oh. Yes, I see what you mean. And in a way, you're right. I've definitely been to a great many Christmas house parties where no expense was spared. But you see,' he said, gently taking the warming pan from her as she turned and got to her feet, 'when I was a grubby schoolboy, I always felt I was there on sufferance, wherever I was. And then, when I got older, the same girls who'd been turning their noses up at me all their lives suddenly realised I was a catch and began trying to trap me. Don't care for being hunted down like a...coursed hare,' he finished bitterly.

'I see.' She picked up the lantern, glanced at the kitchen table and smothered a giggle. He'd surprised her, right after dinner, by sweeping the dishes aside, bending her over the table and lifting her skirts. What followed had been wild and wonderful, if a little shocking. 'It has been the best Christmas Day I've ever had, too.' It had been just as well the table was so sturdy. They'd have shattered a less robust piece of furniture.

And probably carried right on, in its splintered ruins, until they'd finished what he'd started.

'I meant what I said, you know,' he said with a mischievous twinkle in his eyes as he followed the direction of her gaze.

'What about?' She'd lost the thread of the discussion while she'd been reliving the way his hands had taken command of her body, while his lips pressed hot kisses into the nape of her neck.

'About wanting to make love to you in every room in this house.' As if to prove his point, when they reached the door of the room they'd slept in the night before, he kept on walking.

'There must be a dozen bedrooms along this corridor alone.'

'They...they won't be very comfortable, though,' she pointed out, hanging back.

He turned and looked at her keenly.

'It isn't fair to expect you to put up with another night on a hearthrug, is it? Very well,' he said with an exaggerated sigh. 'Let's be practical.' He turned back and entered what she'd come to think of as their bedroom.

'For now,' he said firmly, shutting the door behind them. 'But I give you fair warning that once the Brownlows get here, I shall have them make up every bed, in every room, so that we can try out whichever takes ours fancy, whenever,' he said, thrusting the warming pan under the quilt, 'it takes our fancy.'

Whenever? Oh, yes. She liked the sound of that. Funny, but she'd never thought of herself as a spontaneous sort of person. But then she'd never had the chance to find out who she really was, or what she really liked. She'd been too busy just surviving.

But from the moment she'd married Lord Havelock— or at least, the moment he first started to get undressed, she'd decided she liked being able to make love whenever the fancy took them.

'But for tonight,' he said, taking her in his arms, 'I shall make up for the fact we have to stay in here, by showing you…something new.'

'Something new?'

What more could there be? He'd started by teaching her that people could make love in broad daylight. And gone on to demonstrate that they didn't even need to lie down.

Her stomach flipped over in anticipation as he took her hand and led her to the bed. The look in his eyes made her legs tremble.

'What,' she whispered, 'do you intend to do to me?'

'Drive you wild,' he whispered back.

Chapter Eleven

On the morning of the twenty-eighth, while they were still eating breakfast in the kitchen, the back door flew open and a middle-aged couple burst in, bringing with them the inevitable gust of rain-laden wind.

'My lord, I'm that sorry,' the woman began to apologise. 'Had we any idea you was coming, we'd not have gone away. To think of you having to make do, at Christmas of all times.'

'My Lady Havelock,' drawled Lord Havelock icily, 'allow me to present, finally, Mr and Mrs Brownlow. The caretakers of Mayfield.'

She managed, but only just, to follow her husband's lead and not get to her feet and welcome the couple into the home as though they were guests. But she felt most uncomfortable when the one bowed while the other curtsied to her.

'You look as though you've done very well, considering,' said Mrs Brownlow, her eyes darting about the kitchen before coming to rest on Mary, who suddenly became very aware of the shabbiness of her gown and the fact that she'd not bothered taking off her apron when she'd sat down to breakfast. It felt as though Mrs Brownlow was sizing her up for the position of cook, rather than lady of the house. And that, given the choice, Mrs Brownlow wouldn't have granted her either position.

'But now we're back, you won't need to bother yourselves with all this sort of thing any longer,' she added with a sniff, before going to the stove, opening the doors, rattling the poker about inside, then shutting them with more noise than was anywhere near necessary.

'I notice you've decided to make use of the green-silk room,' said the woman, taking the tea caddy from the shelf where Mary had left it and restoring it to the higher one where she'd first found it, but which was so awkward to reach. 'Saw the smoke from the chimneys as we was coming up the drive,' she added, which explained how she'd worked out where they'd slept, without anyone telling her.

But then Mrs Brownlow stilled, catching the full force of Lord Havelock's scowl.

'We was that relieved,' she said, veering from her display of competence to ingratiating sweetness, 'you hadn't tried to take over the rooms what used to be his late lordship's and his wife's. None of the rooms in that wing have been touched since I don't know when. Need a real good spring clean before they will be fit for use.'

Mary could have told her, had she paused to draw breath, that she could tell exactly how competent she was, from the state of the larder, the kitchen and the wing that had been let out to raise revenue. And that she didn't have anything to worry about. Lord Havelock might have a ferocious scowl, but he wasn't the kind of man who'd turn someone off for not somehow sensing he was about to marry and descend on his ancestral home.

'And we'll need to get the chimneys swept before any-one attempts to light a fire in any of the rooms. Probably got several years' worth of birds' nests in them by now.'

At her side, Lord Havelock froze, his cup halfway to his mouth. From the way his face paled, and the muscles in his jaw twitched, she guessed he'd just had a vision of setting the chimney on fire and burning his house down around his ears on the very first night he took up residence.

'Now, you don't need to sit in the kitchen any longer, not now we're back,' said Mrs Brownlow, laying her hand on the teapot, then whisking it off the table with a rueful shake of her head. 'Mr Brownlow will light the fire in the drawing room.' She shot a speaking look at her husband, who scurried off in the direction of the coal store. 'It will be warm as toast in next to no time. And I'll bring you a fresh pot of tea in there.'

Lord Havelock set his cup down and got slowly to his feet.

'See that you do,' he drawled. His attempt at nonchalance was good enough to deceive the Brownlows, but not Mary. She could tell he was still reeling from that casual reference to highly inflammable nests, which often did get lodged in chimneys.

'Lady Havelock,' he snapped. 'Remove your apron and leave it behind. I sincerely hope never to have to see you in it again.'

Well, he had to give vent to his feelings somehow, she supposed. Lowering her head, in token meekness, she untied her apron strings. But she had to press her lips together to stop a smile forming. She kept her mouth firmly shut all the while Lord Havelock led her to the drawing room.

But once they were standing in the middle of the cold, inhospitable room, it struck her that they were behaving more like two naughty children caught out by their governess, than the lord and lady of the house.

And the giggles that had been building finally began to bubble over.

'What are you laughing at?'

Lord Havelock turned to her, his brows drawn down repressively.

'N-nothing,' she managed in between giggles. 'E-everything,' she admitted, dropping on to the nearest sofa and pressing her hand over her mouth in a vain attempt to stop.

'There's nothing funny about nearly burning the house down.'

'Y-you didn't, though. There must not have been,' she said in a vain struggle to both reassure him and bring herself under control, 'any n-nests up the ch-chimney, after all.'

'Don't say that word!' He planted his fists on his hips and glared down at her.

'Which one? Ch-chimneys? Or n-nests?'

She was laughing so hard by now that she had to wipe away the tears that had begun to run down her face.

'Neither,' he snarled, though his eyes had lost that dead, hollow look. 'Both.' As though coming back to life, he began to stalk towards her. 'Do you hear me, woman? You are never, ever, to mention birds' nests, or chimneys, to me again.'

His words were firm, but his lips were starting to twitch, too.

'Or…' she said, gratitude that he was a man who didn't take himself too seriously surging up within her on a tidal wave of joy. 'Or what?'

He was almost upon her now and his eyes were smouldering with such heat it made her want to lean back into the sofa cushions and open her arms to him.

'Or,' he growled, 'face the consequences.'

With a little shriek, she leapt up off the sofa just before he lunged for her. For the next few minutes, he chased her round and round the sofa, uttering dire threats of what he would do if he caught her, which he could have done any time he chose since she was laughing too hard to properly control her movements.

And then the door opened and Mr Brownlow appeared with a full coal scuttle. And came to a dead halt at the sight of his master and mistress playing chase.

'Dashed cold in here,' panted her husband as Mary froze in place. 'Just keeping warm, with a little exercise.'

The look on Mr Brownlow's face, the knowledge that had he come in a few seconds later he would have caught them rolling about *on* the sofa rather than running round and round it, was too much for Mary. With a shocked little cry she darted past the scandalised caretaker and out into the corridor, where she made for the stairs.

She heard her husband's footsteps pursuing her, but this time she wasn't playing. She really did just want to run away and hide. Without thinking, she made for the only room in the house where she would feel safe. The bedroom in which they'd slept the night before. The embers still glowed in the grate, making the room less chilly than any other, except the kitchen.

Lord Havelock reached it only a few seconds behind her. Before she could even turn round, he'd grabbed her by the waist.

'Got you,' he cried, propelling her across the room and flinging her down on to the bed.

'Now, my girl, we'll see how long you can keep on laughing at me,' he growled. Not that she felt like laughing any more. All the humour had gone out of the situation.

'What is it? What's the matter?'

She hadn't realised she'd communicated her chagrin to him. But she'd definitely tensed up and he'd noticed.

'I…I'm sorry,' she said, tears starting to her eyes as he reared up and looked down at her in confusion. 'It was just…' She gulped. 'I can't believe I forgot Mr Brownlow was on his way to make up the fire in there. A few more moments, and he would have found us… He would have found us…' She couldn't go on. Her face flamed though, at the knowledge she'd been about to let her husband catch her and tumble her to the sofa he'd been chasing her round. And let him commence the perfectly thrilling punishments he'd been threatening.

He started to chuckle.

'It isn't funny.'

'But it is, though. Far funnier than almost burning the house down around my ears. And you, madam…' he gave her a squeeze '…couldn't stop laughing about *that*.'

He kissed her brow in a comforting sort of way. And then her mouth, as his fingers sought the ties of her bodice.

'Surely you cannot still be thinking about…about…' Oh, but he most definitely was. And the minute he slipped his hand inside her gown, she was thinking about it again, too. Not just thinking about it either, but wanting it.

'Since we've been married,' he groaned, pushing aside an inconvenient swathe of material so that he could get at bare skin, 'it seems to be damn near all I can think about.'

'B-but we can't.'

'I don't see why not. Mr Brownlow already knows what we've come up here for.'

'Oh, surely not!'

'Of course he does. He almost caught us at it in the drawing room, don't forget.'

'As if I ever could,' she cried in mortification.

'Mary,' he said more gently, stroking the hair from her forehead. 'You don't really want me to stop, do you? Not…now?'

He ran his hand up the outside of her leg, pushing her skirt out of the way. A thrill shot through her, making her heart beat faster, her insides melt and her hips squirm.

'It would be a positive crime to disappoint Mr Brownlow.'

'Oh, don't speak to me of him,' she whimpered, torn between giving way to the delicious sensations he was rousing and the notion that she oughtn't, she really oughtn't, behave like this any more, not now they had indoor servants.

'Not another word,' he agreed affably. 'In fact, I'm sure I can put my mouth to much better use.'

He did. He set about making love to her with such skill that before long her world shrank to the size of one bed, and the only two people left were the two people on it. What had started out downstairs as playful rose swiftly again to a crescendo of desperate need. The urge to scream when her release came was so overwhelming she didn't know how to deal with it. In the end, she pressed her mouth into his shoulder to muffle the cry.

Afterwards, they lay together panting and just look-

ing into each other's eyes in a kind of mirrored awe. She
was shocked at herself for responding to him with such
ardour, in spite of her awareness that the servants must
know what they were doing.

And he must be wondering what kind of a woman
he'd married. One minute she'd been saying she felt
self-conscious. That she really couldn't…do *that*. The
next she'd been tearing at his clothes in a kind of frenzy,
wrapping her arms and legs round him, and coming to
such a cataclysmic release she'd…she'd bitten him. She
could see the teeth marks on his shoulder!

'Oh, what have I done?' She raised trembling fingers
to his shoulder. Then pressed penitent lips to the red-
dening crescent.

She'd made him feel like a god, that's what she'd
done. He'd never been with a woman who responded to
him the way she did.

'It's nothing.' He shrugged with feigned nonchalance,
whilst desperately trying to stifle the unfamiliar, and
slightly disturbing, emotions welling up inside him.

'It isn't nothing. I've left a bruise….'

'A mark of passion. Such things happen between lovers all the time.'

He winced at the look on her face. He'd been trying to
make light of a moment he was damn sure was going to
live in his memory for a lifetime. Instead he'd made her
think of her wondrous passion as something…tawdry.

Sitting up, he turned his back on her and thrust his
fingers through his hair in annoyance. He should have
just admitted he liked it. He could have done so in a teas-
ing kind of way, so that she wouldn't guess how deeply

she'd moved him, couldn't he? And then she would have smiled and…

God, but it was damn complicated, being married. The good moments got all snagged up with darker feelings until he couldn't unravel the tangle.

'Look, Mary…' He sighed with exasperation. 'If ever you do anything I don't like, I will be sure to tell you. No need to get worked up over such a little thing.'

'I…I'm sorry.'

The tremor in her voice made him turn to look at her sharply. Her little face was all woebegone.

Damn. Why wasn't he more adept with words? His explanation of how his mind worked had come out sounding more like a reprimand. And he'd hurt her. Which was the very last thing he ever wanted to do.

'Look, I warned you before we got married that I'm a blunt man.' In lieu of smooth words, he reached for her hand and gave it a squeeze. 'So this is the truth. I like being married to you.' Far more than he'd thought possible.

'Oh. Well, I like being married to you, too,' she said shyly, returning the pressure of his hand.

He lifted her hand and kissed it.

'There. That's all right and tight, then.' He got up and reached for his clothes. 'Think I'll go for a ride.' Clear his mind. And let her recover.

Because if he stayed he was bound to end up saying something that would make this awkwardness between them ten times worse.

All of a sudden, it seemed to Mary, the place was teeming with servants. When she'd eventually plucked up courage to go downstairs and face Mrs Brownlow, the woman had told her exactly how many she would need to run a house of this size efficiently, then brought them all in. She didn't even go through the motions of letting Mary interview them. She just hired the people she always hired on whenever Mayfield had tenants.

Not that she could fault any of them. Each of them knew exactly what they were supposed to be doing—and each other, too.

She was the only one who seemed to feel like a stranger here. Who wasn't totally comfortable with their role. She was used to *doing* housework, not ordering others to do it, that was half the trouble.

So, as the spring cleaning commenced, even though the new year had not yet come round, Mary took to walking about the rooms with a rag in her hand, and a scarf tied over her head, desperate to find some dirt, or a cobweb, Mrs Brownlow's team might have overlooked.

While her husband rode out early to avoid, she suspected, all the bustle, even though he muttered vague excuses about tenants. And only making love to her at night, behind the closed doors of their bedroom.

'There's a carriage coming up the drive, my lady.'

Mary looked up from the skirting board behind the sofa—where she'd found a satisfyingly thick layer of dust—to see that Mrs Brownlow herself had come with the news, instead of sending her husband.

'You've got visitors. So I'll take that,' she said, snatching the duster from Mary's hand. 'You shouldn't be doing it, anyway,' she grumbled.

Though what was she supposed to do all day, now that her husband didn't seem inclined to chase her round the furniture any longer? Sit on a sofa and twiddle her thumbs?

'I'll have Mr Brownlow...' who'd taken on the mantle of butler '...show them to the drawing room while you go and change into something more suitable.'

'Yes, yes, of course,' said Mary, fumbling the strings of her apron undone and making for the door.

Change? Into what? She supposed she would look slightly better in a clean gown, rather than one she'd been crawling around on the floor in, but not much. Neither of the other gowns she owned were in all that much better condition, after serving as bedding, then withstanding her time as cook and housemaid.

There was her wedding gown, of course. Only was it suitable for receiving callers?

What did the wife of a viscount wear for receiving callers, anyway?

Oh, what did it matter? Surely the most important thing was to make them feel welcome?

And it was no use, she decided—snatching the scarf from her head and stuffing it into her pocket—trying to pretend she was something she wasn't.

She stifled a pang of guilt as she hurriedly tidied her hair before the mirror. Lord Havelock had said he wanted her to be well dressed when the local gentry came calling. He'd said she would have to buy a lot of new clothes.

Only, somehow once they'd got down here, the topic had never come up again. And she hadn't liked to mention it.

With any luck, whoever was calling on her today would be able to tell her where she could find a reliable dressmaker, locally. In fact, it would be a very good topic of conversation. Anyone who knew her husband would have no trouble believing he'd swept her off her feet, and down here, without giving her a chance to buy any bride clothes.

Feeling much better about her gown now she could look upon it as a conversation opener, rather than a personal failing, Mary made her way to the drawing room.

She had only just reached it and taken a seat on one of the chairs by the fireplace, when Brownlow opened the door again.

'Lady Peverell,' he intoned. 'And Miss Julia Durant.'

'Oh!' She leapt to her feet, her hand flying to her throat. She knew that her husband had written to invite Julia to come and live with them, but as far as she knew, he hadn't received a reply.

Lady Peverell, a stylishly dressed blonde who didn't look much beyond the age of thirty, flicked Mary's crumpled, grubby gown a look of scorn, drew off her gloves and made for the chair she'd just leapt out of.

'Oh. Of course,' said Mary, moving out of her way. 'Do come and sit beside the fire,' she said a moment too late. 'You must be dreadfully cold after your journey. Such weather. I expect you'd like tea.'

It was all she could do to cross to the bell pull and ring for a servant, rather than run down to the kitchen and put the kettle on herself. With one withering look, Lady Peverell had made her feel as though she had no right to be in the room. Let alone pose as lady of the house. And as for presuming to the title...well!

'And you, too, Ju—' She pulled herself up, remembering she had no right to *address* her husband's sister by her given name, just because they'd been used to speaking *of* her that way. 'I mean, Miss Durant.'

She sent the girl a timid smile. Which wasn't returned. Miss Julia Durant remained standing just inside the doorway, scowling at her.

Oh, but she looked so very much like Lord Havelock, when things weren't going his way! She had the militant stance and the determined chin. She had the same-shaped hazel eyes, too. And from what she could see of her hair, which was fighting its way out from under her bonnet, the same thick mass of unruly curls that graced his head, too.

Though, she frowned, he had described her as a beauty. A girl at risk from a predatory older man.

Julia could certainly *become* very attractive, once she'd outgrown the spots that marred her complexion, learned not to pout and glower at strangers, and had her hair styled by a professional.

Julia responded to her smile with a look of scorn and a toss of her head. She flounced over to the window and flung herself on to the sill, turning her shoulder to the other occupants of the room.

'You see?' said Lady Peverell, waving the riding crop she held in one hand in Julia's direction. 'You see what I've had to contend with? I have a houseful of guests, but does she care? No. The minute she gets that letter from her brother nothing will satisfy her but instant removal to this godforsaken pile. Won't even wait till Twelfth Night.'

Well, that was very like Lord Havelock, too. He didn't see the need to wait once he'd made up his mind to do something, either.

'And now she *is* here,' Lady Peverell continued, her voice rising both in volume and pitch, 'she's no better pleased. Not that I'm taking you back, miss, so don't you think I will.'

Julia shot her a look of fury over her shoulder, before folding her arms and glaring out of the window again.

'That is the only thing that made me give in to her badgering. The knowledge that at long last I would be able to wash my hands of her! Even though I can see that we've taken you by surprise, turning up unannounced.'

'Oh, no, not at all….' Mrs Brownlow could have any of the bedrooms in the guest wing ready in a trice. 'It doesn't matter in the least that we didn't know the exact date she would arrive—'

'Stuff,' snorted Lady Peverell. 'And this is how it will *always* be once you have her under your roof. Well, I just hope you have a *very* strong constitution. The girl is a complete hoyden. Selfish and self-willed. Totally impossible.'

Mary didn't believe it for one second. From what Lord Havelock had told her, the poor girl had spent her life being passed around like a parcel. The few weeks during which Mary had undergone such treatment had given her a very good idea of how Julia must feel. Especially since her current guardian was doing what her own relatives had done—talking about what was to become of her as though she had no say, no brains, no will of her own.

And no feelings.

She had just taken a deep breath, to explain, calmly and rationally, that Julia would be a welcome addition to the household, when the door burst open and Lord Havelock strode in.

'Gregory!' With a heart-rending cry, Julia leapt to her feet, flew across the room, flung herself into his outstretched arms and dissolved into noisy sobs.

'There, there,' he crooned, rocking her in his arms. 'No need to cry. You're safe now. You're home.'

'Oh, for heaven's sake,' muttered Lady Peverell. 'No wonder the girl is so wild. Nobody can ever do anything with her, because she only has to pour out some tale into your ear and you come rushing in to take her side. She's a spoiled madam and it is all your fault.'

Lord Havelock's arms tightened round his sister's heaving shoulders. He glared at Lady Peverell.

'Then you can have no qualms about leaving her in my care, can you?' He jerked his head towards the door. 'Have a safe journey home. I heard you say how busy you are with your house party. Do not let us detain you.'

Mary's jaw dropped. She knew he had a temper. But was he really going to throw Lady Peverell out, after travelling so far, in such horrid weather? She hadn't even had any tea.

But the peevish Lady Peverell didn't appear the least surprised by his attitude. She just got to her feet and gathered her things together with an air of magnificent disdain.

Shooting the siblings one look of sheer loathing, Lady Peverell turned to Mary.

'I wish you luck,' she said. 'Oh, and before I forget, I brought you a small gift. Here,' she said, thrusting the riding crop into the hands Mary had stretched out, impulsively, to implore her not to leave without at least having a cup of tea.

Mary blinked down at the riding crop in confusion. She couldn't ride a horse, so had no need of such a thing. Of course, Lady Peverell couldn't know that. She raised her eyes, trying to form a polite smile of gratitude.

'I've found,' said Lady Peverell, shooting Julia a look of pure malice, 'it's the only way to keep that creature in line.'

With that parting shot, she strode from the room, her nose in the air.

The smile froze on Mary's lips.

There was a beat of silence.

Lord Havelock was looking at her with cool, assessing eyes. And with a start, Mary realised she was still clutching the riding crop in her hands.

With a cry of disgust, she flung it away. It landed on the floor by the window with a clatter that caused Julia to lift her head from her brother's shoulder and look up.

'I would never,' cried Mary, '*ever* use such a thing. Not on an animal, let alone a person!'

'I know,' he snapped.

There was no need for her to say it. She was such a gentle creature—too gentle for her own good, sometimes.

He'd heard Lady Peverell's tirade well before he'd reached the room, her voice was so strident. And though she'd spoken venomously, he couldn't deny there was an element of truth to what he'd overheard. Julia could be…a bit of a handful. She was a Durant, after all, with the Durant will and the Durant temper.

And he could just see her running rings round Mary, given half a chance.

Well, he'd just have to make sure she didn't get a chance.

He stilled as it struck him that Mary's happiness was now just as important to him as Julia's had ever been. Which was ironic, considering he'd only married her so he could provide a home for Julia. Yet now this had become Mary's home, too. She loved it here. He'd watched her blossom in it. Delight in it.

And he didn't want Julia's moods to ruin it all for her. It would be totally unfair to expect her to deal with Julia—in *this* frame of mind, anyway. Not even Lady Peverell could exert any sort of control over his sister, so how could he expect Mary to take her in hand? Why, she couldn't even keep Mrs Brownlow in her place. The dratted woman had promoted herself to the position of housekeeper and was running Mayfield just as she pleased.

'You needn't be afraid of Mary,' he said to Julia. 'She has the kindest heart imaginable. Honestly,' he said when she continued to cling to him, whilst looking at Mary as though she was some kind of ogre. 'I made sure of it before I married her.'

Mary flinched. Made sure of it? How? They'd only known each other a few days before he proposed.

And yet he'd made that list, hadn't he? A list that ensured the woman he picked would provide a home for his beloved, treasured sister. The girl he was holding in his arms. The girl who'd flown to him. Who called him by his given name without thinking, when so far Mary had never dared be so familiar....

She always had to call him *my lord*, or *husband*, or occasionally, when she felt very daring, *Havelock*. Because he'd never invited her to share the intimacy his sister naturally took for granted.

Though she was sure Julia hadn't meant to, the girl had given her a very brutal reminder of what her place in his life really was.

A means to an end.

'She's been very busy,' said her husband to his sister, 'putting this old place to rights, so you could come home.'

'C-can I have my old room back?'

He shook his head. 'Sorry, Ju. The family wing hasn't been used in such a long time it's still a bit of a mess. But there are any number of rooms in what used to be the guest wing you can choose from.'

When she didn't stop pouting, Lord Havelock chucked her under her chin. 'How about coming and having a look? A couple have good views over the stables.'

'The stables?' Julia stopped crying abruptly. 'I...I suppose that would be...' She sniffed and wiped her tear-stained face with the back of one hand.

'And even better,' he went on, before she had the chance to form her thoughts into words, 'I've got something inside the stables that will put a smile back on your face.'

'A new horse? For m-me?'

'Welcome-home present,' he grinned. 'Saw Panther at Tatt's and knew he'd be just the thing to put the roses back in your cheeks. Want to come and meet him?'

Julia shook off her angry, tearful demeanour the way a dog shakes off water after a dunking.

'Oh, yes, please.'

All smiles and arm in arm, brother and sister left the room without a backward glance. As though Mary didn't exist.

And then Mrs Brownlow came in, with a tea tray. Behind her came Susan, who was the chief housemaid, with another tray, laden with cakes and other dainties.

'Where has everyone gone?' Mrs Brownlow looked most put out to find that her efforts to whip up a tray of refreshments for their unexpected visitors had all been for nought.

'Lady Peverell has gone home. And Miss Durant and his lordship have gone to the stables.'

'And what are we to do with miss's luggage?' said Mrs Brownlow, plonking her tray down on the nearest table with a clatter. 'There's boxes and trunks all over the hall. I can't just leave them there. One of my girls will be tripping over them and breaking her leg, I shouldn't wonder. What room shall I have them taken to?'

'You could have them taken up to the guest wing and placed in…oh, I don't know. How about the room that has all that crimson brocaded wallpaper?'

'It's not really suitable for a young girl, my lady. Far better to put her—'

'Well, one of the rooms that overlook the stables, if you please,' she said more firmly. 'And if she doesn't like it, she can pick another one. You needn't unpack anything. Just move her luggage up there, so it is out of your way.'

'Hmmph,' said Mrs Brownlow, before bustling out with Susan in tow.

Leaving Mary in sole charge of an enormous pot of tea, half a dozen cups and more cakes than she could eat in a fortnight.

Chapter Twelve

'Julia, I think you have something to say to Lady Havelock, do you not?'

Julia hunched her shoulders and lowered her head. 'I'm sorry I was rude to you when I got here,' she muttered.

Good grief. Lady Peverell had said Julia was completely unmanageable, but at only a hint from her brother, she'd apologised for her behaviour. Grudgingly, it was true, but it was far more than she'd expected.

And she was very grateful. She hadn't been looking forward to enduring many more dinners like the one they'd just sat through. It had been bad enough getting used to the formality of the immense dining room anyway, and letting footmen wait on her, but having to try to make conversation with a girl who clearly wanted nothing to do with her, whilst grappling with the reminder of her unimportance to her own husband, had been downright demoralising.

'Think no more of it,' she said. 'It sounds as though you've had a perfectly horrid time with Lady Peverell. Frankly, I was appalled at the way she spoke about you as though you weren't even in the room. If it had been me in your shoes…'

She frowned at the recollection that it had been all too easy to picture herself in Julia's place. Though she'd never had the courage to make a fuss, the way Julia had done, or demand her own way. She'd just meekly allowed people to dispose of her as they liked. She'd let them parcel her off like…like a bundle of dirty washing for someone else to launder.

How she wished she had a tithe of Julia's spirit.

'Well, anyway, I just want you to be happy here. It is your home, after all.'

'I don't remember much about when I lived here before,' Julia retorted. 'I was still quite young when Mama married again and we had to move away.'

And yet she'd requested her old room back, reflected Mary.

'We can soon rectify that,' put in Lord Havelock. 'There are some splendid rides to be had in the area. And now you've made the acquaintance of Panther I'm sure you'd like to put him through his paces. Tomorrow I'll start taking you about and introducing you to people.'

Julia's face lit up.

Mary's hackles rose. He'd never offered to take *her* about and introduce her to anyone. He'd never bought her a horse, either. Not that she had any use for one. But that was beside the point. He simply hadn't bothered.

Lord Havelock smiled back at his sister, then turned to Mary with a troubled frown. It was just as well he'd already reined himself in, in an attempt to spare Mary's blushes after that time Brownlow had nearly caught them out. He certainly wouldn't want Julia catching him chasing his wife through the house and tumbling her on sofas. It wasn't the kind of behaviour he wanted his sister to think was acceptable. And, dammit, it wasn't.

He rubbed his hand round the back of his neck, wondering just what had got into him lately. He'd never been one of those fellows who was led by the urgings of his cock. But ever since marrying Mary, he couldn't stop wanting her. Couldn't keep his hands off her.

True, she'd submitted to every demand he made on her and derived pleasure from every encounter, but didn't he owe her more respect?

He'd been a thoroughly selfish sort of husband, so far. He'd promised her she would always have a room of her own, wherever they lived, that nobody else could enter except with her permission. It was pretty much all she'd asked of him. But had he ever honoured that promise? Had he ever knocked on her bedroom door and asked if he could join her? No.

Well, he could rectify that situation tonight. From now on, he'd be the model of decorum.

He still hadn't provided her with the means to purchase her trousseau, either. Nor had she had the time, she'd been so busy putting Mayfield to rights.

Not that she'd complained. Not once. Not about anything. Most women would have nagged him half to death by now, but she just smiled sweetly and made the most of what little she did have.

'You know, it's past time you saw a dressmaker about getting some new clothes,' he said, guilt making his voice a little gruff. 'I know you've been busy, getting the place ready for Julia's arrival, but surely now you can spare the time to spruce yourself up?'

* * *

Spruce herself up? Spruce herself up! Mary took a deep breath and bit back the indignant response she would have given had Julia not been there.

But then that was just it, wasn't it? This was the second time he'd humiliated her by rebuking her in front of someone else. If he had complaints, couldn't he at least show her the courtesy of waiting to make them until they were alone?

It was bad enough feeling that she half deserved it. She'd known from the look on Lady Peverell's face that the way she dressed was letting him down. But did he really have to chide her like this, as though she was a…a…well, someone who wasn't his equal? When she hadn't complained about any of the things he'd done wrong. Not once.

To add insult to injury, neither he, nor his sister, noticed that she was sitting there, quietly simmering with resentment. They were chattering away happily about people she didn't know and places she'd never been.

After what felt like an hour of being comprehensively ignored, Mary'd had enough.

'I am going to bed,' she said, getting to her feet. And then, because she didn't want to be rude, added, 'Goodnight, Julia,' with a forced smile.

'*I'm* not tired,' Julia declared with a toss of her head.

'It has been a long day,' said Lord Havelock, getting to his feet, as well. 'We'll all go up.'

The three of them mounted the stairs in various states of dudgeon. Julia was pouting at being sent to bed before she was ready to go. Mary was still smarting from her husband's cavalier attitude towards her tonight and tallying up all the other things he'd done to annoy her.

And Lord Havelock looked distinctly uncomfortable at being flanked by two women who were in the sulks.

'What do you think of the room Mary chose for you?' he asked with determined cheerfulness as they mounted the stairs.

Julia shrugged.

'You can always move to another if it's not to your liking. What about this one?' He flung open the door to a room they'd slept in only once. Mary hadn't liked it much. The wall hangings were of a cold greyish-blue, liberally spattered with muddy-hued hunting prints.

'I'm in here, for the moment,' said Lord Havelock, to Mary's surprise, 'but I can soon shift if you prefer it.'

Julia peeped inside, wrinkled her nose and shook her head. 'I like the red room better,' she said.

Heavens, Mary reflected sourly. She'd actually got something right today.

'Good. Mary is in here,' he said, striding to the door of the bedroom she had assumed they would be sharing.

'It's rather poky,' said Julia, taking a quick glance round the room that Mary found so cosy that it had become her favourite. It was easy to keep warm, the chimney didn't smoke and the walls were decorated in a very restful shade of green, with sunny little details in gold here and there.

And then, as one, the siblings bid her goodnight and turned away, arm in arm.

She stared at the door they'd shut behind them on their way out.

What was going on?

And then various snippets of conversations she'd had

began to trickle into her mind. The one she'd had with Mrs Brownlow, only the day before, about how lords and ladies always had their own bedrooms, dressing rooms and sitting rooms. About how her husband would have the ones that had been his father's, while she would have the other, prettier set. How she'd sadly accepted that one day, when the rooms were ready, he would move into his and she into hers.

She'd assumed, until that day, things would carry on as they were. But no. He'd stated, quite firmly, that he would be sleeping in that horrid blue room, while she was to sleep alone in here.

The worst of it was she'd look a complete idiot if she voiced a protest. Because she'd said, before they got married, that she *wanted* her own room. That she valued her privacy.

But privacy, she now realised, was the last thing she wanted. She'd got used to sharing her room with her husband. To sharing her life with him.

No—it was more than that.

Why hadn't she seen it sooner?

She uttered a strained little laugh. Over the years, watching her father's brutality towards her mother, she'd feared the power a husband had over his wife. She'd feared the deliberate oppression of a man bent on ruling his household with a rod of iron. And when she'd discovered her own husband wasn't the kind of man to treat anyone with cruelty, she'd let down her guard completely.

And fallen headlong in love with him.

Which meant he now had the power to hurt her without even noticing. The way he'd done today. Showering his sister with all the affection and attention he would never, ever, give her.

'Stupid, stupid,' she muttered to herself as tears welled and seeped down her cheeks.

Why hadn't she guarded herself against falling in love?

Because she hadn't expected to do anything so stupid, that's why. She didn't even *like* men, as a rule. But Lord Havelock had entered her life like a whirlwind, sweeping her off her feet and into his arms. Totally overwhelming her with his generous, open nature. His spontaneity. His beautiful face and muscular body. His incredible lovemaking.

But now, like the whirlwind of a man he was, he was sweeping right on past her. His focus was all on his sister now. And she was left standing here alone, pining for a man who'd been completely honest about what he wanted from her from the start. And that didn't include *affection*, let alone love.

She'd excused him for not chasing her all over the house now that it was teeming with servants. Had told herself she was imagining he was being a bit more restrained when he came to bed.

But he wasn't the type of man to exercise restraint. He did whatever he wanted, whenever he wanted.

He was bored with her, that's what it was. Why else would he have moved into a room of his own?

Unless it was because, from his point of view, the honeymoon was over.

Hadn't he warned her that his ardour wouldn't last very long? Oh, he'd couched it in terms of them going off each other, but that was what it boiled down to.

She was, after all, only a mouse.

She sucked in a great, shuddering sigh, swiping angrily at the tears she'd been weak enough to shed.

She'd never realised how boring he must have found it, spending the evenings alone with her, until she'd watched his face transformed by the amusing little anecdotes Julia could supply.

He chose that very moment to knock on the door. She only just had time to dash the back of her hand across her face, to swipe away the few tears she hadn't been able to prevent from leaking out, before he came in.

The fact that he was grinning, as though he hadn't a care in the world, felt like a slap to her face. He had no idea how badly he'd hurt her.

Well, of course he hadn't. She wouldn't *be* hurt if she'd managed to stick to the agreement to keep their marriage free from emotion. And she wasn't going to admit she was hurt either, by things he'd consider stupidly trivial.

She drew herself up to her full height and dammed up the flood of tears she wanted to shed behind a façade of pride.

'What,' she said coldly, 'do you want?'

His smile turned downright wicked. 'You know perfectly well what I want,' he said, moving towards her.

But he couldn't want it all that much any more, or he wouldn't have decided it was time to have separate rooms.

She held up her hand, stopping him from coming any closer. How long would it be before separate rooms became separate lives altogether? Before they embarked on the second stage of their marriage? The one where they scarcely saw each other any more?

'It's not what I want!'

Her outburst wiped the smile from his face. 'Is something wrong?'

Wrong? Only the fact that she'd just discovered she no longer wanted a room of her own. That she'd be content to live entirely in *one* room, and cook for him, and do his laundry, and, yes, even wash his dishes without a word of complaint, if only she could be sure she mattered to him. Even half as much as his sister did.

In spite of her determination to avoid the humiliation of bursting into tears, she felt her lower lip start to tremble.

'Wrong?' She managed to produce a laugh and a toss of her head. 'What could possibly be wrong?'

He eyed her up and down dubiously.

'I don't know. But I'd have to be blind not to see that something is wrong. You look, ah…'

Suddenly, she became conscious of the frayed hem of her gown and the patches on her petticoat.

'In need of sprucing up?'

Suddenly, it seemed much easier to let him think he'd offended her with the criticism of her clothing, than to admit she'd breached the terms of their agreement. Temper he would understand. But love? No—to speak of love, when he'd warned her it was the last thing he wanted, would only serve to make her seem utterly ridiculous in his eyes.

'Yes,' she therefore said as waspishly as she could manage. 'You've made your point. Don't worry. I will find a dressmaker locally and smarten myself up so that I don't offend your neighbours with my shabby clothing.'

'Look here—I didn't mean to offend you—'

'You didn't!' And wasn't that the truth? But by flinging her head high, and letting some of her hurt flash from her eyes, she could give him the impression that he had.

'Mary...' He came towards her, hands outstretched, an apologetic expression on his face.

She backed away hastily. For once she let him take her in his arms, she wouldn't be able to hold herself together any longer. She'd break down and sob into his chest. Like the idiot she was. And, being the man he was, he wouldn't rest until he'd winkled the truth from her.

And then her humiliation would be complete.

'That's far enough,' she snapped, holding up her hand to halt him. 'I am not in the mood for...for...'

Actually, that was true, too. She most certainly wasn't in the mood for the decorous brand of lovemaking that only went on behind closed doors, not any longer. Not when she knew he was capable of so much more.

Not when she *wanted* so much more.

His face closed up.

'Forgive me,' he said, looking very far from apologetic any longer. 'I have no wish to annoy you. So I'll take myself off.' He turned on his heel and stalked to the door. 'Goodnight,' he tossed over his shoulder as he went out.

The moment the door snicked shut, her legs gave out, her resolve gave out and the tears flooded out.

How could he just turn and walk away, without making even a token protest? Even a few days ago, he would have done his utmost to cajole her into bed.

But then how could she have hoped to hold his interest? She just wasn't an interesting person. She was a mouse, that was all. That was why he'd picked her. Because there wasn't the slightest risk he would ever feel anything for such a creature.

She wasn't anything special, even if he had made her feel as though she was, for those few, heady days. Of course he'd enjoyed the adventure of the situation. Of foraging for themselves, and letting go of all the restraints society imposed on men and women. It was nothing to do with being stranded, alone, with *her*.

The only reason she'd had his undivided attention, when they'd first arrived, was because there wasn't anyone else there.

For the whole of the following week, every time he knocked at her bedroom door and she turned him away, she told herself she was doing the right thing to make a stand. Not letting him walk all over her and treat her like some plaything he could pick up, or set down, as the whim took him.

Yes—she had the satisfaction of sending him away looking disgruntled. But it was a bittersweet kind of satisfaction. She'd much rather he put up more of a protest. Instead, the way he simply turned and walked away convinced her he just wasn't interested any more, and that the only reason he did persist in coming to her room was because he wanted an heir. It was the second most important reason he'd given for marrying her.

Every day, she grew more and more unhappy, as he made it perfectly plain in dozens of little ways that he didn't return a tithe of her feelings.

He was out practically all day, for one thing, galloping all over the countryside with his intrepid sister. They came back full of stories about the people they'd met and the feats they'd performed, all couched in a kind of jargon that was well-nigh incomprehensible to her.

Not that either of them was unkind to her. They just

made her feel like the odd one out, so alike were they. It wasn't just in their looks. They were both happiest outdoors, on horseback, wearing clothes that didn't fetter their movements.

Whereas she didn't like going outside at all in winter. Having known what it was to fear being homeless, she relished being able to sit indoors in front of a blazing fire.

She didn't even need to go into the village to visit a dressmaker. After consulting Mrs Brownlow about who might be suitable, the housekeeper sent for a local woman, who brought fabric samples and pattern books to Mayfield.

The only time Mary left the house was to attend church on Sundays. People flocked round, after the service, for introductions, but Julia was so much more lively that they invariably ended up talking to her, rather than Mary. Especially since they remembered Julia from when she'd been a little girl. Anyway, Mary felt downright uncomfortable when people curtsied to her and called her my lady, when she still felt like an impostor, so tended to hang back, behind her husband and his sister, and let them bear the brunt of local curiosity.

Apart from Sundays, each day fell into the same dreary pattern. She'd drag herself out of bed after hearing her husband and his sister go out and go down to the deserted dining room to eat breakfast alone. She'd listen to Mrs Brownlow's suggestions for meals, have a fitting, or try on a new outfit, then sit in front of a fire, toasting her toes and wishing she could be content with her new, lazy, luxurious lifestyle.

She could have spent ten times the amount of money she'd laid out on her new clothes and didn't think her

husband would have flinched. Julia was even starting
to return her tentative smiles, once she'd realised Mary
had no intention of trying to change a single thing about
her. She'd even confided, one evening at supper, when
Mary had put on the first of her new gowns, that a lot
of the trouble with Lady Peverell had stemmed from her
attempts to turn Julia into one of those fashionably de-
mure girls who would have done her credit in a ballroom.

Lord Havelock had laughed. 'You're a hoyden, Ju. A
regular out-and-outer. You'd cause havoc in a ballroom.'

He'd had a sort of fond twinkle in his eye as he said
it that showed he was proud of his sister just as she was.

And Mary's spirits sank even lower. *She'd* never
cause havoc in a ballroom. Why, the first night they'd
met, he'd had to virtually drag her out from behind that
potted palm.

No wonder he'd thought she was a mouse.

And still did. Because she was acting like one. Putting up with the way he and his sister overlooked her.
Putting up with his coolness towards her in the bedroom, too.

What had happened to her determination to make a
stand? To her wistful yearning to have some of Julia's
spirit? Hadn't she decided, the day Julia arrived, that she
ought to cease being the kind of woman who let others
post her round the country like a parcel?

Spending the days waiting for her husband to come
home, only to endure his obvious preference for his sister, was draining what little self-respect she'd ever had.

What was the point in hanging around, hoping he
might, one day, come to return her feelings? He'd told
her in no uncertain terms it was the last thing he wanted
from a wife. And how would she attempt to go about it,

anyway? There was nothing about her to attract him. She sat there, night after night, with nothing to add to the conversation apart from domestic trivia that was bound to bore him.

Eventually he would cease knocking on her bedroom door at all. And then what would she do? It made her feel like a condemned woman, waiting for the axe to fall.

And then one night, it all became too much. While she was waiting in her bedroom, half-convinced this would be the night he gave up, her stomach contracted into a cold knot. Sweat beaded her upper lip. For a moment, she thought she might actually be sick.

Head swirling, she tottered to her dressing-table stool and sank down on to it, shutting her eyes.

When the room stopped spinning, she lifted her head and stared bleakly at her wan reflection. She couldn't go on like this. Enduring his indifference was taking its toll on her health.

And the only way she might, just might be able to recover from this hopelessly painful case of unrequited love would be to remove herself from the situation altogether. Surely, if she spent some time away from him, she'd be able to get used to the idea of living separate lives?

And at least she'd be the one doing the separating. She would be able to leave with her head held high, rather than collapsing in floods of tears if he should be the one to go.

So, when he knocked on the door, she didn't bother getting up from her stool. Taking her brush in her hand, she began to swipe it through her hair, to disguise the fact that her hands were shaking.

'Any point in asking if I may stay tonight?' His face

bore the look of resignation he'd adopted after her very first refusal.

'None,' she said tartly, carrying on brushing her hair. 'Though before you go,' she added hastily, as he turned on his heel, 'I may as well inform you that I plan to go to London tomorrow.'

'London?' He swivelled round, his brows drawing down into a knot. 'What the devil for?'

Did his frown mean he didn't want her to leave, after all? Would he ask her to stay? And if he did, would she do it? Would she carry on trying to endure, just so she could be near him?

'I…' Well, she couldn't tell him the truth, could she? That loving a man who was never going to love her back was destroying her.

'I thought I might buy some more clothes. For…for the Season.'

'The Season?' He looked thunderstruck. 'But you've just bought a whole lot of clothes, haven't you?'

'Yes. But…' She did some quick thinking. 'They have been made by a provincial dressmaker. Society people will know.'

'I wouldn't have thought you would want to mingle with society people. Or take part in the Season.'

No. Because he didn't think she would fit in.

Which was true enough, but, oh, so insulting.

'It isn't just for me though, is it? I shall have to start paving the way for Julia to make her come-out, won't I?'

'I don't see that at all,' he snapped. 'I've plenty of aunts and such who have the entrée into the kind of circles where Julia will find a husband, once she gives any sign of wanting to look for one.'

So, he intended to sideline her even when it came to

Julia's come-out, did he? He was going to get some aunt, with the proper connections, to launch her?

Setting down her hairbrush, she half turned on her stool and glared at him.

'You promised me I could do as I pleased, as long as I don't cause a scandal. And I feel like going to London and buying some fashionable clothes. I don't think that is the slightest bit scandalous. Do you?'

'No. But, hang it, Julia has only just got here. You leaving so soon may well cause talk. Couldn't you…wait a bit? And we can all go up together?'

Together? They wouldn't be together. He would be with Julia and she would be hovering on the fringes. Enduring the pain of being the unwanted, unloved wife in a new location, that was all.

And the fact that he was bringing Julia's welfare into the equation was the last straw. Julia. Julia. It was always Julia who mattered. Not her.

Well, two could play at that game.

'And what sort of state is Durant House in, do you happen to know? Will it be fit for her to move into? I really do think it would be better if I went on ahead and checked. After all, one of the reasons you asked me to marry you was to refurbish the place.'

Hoist with his own petard. He turned and walked over to the fireplace, so she couldn't see the devastation her words had wrought. He'd known this day would come. Every time he'd knocked on her bedroom door and been turned away, he'd felt it coming closer.

Even so, he hadn't expected it to hurt so much. Dammit, he'd taken steps to ensure it wouldn't! He'd deliberately picked a woman who wouldn't expect too much from him, who wouldn't nag him for more than he was willing to give. He'd even sat down and spelled out the terms of their marriage, to make sure neither of them would get hurt.

What he hadn't factored in was that Mary would work her way so far under his skin that hearing she wanted to leave him was like having every single bone removed from his body.

Moodily, he kicked at a smouldering log, sending sparks flying up the chimney, when what he really wanted to do was yell, and rampage up and down, and hit something. But he'd learned his lesson, fighting that second duel. As he'd stood there with the smoking pistol in his hand, watching Wraxton fall to the earth with blood gushing down his neck, he'd known he had to change. Never attempting to keep his temper in check had brought him to the brink of killing a man. He'd grown up, that day. He was no longer a child who might be forgiven for lashing out when people let him down, or hurt him.

Though this was the very reason he had got into the habit of lashing out. His temper had kept people at bay. He'd learned early on that all people did was hurt him, if he let them get close.

Lord, what a fool he'd been to have thought his marriage could be any different, because he'd entered into it with such a cool head and with so little expectation. All marriages ended in misery, one way or another.

Fortunately for Mary, the wave of misery he felt drowned his anger completely. It was no use raging at her and forbidding her to leave. She wouldn't understand. He *had* promised her she could come and go as she pleased. That he would let her spend his money as she liked. That he wouldn't kick up a fuss.

And lord knew, she'd put up with him far longer than any other woman had, before losing her patience.

And none of this was Mary's fault. She had no idea she was wounding him. So he would take her departure like a gentleman, not a savage. He would be cool and calm. Polite.

When he eventually turned to her, he'd got himself under control. So far under control that he felt as though ice was flowing through his veins, rather than warm, red blood.

'Just as you wish, of course.' He could hear the ice that was freezing his insides dripping from his words. 'I will furnish you with the direction of my man of business. You must send all the bills to him.'

He sauntered past her and made it to the door. Hesitated. Swallowed.

He couldn't bear the thought of her travelling alone. Of perhaps running into difficulties and having nobody to take care of her. But since she was so independent, so capable, so used to doing everything for herself, she wouldn't think there was any need. 'You will take one of the maids with you,' he bit out. 'You have an appearance to keep up now you are my viscountess. You cannot go jauntering off all over the place on your own. It won't do.'

Chapter Thirteen

Mary didn't feel as if she'd slept at all. Yet the sound of the maid making up the fire and drawing back the curtains the next morning definitely woke her up, so she must have done.

She almost groaned at the thought of facing the day. If only she could pull the covers over her head and hide. Actually, she supposed she could. She could have a tray brought up here, to her room, rather than going downstairs and facing a deserted breakfast table.

While she waited for it to arrive, she heard the sound of hooves trotting past her window. Two sets of hooves. Just as usual. She clenched her fists. While she felt as if her world was coming to an end, her husband and his sister were going out riding. Without a care in the world.

Lord Havelock had exactly what he wanted. Julia was safely ensconced under his roof. Nobody would think it necessary to investigate her hasty removal from Lady Peverell's care. He'd quashed the potential for rumours by marrying.

Yes, he'd got what he wanted, all right. And now she, his wife, was surplus to requirements. In every single way. He'd even made it plain she wouldn't be of any help whatsoever when it came round to Julia's Season.

And very well, it was true that Mary had never had a Season. Didn't know anyone in society. And had no idea how to handle the bevy of suitors that Julia, with her wealth and vivacity, was bound to attract.

She supposed Julia *would* need someone like Lady Peverell, who had at least mingled with the kind of people Lord Havelock would consider eligible, to steer her through that rite of passage. But had it really been necessary for him to rub her nose in all her shortcomings like that?

She was already dealing with the knowledge she wasn't of any practical use around the house any longer. Mrs Brownlow and her team had everything running like clockwork. Even when she consulted Mary about menus it only served to emphasise that Mrs Brownlow knew what were his lordship's favourite dishes, and what was available locally, and who the best suppliers were. While Mary didn't.

Making Mary fully aware how useless she really was.

He'd scarcely notice when she'd gone.

By the time a knock on the door heralded the arrival of a couple of maids bearing her breakfast, her insides were so churned up that the last thing she wanted to do was eat. Throw something, yes, that might have made her feel better. But since the man she wanted to aim the teapot at was probably halfway across the county by now, she couldn't have the satisfaction.

Besides, it hadn't been that long ago when she hadn't known where the next meal might come from. She couldn't squander perfectly good food without suffering a terrible backlash of guilt.

So she accepted the tray, let the maid pour her tea and set a slice of toast on her plate.

And in a cold, leaden voice, instructed one of them to pack her clothes.

'Of course, my lady,' said Susan cheerfully, going to the armoire and lifting down the shabby portmanteau. 'His lordship has said as how you'd be going up to town to buy some new clothes for the Season.'

Oh, had he? Mary took a vicious bite of toast and chewed it thoroughly.

'And I'm to go with you,' she said, setting the portmanteau on the floor in front of the open cupboard. 'Gilbey is preparing the coach,' she added, reaching up for a gown and taking it off its hanger.

Mary's hand froze halfway to her mouth. Gilbey was preparing the coach? 'I'm that excited,' babbled Susan as she draped the gown over the back of a chair. 'I've never been further than Stoney Bottom in my life.'

Mary threw the toast back on to its plate, her stomach roiling. Her husband had given orders to all the servants to hasten her departure, had he? Couldn't wait to get her out of his house and out of his life, in fact.

It felt like a blow to the gut. So real was her pain that she had to fling back the covers and hurry over to the washbasin, over which she heaved for a moment or two before sinking back on to the dressing-table stool, her face clammy with sweat.

'Oh, my lady, are you ill? Shall I cancel the coach? You surely don't want to go anywhere today, if you're poorly.'

Mary shook her head. 'I shall be fine in a moment.' She wasn't ill. Or at least it was only her husband's rejection of her that was making her sick to her stomach.

The nights spent weeping quietly into her pillow. The days spent sitting alone, feeling thoroughly useless.

And she wasn't going to get any better by carrying on in the same way. No—the only way she was likely to find a cure was to get as far away from him as she could and lick her wounds in private.

'Carry on with the packing, Susan.'

'Yes, my lady, if you're sure.'

Rather more soberly now, Susan folded and stowed Mary's new clothes into her old portmanteau while Mary got washed and dressed. Rather shakily.

Her whole body hurt, not just her heart. How could she have let him reduce her to this shivering, quivering wreck of a woman?

Without even trying, that was the most galling thing. He hadn't made any pretty speeches, or given her flowers, or anything. He'd just brusquely told her his requirements, more or less snapped his fingers, and she'd gone trotting after him, all eager to please. Had kept on trying to please him, day after day.

Even though she knew it was pointless.

Because she'd read that horrid list.

A list, she recalled on a mounting wave of bitterness, she'd had to fit, to pass muster. When she'd had to accept him exactly as he was.

Which was completely and totally unfair.

She came to a dead halt in the middle of the floor, pain and resentment surging through her.

If he could measure out her worth according to some stupid list, then why shouldn't she treat him to a dose of his own medicine?

Uttering a growl of frustration, she stormed over to the table under the window where she'd taken to sitting to write her correspondence, pulled out a fresh sheet of paper, trimmed her pen and stabbed it into the inkwell.

What I want from a husband, she wrote at the top of the page, underlining the *I* twice.

Need not have a penny to his name, she wrote first, recalling his stipulation that his bride need not have a dowry.

Can be plug-ugly, she wrote next, recalling how hurt she'd been by his stipulation she need not be pretty, *so long as he will love his wife and treat her like a queen, not a scullery maid.*

Said love will include respecting his wife, being kind to her and listening to her opinions.

Not only will he listen to her opinions, she wrote, underlining the word *listen, he will consider them before he pitches her into a situation she would naturally shrink from.*

Won't deny his wife the right to feel like a bride on her wedding day.

Will appreciate having any living relatives—underlining the word *any* twice.

Need not have a title. But if he has one, it ought to be one he earned. One lieutenant in his Majesty's navy, she explained, remembering her own brother's heroic deeds and his death fighting the enemies of her country, *is worth a dozen viscounts.*

By that time, she'd reached the bottom of the page. And splattered as much ink over the writing desk as she'd scored into the paper.

And had realised what a futile exercise it was.

She wasn't married to a plug-ugly man who treated her like a queen. She was married to a handsome, wealthy lord, who thought it was enough to let her spend his money however she wanted.

She flung the quill aside, got to her feet and went to the bed, on which Susan had laid out her coat and bonnet.

The coat in which she'd got married. With such high hopes.

Before she'd read his vile list and discovered what he really thought of her.

Well, futile it might be, but she was jolly well going to let him know what she thought of him, too. Before she walked out of his house and his life.

Telling Susan she could go and collect her own things, Mary buttoned up the coat and pinned on her hat.

Then snatched up the list she'd just written, stormed along the corridor to the horrid blue room where her husband had taken up residence and slapped the list on to the bed.

And then, recalling the way the list *he'd* written had ended up fluttering across the floor when the door shut, and knowing she was on the verge of *slamming* the one to this room on her way out any second now, she wrenched out her hatpin and thrust it through the list, skewering it savagely to his pillow.

And with head held high, she strode along the corridor, down the stairs and out of his house.

God, but it had been a long day. He'd kept putting off returning to Mayfield, knowing that when he did return, Mary would have gone. But Julia was tired, cold and hungry, and in the end he'd had to bring her back. Had come upstairs to get changed for dinner.

The first dinner of his married life that he'd have to face without his wife at his table.

He had at least the satisfaction of knowing he'd done what he could to make sure her journey would be as easy as he could make it, without actually going with her. She'd been able to use the travelling coach, which had only just come back from the workshop. He hadn't had to hire a chaise, and leave her in the care of strangers. Gilbey was an excellent whip. And she had a maid to save her from impertinent travellers at the stops on the way. He—

He came to a halt just inside the door to his room, transfixed by the sight of a single sheet of paper, staked to his pillow by what looked remarkably like a hatpin.

So she had left a farewell note. He'd wondered if she would. Heart pounding, he strode across to the bed, hoping that she... She what? A note that was staked to his bed with a symbolically lethal weapon was hardly going to contain the kinds of fond parting words he wanted to read, was it?

But it might at least give him a clue as to where he'd gone wrong with her. Why she'd withdrawn from him when, to start with, she'd seemed so eager to please. So eager to please, in fact, that after her first refusal, he'd told himself she must be going through that mysterious time of the month that afflicted every woman of childbearing age. It had only been when she'd kept on refusing to allow him into her bed that the chill reality struck.

She simply didn't want him any more.

Well, hopefully, this note would explain why.

He snatched it up and carried it to the window, so he could make out the words in the fading light of late afternoon.

Only to see the words *What I want from a husband* scrawled across the top of the page.

With the word *I* underlined.

A chill stole down the length of his spine as he scanned the whole page. Because it wasn't just a damning indictment of all his faults. It was worse, far worse than that.

The way she'd set it out, even the way she'd underlined certain words, the very choice of words she'd used—all of it meant she must have read the damn stupid list he and his friends had written, the night he'd decided he was going to start looking for a wife.

A list he'd never meant her to know about, let alone read.

No wonder she hadn't wanted to sleep with him any more. She must be so hurt....

No—that couldn't be right. Heart hammering, he strode along the corridors to the bureau in his father's rooms, where he'd taken to stashing his bills and letters. And found the list locked away, exactly where he'd put it when he'd moved here. Since he had the key on a fob on his waistcoat and that key had never been out of his possession, it meant she must have read it before they reached Mayfield.

And still done her utmost to be a good wife to him. He shut his eyes, grimacing as he recalled one instance after another, when she'd made the best of his blunders while all the while she must have been trying to overlook *this*.

Well, he'd just have to go after her. Tell her he'd never meant to hurt her...

He got as far as the corridor, before it struck him that he'd never done anything *but* hurt her. Blundering, clumsy fool that he was...he'd watched her growing more and more depressed with every day that passed, wishing he knew what to say, how to reach her.

And now he saw that it had never been possible. There was no way he could defend the indefensible.

No wonder she'd left him. *He* would have left him if he'd been married to such an oaf!

He staggered back into his father's rooms, dropped into the nearest chair and put his head in his hands.

What was he going to do? How was he going to explain this to her? Win her back?

Win her back? He'd never had her to win back. Because he'd told her he wasn't looking for affection from marriage.

And this was why.

When men fell in love, it made them weak, vulnerable. God, he hadn't even realised he *had* fallen in love with Mary, until just now, when he'd read her list and realised how much she must hate him. Felt the pain of her fury pierce his heart the way her hatpin had pierced the soft down of his pillow.

His feelings for her had crept up behind him and ambushed him while he'd been distracted by congratulating himself for being clever enough to write that list and pick such a perfect woman.

Why hadn't he seen that picking the perfect woman would practically ensure he *would* fall in love with her?

Because he was a fool, that was why.

A fool to think he could marry a girl like Mary, and live with her, and make love to her, and be able to keep his heart intact.

Let alone keep her at his side.

She'd gone and he couldn't really blame her.

All he could do was hope she'd find the happiness, away from him, that he couldn't give her himself.

And find some way of coming to terms with it all.

Gilbey informed Mary that the roads were too bad to make the journey all in one stage, so they stopped at an inn that wasn't anywhere near as bad as her husband had led her to believe might be the case.

It probably helped that she stalked into the building, still hurt and angry at her husband, and ready to take it out on whoever happened to cross her next. Susan did her part, too, making up the bed in the best chamber with sheets Mrs Brownlow had provided, with such disdain for the hotel's bedding that all the staff treated Mary as though she was a duchess. But all the bowing and scraping from the landlord and his minions could not quite compensate Mary for the knowledge that when her husband had travelled with her, he'd hired a well-sprung, comfy little post-chaise, rather than put up with the antiquated, lumbering carriage that Gilbey had unearthed from somewhere. When she'd travelled with him, she hadn't ended up aching all over and feeling so sick and dizzy that she would have cheerfully curled up on the rug in front of the fire, just as long as she could get her head down.

And then, of course, thoughts of spending nights on hearthrugs in front of fires had churned her insides up so much that she could have been offered the finest, softest feather bed, and it would still have felt like an instrument of torture.

It was past noon by the time Mary reached London the following day. She heaved a sigh of relief when she

finally alighted outside one of the largest, most imposing mansions she had ever seen.

Gilbey, and the horrid carriage, disappeared round
the side of the house at once. Taking the precious horses
to the warmth of their luxurious stables, she supposed.
Susan, carrying Mary's bag, mounted the steps ahead
of her and knocked on the glossily painted, black front
door.

'Lady Havelock, you say?' The butler who opened the
door raised one eyebrow in a way that implied he very
much doubted it. 'We received no notice of your intention to take up residence.'

This was a problem Mary hadn't anticipated, though
perhaps she should have done. It was just like her husband to have forgotten to inform the most relevant people involved.

'Well, I'm not spending another night in a hotel,' she
snapped. One had been more than enough. And she was
blowed if she was going to write to him and tell him his
servants wouldn't let her into the house he'd promised
she could treat as her own. She'd come to London in
part to prove that she could stand on her own two feet.
Survive without him. She wasn't going to crumble, and
beg for his help, at the very first sign of trouble.

'What's to do, Mr Simmons?'

A stern-looking, grey-haired lady came up behind
the butler, who was obstinately barring the way into the
house, and peered over his shoulder.

'There is a person claiming to be Lady Havelock,'
said the butler disapprovingly.

'Well, the notice was in the *Gazette*, so I dare say his
lordship *has* married somebody.'

While the butler and the woman she assumed was

the housekeeper discussed the likelihood of her being an impostor, Mary's temper, which had been on a low simmer all the way to London, came rapidly to a boil.

She'd had enough of people talking about her as if she wasn't there. Of making decisions for her, and about her, and packing her off to London in ramshackle coaches to houses where nobody either expected or welcomed her.

'It's all very well thinking it is your duty to guard my husband's property from impostors,' she pointed out in accents that were as freezing as the rain that had just started to fall. 'But if you value your positions at all...'

'That's 'er, right enough,' a third voice piped up, preventing her from saying exactly how she would exact retribution. 'Leastaways,' said a small boy, who pushed his way between the butler and the housekeeper, 'she's the one wot was wiv 'is lordship when he saved me from the nubbing cheat.'

'Indeed?' The butler's expression underwent a most satisfying change. At about the same moment she recognised the little boy. The last time she'd seen him, he'd been dressed in rags and her husband had been dragging him out of Westminster Abbey by the scruff of his neck.

'My goodness, but you've changed,' said Mary to the boy. He'd not only filled out, but seemed to have grown taller, too. Of course that might have been an illusion, caused by the fact that he wasn't cowering. Or wearing filthy, ill-fitting clothes. And the fact that his hair was clean, and neatly brushed.

'That's wot plenty of grub and a reg'lar bob ken'll do fer yer,' said the former pickpocket, with a grin.

'He means,' put in the butler, having swiped the lad round the back of the head, 'that he is grateful to his lordship for saving him from the threat of the hangman's noose, taking him in and giving him a clean home where he has regular meals. And though we oblige him to wash regularly, I am sad to say that we are still teaching young Jem to speak the King's English, rather than the dreadful language he acquired in the gutter that spawned him.'

The hangman's noose…

Mary's mind went into a sort of dizzy spin, during which time several apparently random items fell rather more neatly into place. Her husband's assurance to his sister that he'd made sure she was kind-hearted, her inability to work out how he could have done so, the lad's pleading for mercy from Mr Morgan and the verger…

And the clincher—this lad's total lack of fear, even when surrounded by his accusers, threatening him with gaol.

'No real fear of the noose though, was there, Jem?' she said acidly. 'It was just a prank Lord Havelock put you up to, wasn't it?'

The urchin's grin widened. 'No putting anything past you, is there, missus?'

The butler swatted him again. 'It is your ladyship, not missus,' he corrected the boy.

It might have been something in Mary's expression as she realised what a fool her husband had made of her, time after time, or the lad's vouching for her character, or her own veiled threat—but for whatever reason, the housekeeper was beginning to look rather alarmed.

'Your ladyship,' she said, pushing both butler and boy to one side. 'Please come in out of the rain. We are so sorry you have caught us all unawares.'

'Yes, indeed,' said the butler, wresting his attention from the boy to his new mistress and permitting Mary to finally step inside Durant House.

The hall was massive. And dark. So dark she couldn't see to the far end of it. That was due in part to the shoulder-high wainscoting, which seemed to suck up what little light filtered in through the few windows that hadn't been shuttered. She couldn't see the ceiling either, no matter how far she craned her neck. But from the echo to the butler's and housekeeper's voices, she judged it was very, very high. On either side of the hall was a dark and ornately carved staircase, which ran by several stages, interspersed with half landings, up under a series of grimly glowering portraits until all disappeared into the murk above a gallery landing.

She wasn't surprised her husband had likened it to a mausoleum.

'We do not, just at present, even have anywhere for you to sit and take tea while we make your room ready,' said the housekeeper nervously. 'Everything is under holland covers.'

Mary wondered how the housekeeper would react if she simply went down to the kitchens and made herself a pot of tea?

But the poor woman had probably sustained enough shocks for one day.

'I dare say you have your very own sitting room,' said Mary. 'Which I'm sure you keep comfortable enough for my needs, for now.'

'Oh, yes, well, I do. Of course I do, your ladyship,' said the housekeeper, torn between relief that her mistress wasn't going to demand another room be made ready at once and consternation at having her invade her territory. 'It's this way,' she said, pragmatism winning.

When Susan scuttled off somewhere with her portmanteau, Mary did her best to calm down. It wasn't fair to take her hurt and anger out on servants.

'Even if we had known you were coming,' said the housekeeper apologetically as she poured the tea, 'I wouldn't have rightly known what room to show you into. The whole place has got that shabby.'

'I know that there is a lot of work to be done here,' said Mary, reaching for a slice of cake. 'It is, in part, why Lord Havelock married me.' Though the reminder depressed her, it seemed to have the opposite effect on the housekeeper.

'Well, now,' she said, perching on the very edge of her chair, 'I'm that glad to hear it. That agent who acts for his lordship—well, I suppose he thinks he has his lordship's best interests at heart, but—'

It was like a dam bursting. The housekeeper had clearly been storing up a lot of grievances. As they all came pouring out, Mary helped herself to a second slice of cake and turned her chair so that she could rest her feet on the fender. Her appetite had come roaring back now she was at journey's end and there was no risk of getting back into that vile coach again. And met a housekeeper who was actually *glad* she'd come. And had a task to perform that would bring benefit to not only her husband, but to all the souls who lived in Durant House.

'I think,' said Mary, once she felt she simply couldn't cram in any more of the delicious fruit cake, 'that you should show me all over the place. So that I can get an idea of exactly what will be required.'

The tour took them right up to suppertime. Mary had known that titled families often owned houses in the town as well as having country estates, but somehow she'd never dreamed her husband would own such an impressive, if sadly neglected one. Neither he, nor his father, the housekeeper informed her, had taken any interest in the maintenance of what had originally been built as something of a showpiece.

Now every room cried out for attention. No wonder he'd moved into a set of cosy apartments and rented this place out. Not only was the amount of work required daunting for a bachelor, it was just too large for one person to live in alone.

Though living here alone was to be her fate, she reflected gloomily.

She felt even more alone when, at suppertime, the housekeeper came to escort her to the hastily tidied dining room and led her to the solitary place at the head of a table that could easily have seated thirty.

As attentive footmen served her course after course, she recalled her bold words about how a lick of paint and rearranging furniture could make any place feel more like home. She almost snorted into her soup. It would take more than that to make this dining room a comfortable place to eat her meals. But since she had no intention of leaving, she would just have to think of something else.

Perhaps there was a smaller, more convenient room in which she could eat her meals. Straight after the last footman had removed the last dish from the table, she went to see if she could find one. And very soon came across a little drawing room off the back of the entrance hall that overlooked the central courtyard around which the house was built. The fountain, which was on the housekeeper's list of repairs, was just outside the window. It would make a very soothing background noise once she got a plumber in to get it working again.

She rang for the housekeeper at once.

When Mrs Romsey arrived, Mary told her that from now on, she wanted to have all her meals served there. And between them, they decided how best to rearrange what furniture there was, to make such a change of use possible.

And then, having started to put her own stamp on the place, Mary suddenly felt bone-weary.

Though she went upstairs, she wasn't yet ready to climb into the bed where she was going to be sleeping alone for the foreseeable future.

Instead, she went into the sitting room that adjoined her bedroom, where she'd earlier seen a writing desk. Mrs Romsey had told her that the desk contained a supply of paper, should she wish to write any letters. Now that she'd calmed down, she couldn't believe she'd left that note for Lord Havelock to find. By letting him know exactly how upset she was, she'd sacrificed what little pride she might have held on to. She'd hoped to leave Mayfield with her dignity intact. Instead, she'd made herself look utterly ridiculous. Emotional and attention-seeking. Why, she'd always despised women who created scenes in futile attempts to get bored husbands to notice them. And wasn't that more or less what she'd done, staking her list of complaints to his pillow in that melodramtic fashion? Oh, if only she'd ripped it up and thrown it on the fire before she left.

A cold chill slithered down her spine and took root in her stomach as she saw that there were far worse things than being secretly in love with a man who didn't handle sentiment well. Forfeiting his respect, to start with. At least before she'd written her stupid list of complaints, she'd had that much.

But there was no undoing it. She'd written it. He'd no doubt found it and read it by now.

And probably despised her for getting all emotional about what was supposed to have been a practical arrangement.

With feet like lead, Mary went to the writing desk and sank on to the chair. She'd known she'd be alone in London, but now she'd made her husband despise her, she felt it twice as keenly.

She'd write to her aunt Pargetter, that's what she'd do. She needn't admit she'd made a total mess of her marriage. She could focus on all the jobs that needed doing at Durant House and ask her for practical advice on that score. She was, after all, the very person to know where she could find everything and everyone she might need.

She carefully refrained from saying anything about her state of mind, but couldn't help ending with just one sentence stressing how very glad she would be to see her aunt and that she would be at home whenever her aunt wished to call round.

Then she rang for Susan, who said she would give the letter to one of the footmen to take round immediately. It was on the tip of her tongue to say there was no need for the man to turn out at this time of night, when it occurred to her that it might be better to have the servants falling over themselves to impress her. Better than having them virtually ignore her, the way they'd done at Mayfield, in any event.

She'd regretted uttering that veiled threat about dismissing staff, upon arrival, because in truth she didn't have the heart to turn a single one of them out, not when she knew only too well what it felt like to get evicted. Particularly not after Mrs Romsey had told her the peculiar nature of their contracts. When there were no tenants her husband's agent had let them all stay on, for bed and board, rather than go to the inconvenience of laying them all off, only to have to hire a fresh set all over again when the next tenants were due, making each of them regard Durant House as their home.

Eventually they'd realise there was plenty of work for them all, since she meant to restore Durant House to its former glory. They'd probably even realise she was too soft-hearted to carry through on her vague threat of dismissals. But for now, at least, they'd treat her with respect.

So it was with a cool smile that she handed the letter to Susan, then wearily succumbed to the maid's suggestion she help her get ready for bed.

She was exhausted. The past couple of days had completely drained her. And yet, once Susan had left, Mary lay wide awake in her magnificent bed. The harder she strove to relax, the more her mind ran hither and thither, the same way the shadows flickered over the network of cracks in what had once been ornately decorated plaster. What was *he* doing, right now? Chatting away happily with his sister, no doubt. Talking about horses and people she didn't know. *He* wouldn't be aching to feel her in his arms, the way she was aching for him. Wishing she could curl into his big warm body. She'd got used to him rolling her into his side and keeping her plastered to him right through the night. As though he couldn't bear the thought of letting so much as an inch creep between them. It had been bad enough sleeping alone when he'd been just along the corridor.

But it was far worse thinking of him in a different building altogether.

For a moment or two she couldn't even recall why it had seemed so important to leave him. So what if he did prefer his sister? Couldn't she have learned to live with that? Couldn't she have put up with him only visiting her in bed from time to time? At least it would have been preferable to this…this distance she'd created. This vast gulf. A gulf he might never deign to cross, now she'd made such a fool of herself.

The thought that the only person she'd hurt, by writing that list and flouncing off to London, had been herself, was so painful that she curled into a ball and cried herself to sleep.

She'd always hated the months between Christmas and spring, but this year those months were going to be almost unbearable.

Each day she'd have to drag herself out of bed to face yet another seemingly endless day.

But drag herself out of bed she did. By the time Susan came in with her breakfast next morning, Mary was up and almost dressed. No matter how low she'd felt during the night, she was not going to lay about in bed all day wallowing in misery. She had a home, she had the security she'd always craved, more money than she'd ever dreamed of. And a title, to boot.

There were many people far worse off than her. And it would be downright ungrateful to dismiss all she did have because she was hankering after the one thing she could not have.

Anyway, it was bad enough knowing she'd made a

mess of her marriage, without drawing attention to the fact and having people pity her.

It would be far better if nobody could guess, by looking at her, that she felt so dead inside.

In fact, it was a jolly good thing Durant House was such a wreck. Restoring it would be a project that would keep her busy, as well as gain favour from her husband. He'd said he would be for ever in her debt if she could make it more like a home....

She gave herself a mental slap. That was no way to get over him. Planning ways to gain his favour! She ought instead to use this time in London to get used to living without him. It was why she'd come, after all. Without him around, prodding at her bruised heart every five minutes with shows of indifference, it would soon start to heal.

Wouldn't it?

Yes. The longer she stayed away from her husband, the easier it would become to be his wife. Hadn't she always suspected that was the only sort of marriage that could work? She certainly hadn't wanted the kind of clinging, cloying relationship she'd seen destroy her parents. That was what had made her tell him, at the outset, that the only man she might consider marrying would be a sailor, because she'd thought that when a man wasn't around, he couldn't hurt his wife.

Well, she knew now that was a load of rubbish. She still hurt, even though she'd created a distance between them. Perhaps even *because* she'd created a distance between them.

And now she couldn't help recalling that those sailors' wives she'd envied so much in her youth for having charge of a man's income without having to put up with his beastly nature, never had looked as happy as she'd thought they should.

Because they were lonely. Lonely and miserable without the men they loved.

When Susan came to take away her breakfast tray, she also brought the news that Mary had visitors.

'Mrs Pargetter. And her daughters. Say they are some sort of relations of yours,' said Susan as if she wasn't totally convinced. 'Mrs Romsey has shown them to the white drawing room.'

'Oh!' When she'd sent an invitation to call whenever they liked, she'd never imagined they would come at once.

As if they couldn't wait to see her again.

Forgetting all her resolutions to behave like a lady and impress the servants, Mary hitched up her skirts and ran along the corridor to the room Mrs Romsey described as white, but which was in reality a patchwork of twenty years' accumulation of stains.

Her cousins, Dotty and Lotty, were poking rather gingerly at the worn coverings on some spindly-legged chairs that looked as though they'd collapse if anyone sat on them. Her aunt was running her gloved finger along the mantelpiece, with an expression of disgust.

Mary had never been so glad to see anyone in her life.

'Mary, my dear!' Aunt Pargetter smiled with genuine pleasure. And then executed a clumsy curtsy. 'I suppose I should address you as my lady now. Old habits die hard.'

'Oh, no. No, you must never call me anything but Mary,' she insisted. 'I don't feel a bit like a my lady.'

She felt her face crumple.

'My dear girl, whatever is the matter?'

And Mary, who'd vowed that nobody, but nobody, would ever know what a mess she'd made of what should have been the perfect marriage, let out a wail.

'I've left him!'

Then she flew across the room, flung herself into her aunt's outstretched arms and burst into tears.

Chapter Fourteen

'Whatever has gone wrong? Has he been cruel to you?'

Mary shook her head. 'No. He has been very k-kind.'
How could she have forgotten the way he'd gone to fetch
coal during the night, shirtless, just so she wouldn't get
cold? Or the way he'd praised her cooking? And told
her she was an angel for putting up with his failings?

'And g-generous,' she wailed, suddenly remembering he'd promised her free rein to decorate this house,
to buy as many clothes as she liked and not worry about
the bills because he'd pay them all.

'Th-that's why I f-fell in love with him,' she sobbed
into her aunt's shoulder.

'But…so…why have you left him then, if he is so
wonderful? And you've fallen in love with him?'

'Because he doesn't love me,' she wailed.

'Of course he does. Why, I've never seen a man so
smitten. He couldn't wait to get you to the altar.…'

'It wasn't because he fell in love with me. It was because he was so sure he *wouldn't*! He only wanted to
marry me so quickly because of…because of…'

'What do you mean, sure he wouldn't?'

'He wanted a certain sort of wife. A woman who wouldn't give him a m-moment's bother. He warned me not to expect affection from marriage. *I'm* the one who changed my mind about what marriage means to me. *I'm* the only one who wants more.'

'Well, if that is true, running away isn't going to endear him to you,' said her aunt tartly, though she was still patting Mary's shoulder in a comforting sort of way. 'If you don't believe he can ever love you, you must surely want him to respect you, don't you? It would have been far better to stay with him and show him what a wonderful wife you can be. That your love needn't make him uncomfortable.'

'I know!' Mary sat up and scrubbed angrily at the tears she couldn't check. 'I know that *now*. Only for a while I completely lost my head. Said things and did things he will never, ever, forgive. I've ruined everything!'

While her aunt had been soaking up Mary's tears, Lotty had poured her a cup of tea and now pressed it into her hands.

'Here. Drink this. And we'll help you come up with a plan to win him round.'

Well, if anyone could, Dotty and Lotty could. They were such adept flirts they could probably make a living giving lessons in it.

'I'm so sorry,' said Mary, wiping her eyes with the handkerchief Dotty gave her. 'I can't think why I've become such a watering pot. I'm not usually prone to tears.'

Aunt Pargetter sat bolt upright.

'Is it possible you are increasing?'

'What?'

'Well, every time I have been in the family way, I became a touch unstable. And this sort of behaviour is most unlike you. I always took you for a very sensible, down-to-earth sort of girl.'

'Increasing…' Mary laid her hand flat on her stomach, and did a few sums. 'It…it might be the case. I haven't…'

Aunt Pargetter nodded sagely. 'Well, then. That is a sure way to win him round. Every time I got in the family way Leonard was so pleased with me he couldn't do enough for me. You have only to write and tell your own husband and I'm sure he will come post-haste to your side.'

'No.' A cold, sick feeling knotted Mary's stomach. 'No, that really would be the end. We agreed, you see, that once I was expecting, he would no longer need to… need to—' She broke off, blushing fierily. 'He said that as soon as I gave him an heir, we could go our separate ways.' She buried her face in her hands. 'If I am increasing, he won't think there's any need to see me again. I'll *never* get him back.'

'Well, then, don't tell him.'

Mary's head flew up. 'But I promised him an heir. Wouldn't it be dishonest to keep him in the dark about something he finds so important?'

'Pish,' said her aunt, making a dismissive gesture with her hand. 'The man clearly needs to be brought to his senses. And you're not going to be able to do it unless you can get him here. Unless you would rather go crawling back to him and beg him to love you?'

Since she'd already vowed never to do such a craven, spineless thing, Mary shook her head vehemently.

'I thought not. But anyway, it won't be exactly dishonest. It is far too soon for you to be absolutely sure you are increasing. I know I detected more than a hint of uncertainty in your voice when I brought it up.'

'Yes. I mean, no. I'm not sure…' Although it was far too early to tell, now that her aunt had mentioned it, it *did* explain her tendency to weep and her ungovernable bursts of temper. And why she'd been feeling alternately nauseous, or ravenous. And it was better than going on believing she'd become physically ill simply because she'd fallen in love and had no hope of her feelings being returned.

Besides, there was the matter of a missing monthly flow. And her husband had been so very amorous, at least to start with. Hadn't she always thought how very virile he was? Yes—it must be true. She *was* going to have a baby.

'He sets great store by getting an heir, you say?'

Blushing hotly, Mary nodded her head. Then she glanced at Lotty and Dotty, wondering how much she could confide in her aunt, with them listening. Both of them were staring at her, wide-eyed, with a mixture of concern and curiosity.

'He said that he wanted to get me with child as soon as he possibly could,' she admitted.

'Then it's likely, if you keep him in the dark about your suspicions, that he will have a good excuse to come to town and keep trying.'

Mary shifted uncomfortably in her seat.

'I can't… It must seem odd, but somehow I can't bear the thought of him steeling himself to visit my bed….'

Her cousins giggled.

'Mary. You are such an innocent.'

'What do you mean?'

'Hush, girls,' said her aunt repressively. Then turned to Mary. 'I do not think it is his feelings about the act that trouble you, but your own. Now that you have fallen in love with him, you shrink from permitting an act that has probably up till recently been only carnal in nature.'

The words struck to her very core. She hadn't been in love with him that first night, had she? When she'd been so hot for him she'd practically ripped off his shirt.

'You are right. I want more than just…enjoyment. Is that very selfish of me?'

'Not in the least. I think most women want much more from their husbands than they ever receive, in emotional terms. Men are just not given to deep feelings.'

'Then what am I to do? How can I learn to settle for… for the little he is prepared to give?'

Her aunt patted her hand. 'Perhaps coming to London without him was the best thing you could have done. If he wants a calm, sensible sort of wife, then you can give yourself the time to calm down. And when he does come after you, which believe me, my dear, he will do, then you must show him you can be sensible. Be the kind of wife he wants. And you will regain the respect you believe you have forfeited.'

Mary twisted the handkerchief between her fingers. What Aunt Pargetter was saying was only what she'd thought herself. And what's more, she did know *exactly* the sort of wife he wanted. He'd written it all down on that list.

At least, he'd written what he *thought* he wanted. She'd soon discovered he didn't really want a modest wife. He enjoyed her eager response to his inventiveness.

The delicate handkerchief ripped.

She could tie herself in knots trying to conform to

the things he said he wanted and be totally wasting her time. And anyway, she couldn't—no, actually, she simply *wouldn't* try to be something she was not, just to keep him sweet. She'd watched her mother do that and look where it had got her!

'No,' she said firmly. 'I am not going to start plotting and planning, and embarking on a campaign to alter the terms of our marriage. After all, I agreed to all those terms, didn't I? I told him I wanted a practical, loveless marriage. It's not his fault I went and fell in love with him, is it?'

'I don't see how you could have helped it,' said Dotty. 'He's remarkably handsome and was so attentive to you.'

'And at a time when you must have felt so alone,' added Lotty.

'Yes,' said Dotty indignantly. 'He practically pounced on you when you were at your most vulnerable.'

Like a predator with a mouse.

But she *wasn't* a mouse.

It was heartening to have the girls blame him for everything, the way she'd been doing up till now. But was it fair to say he was a predator and she'd been his victim? Was it even true? She'd just told her aunt she'd agreed to marry him for practical reasons. And at the time, she *had* seen it as a way to help her aunt and cousins. To help Julia. But had she just used that as an excuse to get close to him? To belong to him?

Oh, lord, she thought, perhaps she had. That was why she'd been so devastated when she'd discovered and read that list. He'd already told her he didn't want a woman who would be looking for affection within marriage. But it hadn't really struck home until she'd read it in black and white.

She'd married him under false pretences. Oh, perhaps not deliberately. And she'd been deceiving herself more than him.

'It's *not* his fault,' she said with resolution. 'I cannot blame him for being what he is. And sticking to the terms we agreed. I shall…I shall just have to pull myself together.'

'We'll help you,' vowed Dotty.

'Yes. We'll keep you so busy you won't have time to mope over the stupid man.'

And every day she would grow more accustomed to her lot. She *would*.

'It looks as though there's enough for you to do in this house to keep you occupied until well after the baby arrives,' added her aunt. 'You did say, in your letter, you needed the names of reliable plumbers, and plasterers, and painters, and upholsterers, didn't you?'

'Yes,' said Mary. She was also going to need the name of a doctor she could trust. And a midwife. And she'd certainly have to buy all those clothes she'd used as an excuse to come up to London without him, or she really would look pathetic.

'Do you know which modiste the most fashionable, wealthiest ladies of the *ton* patronise? If I'm going to live apart from my husband, there's no sense in looking as though I mind.'

'That's the spirit,' said her aunt with a smile. 'Spend his money making yourself all the rage and he'll soon sit up and take notice.'

Would he?

Well, whether he did, or didn't, she was going to get on with her life. She was going to start by making Durant House into a comfortable home for herself and her baby. And she had the confidence she could do it, too, with her family, to wit, these women in the room with her right now, on her side.

Yes. By the time Julia was ready to make her come-out, she would have transformed this place.

She didn't know what had come over her at Mayfield. She didn't know why she'd got so low she even thought she had nothing to offer Julia. She had something very wonderful to offer Julia. An introduction to these three women. Her warm, witty and wise aunt Pargetter and her bubbly, generous-natured cousins. They might not be out of the top drawer like Lady Peverell, but they had something that lady lacked. They would never look down their noses at Julia and would accept her just as she was, the way they'd accepted Mary. They'd make friends with her. Go shopping with her. Giggle with her over her conquests and give her tons of practical advice about how to charm men.

Not only would she make Durant House the envy of every other society lady, but she was going to ensure that Julia enjoyed every moment of her first Season.

And only married for love.

Lord Havelock handed his horse over to a young groom he didn't recognise, wondering where Gilbey had got to. He would have felt better if he could have had a few words with him before he went inside. Found out how Mary was, in a casual sort of manner, without making it obvious he was at his wit's end.

He glowered up at the gloomy façade of Durant House as he strode across the stable yard to one of the rear doors. He'd sworn he'd never spend another night under its roof, but what else was he to do? Mary was here.

And he couldn't stay away from her another moment. He'd got to the stage where he'd rather have her rant and rage at him, or even skewer him right through the heart with a hatpin, than spend one more dreary day without the chance of getting so much as a glimpse of her. Or endure one more restless night, reaching out for her after finally succeeding in dozing off, only to jerk wide awake on finding the space at his side cold and empty.

He paused, with his hand on the door latch. He had no more idea now what to say to her, how he could make things right with her, than he'd had the first minute after he'd read her farewell note. He hadn't come here with a firm plan, but...

Hell, when had he *ever* made plans? Only the once. And look how that had turned out.

With a sense of impending doom, he pushed open the door and went in.

The corridor was deserted, but he could hear some sort of activity going on towards the front of the house. A strange clattering, rattling sound, interspersed with what sounded like shouts of encouragement. And the smell of paint hung in the air.

No matter what she thought of him, Mary was obviously keeping her word about doing up Durant House. The noises were probably that of workmen, doing something in the hall. It certainly needed it. There couldn't be a gloomier entrance hall anywhere in town. What had his grandparents been thinking when they agreed to its design?

'The deuce!'

The words escaped his lips involuntarily as he opened the door from the servants' quarters and stepped into a space that he barely recognised.

It was the light that struck him first. He looked up, astonished to see there were so many windows.

But before he could register what other changes Mary had made, he saw two little boys go thundering up each of the lower staircases that rose to the gallery. When they got to their respective half landings, they flung themselves down on to what looked like little sleds.

'Three,' shouted a footman who was stationed at a midway point of the upper landing. 'Two! One! Go!'

The boys launched themselves down their staircases with blood-curdling yells. Explaining what the odd clattering, rattling sound had been that he'd been able to hear from the stable yard.

Seconds after they landed on piles of what looked like bundled-up holland covers, money changed hands between his footman and a stranger in brown overalls. They'd clearly been taking bets on which boy would reach the ground first.

'Strike me down, it's 'is lordship,' cried one of the boys—whose face looked vaguely familiar—struggling to free his legs from the swathes of material that had cushioned his landing. He rather thought it was Jem, although the pickpocket looked vastly different with a clean face and wearing the Durant livery.

He thought he recognised the other boy, too. He only had to imagine him coated in flour and he would swear it was the youngest Pargetter.

While he was eyeing the boys with something that felt very much like jealousy—because he'd never seen the grand staircases put to better use and only wished he'd thought of tea-tray races down them when he'd been their age—the footman sprang guiltily apart from th